STAR WARS AND CONFLICT RESOLUTION II

My Negotiations Will Not Fail

Published by DRI Press, an imprint of the
Dispute Resolution Institute at Mitchell Hamline School of Law

Dispute Resolution Institute
Mitchell Hamline School of Law
875 Summit Ave, St Paul, MN 55105
Tel. (651) 695-7676
© 2024 DRI Press. All rights reserved.
Printed in the United States of America.
Library of Congress: 2024931999
ISBN-13: 978-1-7349562-1-4

Mitchell Hamline School of Law in Saint Paul, Minnesota has been educating lawyers for more than 100 years and remains committed to innovation in responding to the changing legal market. Mitchell Hamline offers a rich curriculum in advocacy and problem solving. The law school's Dispute Resolution Institute, consistently ranked in the top dispute resolution programs by *U.S. News & World Report*, is committed to advancing the theory and practice of conflict resolution, nationally and internationally, through scholarship and applied practice projects. DRI offers more than 30 dispute resolution courses each year in a variety of domestic and international certificate programs. Established in 2009, DRI Press is the scholarship dissemination arm of the Dispute Resolution Institute which brings significant conflict resolution work to a broad audience. For more information on other DRI Press publications, visit https://mitchellhamline.edu/dispute-resolution-institute/dri-press/

"Star Wars" is for literary effect only, and is not intended to mislead or to imply sponsorship or endorsement by any entity or person involved in creating, producing or exploiting "Star Wars" branded products or services.

Cover design by Karin Preus/Acorn Design. Images by Gerd Altmann/Pixabay contributed to the cover collage.

Visit us at https://www.starwarsconflictresolution.com/

STAR WARS AND CONFLICT RESOLUTION II

My Negotiations Will Not Fail

Edited by
Jen Reynolds & Noam Ebner

DRI Press
Saint Paul, Minnesota

Table of Contents

Introduction vii
   Jen Reynolds & Noam Ebner

Prequel Trilogy

Chapter 1: A Larger View of Negotiation:
   When Failure Is Success 1
   Jen Reynolds & Noam Ebner

Chapter 2: Leaders as Negotiators: Padmé vs. Palpatine 13
   Jan Smolinski & Remi Smolinski

Chapter 3: Are the Jedi Peacekeepers? 25
   Avideh K. Mayville

Chapter 4: The Gungan/Naboo Alliance: A Case Study 41
   Jeroen Camps & Maja Graso

Chapter 5: How Mediation Might Have Saved the Galaxy 53
   Amber Hill Anderson

Rogue One

Chapter 6: Rebellions Are Built on Hope . . .
   But A Little Kairos Can't Hurt 65
   Kimberly Y. W. Holst

Chapter 7: The Empire Is a Terrible Place to Work
   (But So Is the Alliance) 77
   Amanda Reinke, Paul Story & John Martin

Original Trilogy

Chapter 8: Negotiating Like a Sith 91
   Troy Stearns

Chapter 9: You Can Learn the Jedi Mind Trick! 103
   Zach Ulrich

Chapter 10: Is Luke a Hero? The Consequences of
   Choosing Between Goals 115
   Emily A. Cai & Deborah A. Cai

Chapter 11: Chewie Deserved a Medal: Implicit Bias
   in a Galaxy Nearby 127
   Josefina M. Rendón

Chapter 12: Join Us or Die: Absolutism in Conflict 139
   Alon Burstein

SEQUEL TRILOGY

Chapter 13: The Intuitive Force and the
   Wisdom of Feelings 151
   Michael T. Colatrella Jr.

Chapter 14: Why the Uneti Tree Had to Burn:
   Luke Skywalker Gets to Yes with Himself 163
   Sherrill W. Hayes

Chapter 15: Making the Force Live: Sources of
   Negotiation Power 175
   Olivia Hernandez-Pozas & Orlando R. Kelm

Chapter 16: The Light Side, the Dark Side, and
   the Third Side 187
   Danielle Blumenberg

Chapter 17: Does Jedi Training Reduce Stress? 199
   Jill S. Tanz & Robert R. Tanz

Chapter 18: Flyboy! Traitor! Unpacking the
   Poe/Holdo Conflict 211
   Rachel Viscomi

Contributors 223

Introduction

Jen Reynolds & Noam Ebner

Conflict is always with us. Couples will always argue whether to vacation in a ritzy Coruscant penthouse or by a dreamy, romantic freshwater lake on Naboo. Co-workers will always argue over who gets the corner office (designing the Death Star as a globe was an effort to stamp this ages-old conflict out, and that place saw some of the worst workplace conflict ever). Those same squabbling co-workers will always still join forces in muttering complaints about their managers. The courts will always take longer to decide things than the Senate, there will be separatists in every Republic, and full-scale wars will always break out even though we know that wars not make one great.

When we published our first book, *Star Wars and Conflict Resolution: There Are Alternatives to Fighting* (nicknamed Episode I), we were amazed by the support it received from the conflict resolution field and much further abroad. Since then, we have done dozens of conferences, guest lectures, webinars, podcasts, and panels at Comic Cons. Many people proposed ideas for new chapters (even, new books!), and many others offered their support for the project in any number of ways. And everywhere we go we've been thrilled by the response we've received: namely, that we *do* need to know more about managing conflict and negotiation, and there's no better way to learn than through *Star Wars*.

So here we are, introducing Episode II, *Star Wars and Conflict Resolution: My Negotiations Will Not Fail*.

As before, our authors are all conflict experts from practice or academia, with some from both worlds. They have produced a fascinating lineup of conflict concepts and resolution tools. Some chapters cover familiar ground while taking things in new directions, and others introduce new topics entirely. Just as with the previous book, you can pick this one up without having ever read anything else on conflict resolution (including our first book) and come out the other end knowing more about conflict resolution than before. And more about *Star Wars*, too.

We continue to focus on the live-action movies but this time around, we've organized the book's content around the saga's movie trilogies, with chapters focusing on conflict and negotiation topics in the prequel trilogy (*The Phantom Menace*, *Attack of the Clones*, and *Revenge of the Sith*); in the original trilogy (*A New Hope*, *The Empire Strikes Back*, and *Return of the Jedi*); and in the sequel trilogy (*The Force Awakens*, *The Last Jedi*, and *The Rise of Skywalker*).[1] We also have two chapters on *Rogue One*.[2]

At this point, we must explain a choice we made, one of the riskiest of all choices for *Star Wars* aficionados. After much deliberation, we decided to go with chronological (not release) order, with the prequel trilogy (1999-2006) first, the sequels (2015-2019) last, and the original trilogy (1977-1983) in between them. *Rogue One* (2016) is in place right before the original trilogy. Please restrain your rancors! We take no position on the correct or "real" order of the films, and we encourage our readers to read the book in most natural order for them. You've got to follow your own path; no one can choose it for you.

That said, no matter how you read this book, you'll come to the same conclusions. In *Star Wars*, as in our own lives, life is filled with conflict and negotiations often fail. Overcoming differences, resolving disputes, and bringing peace and justice to the galaxy are no small tasks. Throughout the saga, more often than not, clash-

---

[1] We occasionally refer to other parts of the *Star Wars* universe, canon and non-canon: the animated and live-action TV series, novels, and more. We do so in footnotes, so as to keep the main text focused on the movies. If you're into the expanded universe, always follow the footnotes, just as you've done now. You've taken your first step into a larger world! Wasn't this a fun little training exercise, with no one needing to get zapped by a floating ball, shot at by a roomful of clones, rated as the worst trainee ever by a droid who has literally seen them all, or carry a little green guy making snide comments on your back?

[2] Unfortunately, no chapters in the book focus primarily on *Solo: A Star Wars Story*. But we've got a good feeling about next time.

Introduction

ing interests and worldviews lead to fierce competition: all-out war, starfighter dogfights, and lightsabers twirling, vooshing, and crackling as they meet. Many of these situations could have been prevented with better skills at negotiation and relationship-building. Blowing up a Death Star, after all, only results in a counterattack and the building of a bigger Death Star. Relationship repair, trust-building, persuasion, and conciliation, on the other hand, can bring an end to destructive conflict. If you already knew this, then . . . you were right.

In the summer of 1977, in different regions of the United States, we each went into a movie theater and never fully came out. We both went to law school, and we both practiced the aggressive negotiations and diplomatic solutions that are the stuff of *Star Wars*. As time went by, we moved toward constructive negotiations and creative solutions to conflict, practicing as mediators and conflict coaches. As professors, we teach the art of cooperation and creative conflict resolution in law and business schools—landscapes naturally oriented toward competition and even fierce conflict—bringing a new kind of balance to the Force.

For the longest time, we've dreamed of promoting this balance through books connecting *Star Wars* and conflict resolution, and we have been incredibly lucky to find partners in this effort. Each of our authors is a subject-matter expert who takes *Star Wars* so seriously they make Yoda look like a stand-up comedian. Our deepest thanks to these stellar contributors. And to everyone who said, "Count me in for next time!" – we're keeping tabs. May the Force be with you until then.

We are so grateful for the tireless work of Gold Squadron, our group of brilliant research assistants: Ethan Brody, Max Lentz, Elizabeth Mayans, Sarah Takessian, and Pavan Tolani. These law students at the University of Oregon School of Law provided invaluable support in the creation of the book. They proofread and fact-checked every chapter—every line—of this book, keeping our references to the source material as precise and faithful as possible and making sure we had the right number of c's in sarlacc and sabacc. We are thankful for these Padawans' outstanding work and we will watch their careers with great interest.

Our publisher, DRI Press at Mitchell Hamline School of Law, is the Obi-Wan to our Anakin, the Chewbacca to our Solo, and the Finn to our Poe. DRI director Sharon Press has believed in our project from day one. Debra Berghoff's amazing work throughout pre-production, editing, and post-production is what put these words on the page and the book in your hands. Karin Preus created the stunning artwork for the book's cover. We treasure their guidance, partnership, and friendship.

Our families have been tremendous wells not only of love and support, but also of *Star Wars* expertise. Jen is so grateful to her family—Forrest, Abby, Mason, and William—for many reasons, not the least of which is their willingness to watch and discuss the seemingly unending number of *Star Wars* shows surging into the popular culture. William and Mason in particular have become incredible analysts of negotiation in the *Star Wars* franchise; they will be ready for the trials soon.

If Yiffie is Noam's Sanctuary Moon, Tuli, Aury, Ben, and Dandon (Ebner-Winkler), are the Ewoks knocking over Imperial walkers, bringing interesting guests home for dinner, banging on stormtrooper helmets meaningfully, and providing their enthusiastic support to crazy causes such as this book. They all let him C-3PO the story of the Rebellion again and again, complete with sound effects, correcting him gently when he forgets something. Noam continues to be grateful to his parents, who took him to see *Star Wars* a long time ago, and remembers every trench run taken with Moshe Ebner and Estherlee Kanon.

Many other family members, friends, colleagues, and students have helped and supported us along the way, far too many to list. Please know that our memory banks have not been wiped. We are endlessly thankful and think about you gratefully and often, especially on every Life Day. We had each other, and that's how we won.

Introduction

As always, we are thankful to you, our readers. We don't know who you are, but just know that we had you in mind long before you knew we existed, sort of like Ben Kenobi thinking about Luke and waiting for the opportunity to train him. Passing on what we have learned to you, about conflict and conflict resolution and *Star Wars*, is the best part of our professional lives. Connect with the project at www.StarWarsAndConflictResolution.com and tell us about your own *Star Wars* and conflict resolution journey.

Lock in the auxiliary power, everyone, we're gonna do this Kessel Run in under eleven parsecs. And then, we'll round down.

PREQUEL TRILOGY
This is where the fun begins

1

A Larger View of Negotiation: When Failure Is Success

Jen Reynolds & Noam Ebner

> *I will not let this Republic, which has stood for a thousand years, be split in two. My negotiations will not fail.*

It's not easy to take over an entire galaxy, but Sheev Palpatine is up to the task. For decades, Palpatine engages in the most careful planning imaginable, layering strategies upon strategies, making back-up plans for his back-up plans, patiently moving all the pieces into place. Leading a double life, as Chancellor of the Republic and as Darth Sidious of the Sith, he plays all sides against one another, as he strives for absolute (even unlimited!) power.

Palpatine's treachery is on full display in *Attack of the Clones*, when he meets with the Jedi delegation to discuss the Separatist threat and memorably declares: "My negotiations will not fail." At first blush, this sounds like the rallying cry of a leader who will work for peace and prosperity through diplomacy and not through violence. But we've all seen the entire prequel trilogy once or twice by now, so we know that Palpatine is running a long con here. He needs to persuade the Jedi and other Republic power players to continue to support him so that he can buy enough time to ready the clone army (which he arranged) for the impending Separatist attack (which he ordered), thus kicking off the Clone Wars (which he wants) and creating the conditions for Anakin to be turned (which he needs). With Anakin at his command, Sidious can eliminate any remaining opposition before taking over as Emperor.

It is a testament to Palpatine's evil genius that he can make such a statement and have it be at once both true and false. He allows the Republic to be split into two, but only so that he can forge it back together into an Empire he alone controls. His negotiations fail because he wants them to. Indeed, failed negotiations are a necessary precondition for Palpatine to achieve his ambition; and in this way, his apparent failures pave the way for his success.[1]

They will have no choice but to accept

Long cons aside, let's take Palpatine's declaration at face value. What does it mean to say that your negotiations will not fail?

It's an odd statement. Negotiation is a process that people undertake because they need something from the other and can't unilaterally impose their will on them. To get that something, they must get the other person to agree. Although sometimes one party might seek to influence the other's decision through coercion, pressure, competitive dynamics, or other factors to wind up with a bigger piece of the pie, there is always uncertainty around whether parties will come to agreement at all. In other words, because neither party can completely control the other in negotiation, it is impossible to say that negotiations *will not* fail. You can't ensure success in negotiation any more than you can stop the suns from setting.[2]

But Palpatine said it, and the Jedi didn't seem concerned that their esteemed chancellor had suddenly begun dealing in absolutes. Perhaps they thought Palpatine was engaging in conventional aspirational statements, meant to bolster their trust and loyalty. Or they may have assumed that Palpatine meant the Republic had a strong bargaining position, with abundant resources capable

---

[1] And back again, when his greatest success—the creation of Darth Vader—ends up throwing him down a reactor shaft of the second Death Star.

[2] Just ask Nute Gunray. He must have had the same sense that his negotiations would not fail each time he told Queen Amidala to sign his treaty. And yet, even if he could take her throne by force he could not "win" a treaty by force; she could always withhold her agreement.

of meeting the interests of all its wavering systems. Certainly Palpatine could have been engaging in typical politician-speak, the sort of statement that brings the conversation to a close and cuts off further debate. Along these lines, the statement itself—with its undertones of arrogance and superiority—may have been unintended, a slip of the tongue that briefly revealed Palpatine's ultra-competitive Sith personality.

Whatever the reason, a statement like "my negotiations will not fail" tees up the familiar question of how we define success in negotiation—along with the natural follow-up questions of what negotiation failure looks like and how we can avoid it.

Let me help you to know the subtleties

Defining negotiation success can be tricky, given that negotiation is a subjective process: people perceive the essence of the process differently and experience it differently. Some see negotiation as a struggle over a fixed resource. They will often define success by focusing on the *economic outcomes* of the struggle (who got what), often becoming sidetracked by *comparative outcomes* (who got more). Others may look beyond outcomes, defining success more generally by the *overall experience* of the struggle (how did it feel). Whether you succeeded in negotiation thus depends on criteria that are simultaneously broad and subjective. Did you get what you wanted, or at least one thing you wanted? Did it feel fair, or at least not devolve into fighting? Did you feel like you "won" the negotiation, maybe by getting the other side to do worse than they had hoped?

Such definitions of success are problematic, for at least two reasons. First, these definitions are easy to manipulate. Imagine you encounter a "soft" or accommodating negotiator, someone who wants to avoid confrontation. You can do your best Sebulba impression, badgering and bullying the other person until they agree to your demands in exchange for you treating them nicely. Likewise, if you are dealing with a "hard" or competitive negotiator focused on winning, you can agree to something they ask for that you don't care about, perhaps acting defeated and chagrined afterward, so that they feel especially victorious. If young Anakin would have kowtowed to Sebulba (instead of escalating their rivalry with "I'd hate to see you diced again"), Sebulba may have felt less inclined to bother sabotaging Anakin's podracer.[3] Whenever a negotiator defines success by their personal experience of the encounter—like friendly feeling, winning/losing, or fairness—the other negotiator can exploit that definition to their advantage.

Second, these definitions of success are incomplete. Negotiators who focus on economic or comparative outcomes, for example, may be looking only at the bottom line. In doing so, they might ignore the indirect costs or losses they may have suffered, including things like broken trust or shattered relationships. Similarly, focusing on overall experience may provide a useful emotional snapshot for negotiators after the negotiation is over, but the "feels" alone do not provide an objective measure of what negotiators have achieved. In short, when negotiators view success only in terms of outcomes or experience, they do not get a sense of how well the negotiated agreement meets the interests of the parties, whether the agreement is better than available alternatives, or if the agreement represents the best possible arrangement the parties could devise, given their time and resources.

And to the extent that negotiators are motivated by both types of success—that is, they are focused on both comparative outcomes as well as personal experience—figuring out whether the negotiation was successful can become even more difficult. Imagine a competitive negotiator, someone who wants to win every time. Such a person may get an objectively good deal but still be disappointed with the outcome, because they feel (subjectively) like they should have gotten even more. Or maybe this person ends up with an objectively bad deal but is nonetheless pleased with the outcome because they managed to harm their counterpart in some way. Indeed, our self-serving biases push us to choose the measurement that casts us in the most successful light. When definitions of success are too subjective, you get to decide what

---

[3] Sebulba and Anakin's rivalry is not a negotiation, of course, but it illustrates how competitive people can stoke conflict by engaging in aggressive ways.

qualifies as success after the fact. In this respect, your negotiations will not (in fact, cannot) fail.

Remember back to your early teachings

Let's examine another definition of success by returning to what we know about negotiation. Negotiation is an opportunity to interact with someone who may (or may not) be able to help you achieve one or more goals. The process of negotiation touches on substantive, relational, and process concerns; but at the end of the day, negotiation success is determined by two things: interests and alternatives.

Interests are the cornerstone of negotiation. We negotiate to address interests (defined broadly here as needs, wants, concerns, values, hopes) that we cannot satisfy without the help of others. In negotiation, we often express these interests by taking a *position*. When Qui-Gon speaks with Shmi after testing Anakin's blood, he takes the position that he should train Anakin. Qui-Gon can't just leave with Anakin; he must negotiate with Shmi (and Watto, for that matter). Note that Qui-Gon's position here is the culmination of many underlying interests: energizing the Jedi Order; defeating the dark side; bringing balance to the Force; protecting people from injustice, generally speaking; protecting Anakin, more specifically; helping Anakin reach his potential; increasing his own mastery of the Force; and so on. And who knows? Qui-Gon may also be thinking about paving the way for his own retirement, or about one-upping the other Masters, or about gaining more influence over the Order's direction. Whatever his interests may be, they lead him to take the position that he should teach Anakin the ways of the Force.

For her part, Shmi doesn't put up much of an argument. Her interests are primarily centered on Anakin's well-being and happiness, and she sees Jedi training as a step in the right direction. So she takes the position that Anakin should go with Qui-Gon if he chooses to. But imagine if she had objected to Qui-Gon's proposal, asserting the position that she wanted Anakin to stay. If the negotiation were all about positions, then the two may have found themselves at an impasse or (even worse) Qui-Gon may have asserted his superior leverage, which could have led to a lose/lose outcome for all involved. But when negotiators look through positions to the interests underneath, they often see some shared interests and some room for possible trades. This is the nature of integrative or interest-based bargaining, where negotiators refrain from haggling over positions and instead seek to unearth each other's interests to come up with creative agreements.

An interest-based conversation between Qui-Gon and Shmi would have given them an opportunity to share possible visions of what Anakin's future may look like. They would have discovered that they shared common interests around Anakin reaching his potential in a safer and more just universe, which could have gone a long way toward helping Shmi agree to let Anakin go. And who knows? Maybe getting more of Shmi's interests on the table, which surely included not being a slave, would have prompted more thinking about how to free both Skywalkers, not just one (which may have avoided all kinds of trouble). This kind of *value creation* is a hallmark of interest-based negotiation. Only by sharing our interests can we generate creative and value-rich solutions.

Even competitive or selfish negotiators who do not care about their counterparts would do well to keep interests in mind. Getting another person to agree is easier if the deal meets their interests, and coercive behaviors (including Jedi mind tricks) may not lead to durable or implementable agreements down the road.

Leave him, or we'll never make it

Yet it isn't enough just to know your own interests and find out those of the other side. When it comes to defining negotiation success, we must also consider *alternatives*.

Alternatives are not the same as options. Options are the range of possible agreements, or components of agreements, between two negotiating parties. For an option to become part of an agreement, both parties need to agree on it. In negotiating with a system considering leaving the Republic, for example, Palpatine could offer the system better treatment, fair taxation, a choice spot for its delegates in the Senate close to the concession stands, and such like. These are all options. The system's representatives, for their part, might demand a public venue for airing its grievances, more voice in Galactic decision-making, or less bureaucracy in dealing with its needs. These are also options. All of these various proposed options could end up as components of an agreement between Palpatine and the systems. Once both parties agree to them, they are upgraded from options to agreements. However, if one party rejects them, pulling an Amidala by refusing to sign a treaty, these options have no standing; no party can impose them unilaterally.

Alternatives, on the other hand, are the range of actions each party might take, *on their own*, if there is no agreement on a set of options that satisfies their interests. If Palpatine and the representatives cannot agree, both parties have alternatives away from the table. The system representatives can declare their system neutral, join the Separatists, stop paying taxes, or declare war on the Republic. Palpatine can blockade the system's trade routes, impose financial sanctions, whistle up a clone battalion to attack the system, or let them leave and find a richer system to recruit to the Republic. Each party can turn to their alternatives unilaterally.[4]

Thinking through their alternatives to reaching agreement in a negotiation helps negotiators gauge how badly they need this particular deal to happen, which in turn can make it easier to assess whether a particular concession is warranted or whether a proposal is acceptable. Will our interests be better satisfied by reaching agreement, or should we leave this negotiation and pursue a different path?

You are the best choice by far

Engaging in negotiation with a galaxy full of away-from-the-table alternatives can be confusing. Which alternative should you compare the proposed deal against? An important rule of thumb in negotiation is that when you are thinking through your alterna-

---

[4] We're not discussing the justifications or ethicality of these alternatives, just clarifying and applying the term itself.

tives, you should evaluate each alternative in terms of your own interests. This will help you identify your Best Alternative To a Negotiated Agreement, or BATNA.[i] Your BATNA is the alternative you will *actually* turn to if the negotiation ends with no deal.[5]

The best alternative that many star systems could see to Palpatine's entreaties or offers to keep them in the Republic was an offer from Palpatine's seeming competitor, Count Dooku. While all Palpatine could offer was minor improvements to a failing system, Dooku promised real change, change that would satisfy a disgruntled system's deepest-held interests. It should come as no surprise that many systems chose to cut off negotiations with the Republic and go with their BATNA (accepting Dooku's offer). We do the same in many ordinary bargaining contexts, like negotiating the terms of a new job.

One use to which we may put our BATNA is within the negotiation itself. We might share our BATNA with our counterpart, using it as leverage to get them to offer us an improved option. Let's say you are renting a TreeBnB for a relaxing week on Kashyyyk. You consider two identical condos, one owned by Brewbacca and the other by Twobacca, each with a perfect view of the treetop square where the Life Day ceremonies are to be held. If Brewbacca demands a high price and Twobacca offers his condo for less, renting Twobacca's tree condo is your BATNA, your best alternative to continuing to negotiate with Brewbacca. In this way, your BATNA provides further grist for negotiating: "Brewbacca, please don't pull my arms off but I gotta tell you, Twobacca has offered me a similar place for over twenty percent cheaper. Make me a better offer, or I'll go with him."[6]

Another use of our BATNA is to help us determine whether to accept a proposed deal. If price is the most important consideration

---

[5] Working with alternatives, spelling is critical. While negotiating, there are two things you don't want to confuse: BATNA and BANTHA. A *BATNA* is your Best Alternative to Negotiated Agreement. A *BANTHA* is a woolly, horned, elephant-sized creature native to the sunny planet of Tatooine. We suggest—nay, *urge*—you keep these in separate pockets.

[6] Using this method may seem to require a great deal of courage but remember, you usually will not be negotiating with Wookiees.

for you, and Twobacca's condo (your BATNA) is cheaper, moving to your BATNA may meet your interests better than accepting Brewbacca's more expensive proposal.

Remember, if your BATNA is better than the proposed deal, you should always consider walking away. Walking away in this situation is not a failure. Indeed, some negotiations *should* fail. Put another way, sometimes reaching agreement in a negotiation is a failure rather than a success. Agreeing to a deal that doesn't satisfy your interests is not a negotiation success, especially if you could have gotten a deal that could have served your interests better by leaving the negotiation and going elsewhere. Successful negotiators constantly ask themselves whether the deal on the table satisfies their interests and is better than their best alternative (BATNA). In negotiation, no deal is better than a bad deal.

The thought of losing you is unbearable

That said, even seasoned negotiators sometimes appear to forget about their BATNAs and end up with bad deals instead. To nutshell some very sophisticated inner workings of our minds, we're wired to believe that as long as we're in a negotiation, we *need* to reach agreement and impasse is failure. We may have "sunk costs" driving us to close a deal: we've spent a week trying to negotiate this system back into the Republic and a ton of coaxium to get here, so are we going to throw all that away and walk? Or should we give them that one last concession, so that we can go back to Coruscant and announce that we've achieved peace in our time? Additionally, manipulative negotiators have an array of endgame moves that can rush a counterpart toward agreement, and sometimes the final details of a deal can slip by so fast you don't fully consider them. Having a good sense of your BATNA will protect you from these negotiation "successes" that will come back to bite you like an even bigger fish. Knowing your BATNA helps you measure when you would be a *successful* negotiator by letting this negotiation fail, or by being the one to declare that it has failed before moving along.

Mace Windu, for his part, keeps an eye on alternatives. He isn't blinded by Palpatine's fierce determination and confidence in his negotiation abilities, and he provides Palpatine wise counsel around the possibility of more star systems joining the Separatists:

PALPATINE: My negotiations will not fail.
WINDU: But if they do, you must realize there aren't enough Jedi to protect the Republic. We're keepers of the peace, not soldiers.

In this scene, Mace Windu tries to teach Palpatine an important negotiation lesson: Not only must you have your BATNA prepared before walking into any negotiation, for all the reasons we've discussed, but this backup plan must be realistic, thought through, grounded, and actionable. If your BATNA is just a general idea—untested, vague, or wishful thinking—you don't have a BATNA. You have a phantom BATNA.

The phantom BATNA can lead negotiators into making poor decisions because phantom BATNAs can create unwarranted confidence, lead to fictional comparisons, and provide no real leverage. Back to Brewbacca's condo. If you hadn't identified Twobacca's condo as a realistic alternative but instead just assumed or hoped you'd find on the holonet a cheaper place that was basically as good as Brewbacca's spot, you would be working with a phantom BATNA. Your alternative in the TreeBnB negotiation is a fantasy—it is not grounded, verified, or actionable. Whether you reach a deal or not, there's a good chance your negotiations will have failed.

Another trap that new and experienced negotiators can fall into is focusing too much on their WATNAs, or Worst Alternatives To a Negotiated Agreement. The WATNA is the worst you fear could happen if your negotiation does not reach a deal. When Mace Windu advises Palpatine that the Jedi cannot serve as soldiers, Palpatine does something that all good negotiators should do. Rather than quickly imagining that the most catastrophic outcome will happen ("Oh no! War is sure to break out! We're all going to die!"), he conducts a realistic assessment by asking Yoda to tell him the odds. Likewise, negotiators should think through their WATNA to know the stakes, to obtain a sense of proportion, and to identify any possible corrections—not to scare themselves into making unnecessary concessions or quick agreements. Too often we focus on the (extreme) negative and let our fear of the WATNA cripple us in negotiation. We worry that if we ask something of the other side, they'll walk away. That if we ask for a raise, we'll get fired. Sure, those are scary outcomes, but what are the chances those will happen? Often, the chances are low.

Everything is going as planned

In the prequels, Palpatine's negotiations never failed because he was secretly holding all the cards. Every move he made furthered his heads-I-win, tails-you-lose strategy that he had been planning for years. The Force must have been particularly shrouded the day the Jedi heard Palpatine claim that his negotiations would not fail. Any negotiation expert would have known in an instant that something was off, dark side or no dark side.

Success in negotiation is not a matter of confident declarations, and it's not about whether a deal is reached. In interest-based negotiation, we can measure success and failure along two spectrums: interests and alternatives. Did the outcome satisfy the interests of the parties? Was the outcome better than our best alternative, or BATNA? The key to determining success and failure in negotiation is separating "success" from agreement and "failure" from impasse.

Palpatine was an expert in this regard. He knew that success in negotiation sometimes means arriving at a deal and sometimes means walking away with nothing. We too should remember that if the other party offers us a deal that meets our interests and is better than our BATNA, we are in good shape. If the other party quits the negotiation because we will not settle for a deal that leaves our interests unfulfilled, we have staved off the failure of binding ourselves to a bad deal. If turning to our BATNA improves our situation beyond that, we are further out of the failure zone. If our BATNA satisfies our interests, we are solidly in the positive zone. Moreover, if we are the party that chooses to walk out of a deal that doesn't satisfy the interests of the parties or that isn't as beneficial as our BATNA, we have succeeded.

Where Palpatine went wrong, of course, was his failure to appreciate how the deeply-held interests of other parties might stymie his ambitions; a failure that eventually weakened the reliability of Palpatine's all-purpose BATNA ("Agree to this, or Darth Vader will come for you") and left him vulnerable. His failure is a reminder that our focus determines our reality, and also that negotiation is ultimately a cooperative enterprise. If you focus only on what you want, you may set yourself up to fail. If you instead focus on interests—yours and the other side's—and remember to compare possible deals with your BATNA, you may wind up getting what you need. In an uncertain galaxy, that's a lot.

References

[i] Fisher, R. & Ury, W. (1991). *Getting to yes: Negotiating agreement without giving in* (2d ed.). Houghton Mifflin Company.

Leaders as Negotiators: Padmé vs. Palpatine

Jan Smolinski & Remi Smolinski

The *Star Wars* universe is a treasure trove of wisdom on leadership and negotiation. From the sun-soaked dunes of Tatooine to the bustling skyscrapers of Coruscant, individuals from all walks of life find themselves embracing the mantle of leadership. Yet, as we follow the leaders through the galaxy, we realize that they are not all cut from the same cloth. Some possess the remarkable ability to guide us to the furthest reaches of our potential, while others leave us questioning our loyalty to the cause.

From the picturesque planet of Naboo, a haven of natural beauty and refined culture, two influential figures emerge: Padmé Amidala and Sheev Palpatine. Both are leaders, but not the same kind of leader. Padmé demonstrates a *servant leadership* style. She is motivated to do the best thing possible for her people and to be as fair to them as she can. Her decisions are influenced by what is best for her constituents and will represent their priorities well. She cares about democracy, the rule of law, and good living standards for everyone—to the point that she will sacrifice her own life for them. Palpatine, on the other hand, represents an *authoritarian leadership* style. While he is good at understanding the needs of others, he seldom changes his own plans as a result. Rather, he uses this understanding to manipulate people and maintain his position. Even when he uses the language of servant leadership, as he does when accepting emergency powers as Chancellor, he is simply consolidating his own authoritarian power. Most, if not all, of his motivation in assuming office, building relationships, and supporting others, is selfish.

Servant leadership and authoritarian leadership are polar opposites. Yet throughout the films, Padmé and Palpatine exhibit some surprising similarities as leaders. Both possess an intrinsic understanding of the power of empathy, communication, and negotiation. It is through these captivating qualities that they inspire and forge connections with others and navigate the intricate currents of galactic diplomacy.

In the seminal book *Real Leaders Negotiate*, Jeswald Salacuse introduces a framework for understanding leadership styles and negotiation skills.[i] This chapter will examine the leadership approaches of Padmé and Palpatine using Salacuse's framework, specifically focusing on similarities and differences in the following dimensions of leadership: caring about the interests of others, taking time to negotiate relationships, finding the right leadership voice, and negotiating a common vision.

Leadership doesn't happen in the abstract; leaders lead real people and have an impact on their lives. When looking to understand leaders, we need to look at their followers as well. And indeed, at its core, the prequel trilogy offers both perspectives: it is about the fundamental conflict between two visions of leadership, and this conflict is embodied by Anakin Skywalker's struggle to decide which leader to follow. Anakin must choose between continuing along the Jedi way and maintaining his allegiance to the Republic, the path represented by Padmé; or succumbing to the power and promise of the dark side, as represented by Palpatine.

Caring about the interests of others

True leaders exemplify empathy and care for the interests of others, understanding their needs and empowering them to reach their full potential. In his book, Salacuse observes that: "[t]he basis of any relationship is some perceived connection that exists between leader and follower . . . it may be psychological, economic, political, or cultural" (7). By establishing strong connections with their followers, leaders can create a supportive environment where everyone is motivated to contribute to the greater goals of the organization.

As noted above, Padmé has a servant leadership style centered around genuine empathy and care for others. Throughout her political career, first as Queen of Naboo and later as a Senator, she formulates her goals based on the needs of her constituents, constantly demonstrating her commitment to understanding and addressing their concerns. In her personal relationship with Anakin, Padmé shows compassion and understanding toward his troubled past and intrusive thoughts. She patiently supports him through his journey of healing from past traumas, becoming a reliable source of strength for him. This support allows Anakin to focus on his duties in the war, knowing that he has Padmé's unwavering love and support upon his return to Coruscant. In this way, Padmé's empathy not only provides comfort to Anakin but also enhances his ability to work towards their shared goal of liberating the Republic from the Separatist threat. Importantly, Padmé's care and support for Anakin are genuine and motivated by her personal connection to him, with any greater goal arising as a secondary outcome.

Yet Anakin ultimately chooses not to follow Padmé's advice, instead turning to Chancellor Palpatine on many occasions. From the perspective of leadership dynamics, this misjudgment on Anakin's part could be because he experiences Palpatine as empathetic, possibly even more empathetic than Padmé. In *Revenge of the Sith*, Palpatine listens attentively to Anakin's needs and concerns. He asks probing questions around Anakin's experience on the Jedi Council, learning that Anakin feels unfulfilled and unappreciated for his great achievements in the Clone Wars. Palpatine also shows compassion when he hears about Anakin's terrifying visions of Padmé's death in childbirth. In these ways, even though his motives are evil, Palpatine demonstrates empathy and care, gaining Anakin's trust. Additionally, because Palpatine has listened so carefully, he is able to offer ideas and suggestions that cleverly address Anakin's worries. He designates Anakin as one of his closest confidants and compliments him on his bravery. And by telling the story of Darth Plagueis the Wise, a feared and powerful Sith Lord who could save others from death, Palpatine plants the seed for Anakin to switch loyalties. Palpatine's skillful display of understanding and support make Anakin eventually choose Palpatine over the Jedi, enabling Palpatine to take complete control of the Republic.

In other words, Palpatine succeeds at enlisting Anakin as a follower and supporter because he is able to intertwine his own interests in gaining control of the galaxy with Anakin's interests in being appreciated and protecting his loved ones. He paints a picture in Anakin's head that encompasses all of their deepest desires. Of course, once this greater goal is achieved, Palpatine allows Anakin's wishes to fall by the wayside. The Emperor does not need to pretend to care about Darth Vader in the same way that he pretended to care about Anakin.

Taking time to negotiate relationships

Real leaders understand the importance of investing time and effort in negotiating and nurturing relationships. As Salacuse points out, leaders recognize that building trust and establishing a solid foundation of rapport and understanding are crucial for fostering effective collaboration in the future. He further elaborates that "[t]he relationship between leader and follower often tends to create trust in the leader. Trust . . . is essential to leadership" (7). By prioritizing relationship-building, leaders lay the groundwork for successful teamwork, open communication, and mutually beneficial outcomes.

Padmé is a skilled negotiator when it comes to building relationships. She effortlessly forges genuine friendships with her allies in the political arena, with notable examples being Bail Organa and Mon Mothma. Their bond is so strong that Bail offers without hesitation to adopt Padmé's daughter, Leia, following Padmé's tragic death in childbirth. What sets these relationships apart is that they go beyond mere means to achieve professional goals but instead are rooted in shared values, trust, and genuine connection. Padmé understands that in order to make progress, she should not simply surround herself with powerful individuals and move within their circles; instead, she seeks out people whom she admires and genuinely enjoys being around. It is the power of these connections that allows for fruitful collaboration in her political endeavors.

Further, when it comes to relationships, Padmé recognizes the importance of taking her time and not rushing into things. This is evident not only in her approach to building relationships with allies but also in her relationship with Anakin. She invests ample time and effort in getting to know him on a deeper level. Unlike Anakin, who is eager to dive headfirst into a romantic relationship, Padmé demonstrates her clear-mindedness by thoughtfully considering the implications and whether it is the right course of action. This discerning approach to relationships reflects Padmé's astute analysis of the world around her. She does not let impulsive desires guide her decisions, but instead exercises thoughtful consideration. This level-headedness and her willingness to invest time and effort in building connections are integral to her success in both her personal and political life.

Palpatine, too, is an expert at building relationships. His approach to taking over the Republic and getting close to Anakin showcases a remarkable display of emotional intelligence, patience, and strategic planning. Rather than rushing into action or ordering people around, he meticulously positions the dominoes one by one, adhering to his carefully crafted ideas. Palpatine methodically integrates himself into the system, first assuming the role of a politician, orchestrating a crisis, and then seizing the opportunities it presents, ultimately ending up elected Chancellor and acquiring extensive emergency powers. Remember, he does none of this by force; rather, his relationship with Padmé leads him to the Chancellorship, and his relationship with Jar Jar Binks results in his gaining emergency powers. By meticulously building long-term connections, Palpatine creates a web of influence and loyalty, paving the way for the realization of his goals. His strategic patience and astute manipulation of relationships are key elements in his carefully planned rise to power.

Indeed, Palpatine's relationship-oriented approach—truly a masterclass in the art of cultivating strong ties and relationships over an extended period—is the only way he could have drawn Anakin to the dark side. Anakin craves intimacy and community, having lost both his mother and, in Qui-Gon, his father figure.[1] In building a close relationship with Anakin, Palpatine exhibits unwavering patience. He bides his time, waiting for Anakin to mature and become disillusioned with the Jedi Order. As a mentor, Palpatine strategically inserts himself into Anakin's life, providing support and resources and gradually gaining Anakin's trust. One of Palpatine's masterful maneuvers involves deliberately placing himself in a hostage situation aboard a Separatist ship. In this cunning move, he stokes Anakin's anger and loyalty before manipulating events to provoke him into killing Count Dooku.[2] Anakin initially feels guilty about the act, but Palpatine is right there to comfort and reassure him. Through these calculated actions, Palpatine furthers his own agenda by deepening the bond with Anakin.

Finding the right leadership voice

Finding the right leadership voice is crucial for effective leaders. Salacuse argues that the way we communicate with others carries a profound message about the level of care and consideration we have for them. He stresses that communication is the essence of leadership: "[c]ommunication is fundamental to building relationships and therefore the ability to lead. Indeed, leadership could not exist without communication" (9). Additionally, the setting in which we choose to engage with individuals holds significance, as it reveals our intentions and the extent of our commitment and involvement.

---

[1] For more on Anakin's identity needs, see Blumenberg, chapter 4, in *Star Wars and Conflict Resolution: There Are Alternatives to Fighting* (Ebner & Reynolds eds., 2022).

[2] Another aspect of Palpatine's strategic approach to relationships was knowing when to end them. Just ask Dooku. Or the Separatist leaders. Oh wait, you can't.

In *The Phantom Menace*, Padmé exhibits a remarkable understanding of selecting the right leadership voice and negotiation setting. When seeking the support of the Gungans against the invasion of Naboo, she chooses to abandon her cover, drop to her knees, and beg Boss Nass to join forces with her. By demonstrating her commitment to and trust in Boss Nass, Padmé successfully convinces the Gungans to create a diversion. Then, as she leads her troops to retake the palace, she adjusts her leadership voice accordingly, motivating her troops to perform at their best. Padmé's ability to adapt her tone and position during negotiations becomes evident when she has the Trade Federation leaders surrounded. Swiftly switching to a position of strength, she asserts her upper hand without becoming emotional or aggressive, showcasing an astute command of negotiation dynamics.

This intuitive understanding of choosing a leadership voice and negotiation setting extends to Padmé's interactions with Anakin on Naboo. She creates the right atmosphere to engage Anakin through storytelling and attentive listening, further strengthening their connection even as she pushes back on some of his anti-democratic statements. Of course, perhaps her choices in these encounters are less about leadership voice and more about falling in love. Even so, it may be that people with benevolent leadership styles utilize these tools as well, for benevolent purposes, in all their relationships.

Power-hungry Palpatine also takes a thoughtful and dynamic approach to leadership voice. He demonstrates a high level of control over all his interactions, particularly those with Anakin. He intentionally invites Anakin into his private chambers, asking others to leave, to establish an environment of exclusivity and confidentiality. This deliberate act of the Republic's chancellor making time specifically for Anakin instills a profound sense of importance in Anakin, who along with intimacy and community also craves recognition. On another occasion, Palpatine invites Anakin to join him in the VIP box at the opera, creating a comfortable and pleasant space for their discussions. Palpatine's meticulous approach to interacting with Anakin underscores his strategy of making Anakin feel exceptionally valued and essential.

Throughout the prequels, we see Palpatine strategically engaging with different forums: addressing the full Senate, speaking with small senatorial groups, meeting with delegations from a single system, interacting with Jedi leadership, or having one-on-ones with individuals. In each, he finds the right voice to make everybody feel respected while clarifying his own position and expectations. Of course, as Darth Sidious, he uses a very different range of leadership voices to get others to follow him.[3]

Negotiating a common vision

Organizations consist of individuals with personal needs and expectations, including those concerning the leader, her role, and the purpose and strategy of the organization. These needs and expectations usually cover a wide spectrum of possible alternatives. Salacuse explains that "[o]rganizations look to their leaders to help determine that sense of direction and then ensure that their members move towards it" (65).

Padmé excels in creating shared visions that inspire others to think critically and take action. As a prominent member of the Loyalist Committee, an advisory council to Chancellor Palpatine, Padmé fearlessly exposes Palpatine's political maneuvers as power grabs, encouraging her close political allies to join her in opposing such injustices. And her approach extends beyond her interactions with politicians. She consistently presents and defends a democratic vision of the Republic when engaging in discussions with her closest confidants. Whether it's rallying Anakin around the importance of genuine public servants and the parliamentary process, or enlightening acquaintances like Obi-Wan and Jar Jar Binks, Padmé passionately emphasizes the power and value of democratic principles. "Have you ever considered we may be on the wrong side?" she muses to Anakin, demonstrating more con-

---

[3] The crossover between these two voices is his command to Anakin to kill Count Dooku. Palpatine was jovial and encouraging beforehand and comforting afterward. But it was Sidious who snapped: "Do it!"

cern about the underlying realities of the situation than about her own investments or political reputation. Her ability to articulate her ideals and express both criticism and self-doubt is rooted in her profound belief in the importance of collaboration and inclusive governance.

Indeed, there is substantial reason to believe that Padmé's ability to forge a shared vision played a pivotal role in sustaining her enduring romantic connection with Anakin. Given their respective callings, they were frequently separated during the Clone Wars, a separation that grew more poignant with their marriage and the anticipation of parenthood. Padmé's reaffirmation of their mutual aspirations for galactic peace and prosperity while they lived on Coruscant, and her plea for Anakin to leave everything and escape with her as he began descending to the dark side, served as significant components of this shared vision.

In a fleeting moment on Mustafar, as he holds Padmé in his embrace, Anakin's eyes momentarily go back to their usual shade of blue, and he looks like he genuinely considers retiring from fighting and living a simple life with his new family. However, this transitory glimpse vanishes as he catches sight of Obi-Wan. Padmé, at her best, possessed the ability to encapsulate Anakin within her vision. However, at her lowest, while mourning the demise of the Republic and the love of her life, the influence of Palpatine's vision on Anakin prevails.

Like Padmé, Palpatine also has the ability to articulate and, at least before emerging publicly as the Emperor, negotiate a shared vision. In his adherence to the Sith Rule of Two, Palpatine demonstrates a remarkable ability to inspire and recruit new apprentices who align with his vision of a galaxy dominated by the dark arts. Throughout the prequel trilogy, he trains a series of individuals, including Darth Maul, Count Dooku, and Anakin Skywalker, convincing them to join his cause by vividly illustrating the potential outcomes they can achieve by standing at his side.

For example, Palpatine presents to both Dooku and Anakin a compelling alternative to the disappointments they experienced within the Jedi Order and the Republic. He offers them a tantalizing vision of a new galaxy, one where they have the power to rectify the flaws they perceive in the current system. Palpatine's persuasive prowess lies in his ability to articulate a clear path forward and skillfully negotiate the roles his followers will play in the realization of this vision. This shrewd approach enables him to identify the perfect fit for each apprentice and ultimately achieve his objectives with Anakin.

Palpatine's talent for shaping the narrative and outlining a promising future not only entices his apprentices but also establishes a sense of purpose and direction for their lives. By showing them the potential rewards and providing a persuasive vision, Palpatine cultivates a following of powerful and devoted individuals who play pivotal roles in his grand scheme. Palpatine's ability to inspire and recruit is a testament to his charisma, understanding of the human psyche, and manipulative skills. He leverages the desires, ambitions, and grievances of his apprentices, molding their aspirations to align with his own. Through his manipulation and careful negotiations, Palpatine secures his Sith disciples under a common vision, ensuring the continuation of the Sith legacy and his own pursuit of galactic domination.

"So this is how liberty dies. With thunderous applause"

It may seem counterintuitive to compare the leadership styles of Padmé and Palpatine—and it may seem even more counterintuitive to realize that they are effective and skilled as leaders in very similar ways. Yet we know that Padmé and Palpatine are not the same kinds of leaders. Even when they employ similar leadership strategies, the differences in their values and goals ultimately bring different results to their followers. Salacuse points out that leaders are rarely chosen for their competencies alone, but rather that a person's goals and intentions also play a large role.

Palpatine is incredibly methodical and patient in his authoritarian leadership and has everything planned out to the smallest detail. He understands the needs and desires of others, but only uses this knowledge selfishly to further his own agenda. Palpatine's approach inspires Anakin to follow him for a long period of time. Yet in the end, Anakin destroys Palpatine. Palpatine never had Anakin's best interests in mind, and he never cared about Anakin being happy or fulfilled in life. All Anakin ever was to him was a chess piece in his game. Leaders like that may inspire us at times but, as Anakin discovers, they always leave us stranded when we need them the most.

Padmé, also methodical and patient, seeks to empathize so that she can help others, not to gain a selfish strategic advantage. She is the embodiment of empathy towards even the most troubled people, and she serves as an example of leading with everyone in mind. She does not use people but instead shows genuine interest in them and tries to do well by them. Padmé adapts quickly to what's happening around her, taking a more hands-on style when the situation demands. This skillful mastery of leadership and negotiation, paired with her strong values and relationships, are the basis for her successful leadership as well as her strong bond with Anakin.

Leading like Padmé exacts a toll on individuals. In pursuit of his selfish goals, Palpatine ascends to power in the galaxy with almost effortless ease. In stark contrast, Padmé meets an early demise, burdened by sadness, exhaustion, and disappointment in her once-trusted Anakin. Compassionate leadership is challenging and requires significant effort and energy. Fairness, attentive listening, and advocacy for the voiceless may pose formidable challenges, even when aligned with our intrinsic values. Ultimately, in another fascinating parallel, Padmé—like Palpatine—also is destroyed by Anakin. While her passing is tragic, her legacy endures beyond death; the bond she forged with Anakin lasts even through his Darth Vader years, contributing to his redemption and return to the path of light.

Within the cosmic dance of power struggles, Padmé and Palpatine serve as contrasting exemplars who teach us that capable leadership alone is insufficient. True leaders—leaders who are able to build thriving organizations and movements—must possess the virtue of selflessness, serving and mentoring those they guide. Leadership is an ever-evolving journey of understanding, with empathy guiding every step. Through this lens, true leaders demonstrate that genuine strength lies not in ruling with an iron fist, but in guiding with an open heart.

Along with these lessons in leadership, the *Star Wars* saga sounds a dire warning of the dangers of uncritical followship. Both sides in the galactic conflict, the Republic and the Separatists, built up armies of obedient soldiers—clones and droids, respectively—designed to never question authority. Anakin himself often seemed naive and impressionable, soaking up the values of others like a sponge. In our own lives, there always will be people around us uniquely poised to make an impression on us, and we must be mindful of the values of those who gather us into their circle.

Applied in our own galaxy and that other one far, far away, the conclusion is simple to agree with yet hard to put into practice: whether we are leaders or followers, we need to remember to always reflect and question our beliefs and reassess our resulting actions if necessary.

References

[i] Salacuse, J. W. (2017). *Real leaders negotiate! Gaining, using, and keeping the power to lead through negotiation.* Springer.

Are the Jedi Peacekeepers?

Avideh K. Mayville

In *Attack of the Clones*, Count Dooku's Separatist movement gathers support and threatens to tear the Galactic Republic in two. Fearing a Separatist attack, many in the Galactic Senate seek to establish an army to defend the Republic. Chancellor Palpatine (seemingly, at least) puts them off, insisting that he will resolve the situation through negotiations. Jedi Master Mace Windu is careful to clarify the Jedi role to Palpatine: "You must realize there aren't enough Jedi to protect the Republic. We're keepers of the peace, not soldiers." But are Jedi really keepers of the peace? And what is a peacekeeper anyway?

In our galaxy, "peacekeeping" is a relatively new role tied to the creation of the United Nations. Emerging from the ashes of World War II, fifty countries gathered in 1945 to establish the UN as an international organization with a mandate to maintain international peace and security, protect human rights, and facilitate cooperation to resolve global issues. The UN has no army, so specially trained *peacekeepers* serve as the operational arm of the UN Security Council and have evolved over the years into an impartial and diverse "moral force." Like Jedi, who hail from all species and planets across the galaxy, the ranks of UN peacekeepers consist of military, police, and civilians from multiple member-state countries. They help maintain peace by preventing the outbreak of violent conflict in warzones and bringing about mediated resolution to conflicts.[i]

This all sounds a bit like the Jedi of the prequels—except that unlike UN peacekeepers, who came into being after the creation of the United Nations, the Jedi Order long preceded the existence of the Galactic Republic. The Jedi were an ancient monastic organization unified by belief and observance of the light side of the Force. Only later did they come to serve the Galactic Republic as guardians of peace and justice, something like UN peacekeepers.[1] But the indiscriminate layering of roles and responsibilities onto traditional Jedi culture ultimately proved disastrous.[2] The inability of Anakin and other Jedi to reconcile the Jedi Code with the competing demands associated with keeping the Republic's peace led to the devastation of the Order, the downfall of the Republic, and the rise of a Sith-ruled Empire.

In this chapter, we examine how the Jedi sought to (or were sometimes compelled to) intervene in conflicts as "keepers of the peace," leading up to and beyond the Clone Wars. Comparing the Jedi's interventions to the peacekeeping operations of the United Nations, we can evaluate the Jedi in their peacekeeping role and gain greater insight into the identity-based fissures that emerged at individual and institutional levels throughout the prequel trilogy. Do the Jedi peacekeepers meet the standards set for UN peacekeepers? Let's see!

Turmoil has engulfed the Galactic Republic

The *Star Wars* galaxy is a vast and complicated place, much like our own world. At the time of the prequels, numerous star systems shared sovereignty over a multitude of planets from the Core Worlds to the Outer Rim, with many spaces of lawlessness throughout. Maintaining peace across thousands of systems with varying degrees of rule of law and access to resources was challenging. Some star systems and industrial corporate powers were loyal to the Republic. Others joined the Separatist Alliance, which eventually split from the Republic during the Clone Wars. Still

---

[1] As Ben Kenobi explained to Luke in *A New Hope*: "For over a thousand generations the Jedi Knights were the guardians of peace and justice in the Old Republic."

[2] For more on the often conflicting roles played by the Jedi, see Anderson, chapter 5.

others maintained their own individual independence and political neutrality. This is the broad and overarching *conflict context* of the prequels.

Narrowing our focus to the specific institutions and systems in which the Jedi operated, we learn early in *The Phantom Menace* that the Galactic Republic has been taxing major trade routes to outlying star systems, and in response, the "greedy" Trade Federation has blockaded the small planet of Naboo. Taxation and access to trade routes are a typical source of conflict in our world as well. Trade across vast territories governed by multiple entities can be hazardous, so trade routes must be maintained and secured to keep traders from being robbed by opportunistic pirates or bounty hunters. The Trade Federation, which is not a state or star system, but an interstellar shipping and trade megacorporation, has a seat in the Galactic Senate. In allowing powerful corporate entities to exist as equal actors to states within a legislative body, we can already see how the Galactic Republic differs from the UN as a governing institution.

The UN does not allow multinational corporations or private sector companies to be official Members of the UN. Only countries (states or governments) can become UN Members. The UN does allow Observers, which includes two non-member States (Vatican City and Palestine) as well as intergovernmental or international non-governmental organizations like councils, communities, and agencies, which can represent economic and business interests. For instance, the International Labor Organization and the European Union are UN Observers, but global companies or megacorporations such as Meta or Amazon are not. While megacorporations and the private sector may lobby, partner, and otherwise advance their interests with UN Member states and Observer entities, they cannot be granted Member or Observer status and therefore are prohibited from playing an official role in global governance or legislation. Why does this matter? Because it separates the business of profit-making from the task of governance and the maintenance of order, peace, and rule of law. This separation is important, given how susceptible to corruption governments can become, from Geneva to Coruscant. As Qui-Gon Jinn wisely said, "Greed can be a very powerful ally."

Okay—so we can see how the governing institutions of *Star Wars* are different from our own in this conflict context, and we can also see how this difference complicates the nature of an intergalactic trade tax dispute since the Trade Federation is actually a (wavering) member of the Galactic Senate, the very body that passed this trade tax. When the leader of the Republic, Supreme Chancellor Valorum, dispatches Qui-Gon and Obi-Wan Kenobi to negotiate with Trade Federation Viceroy Nute Gunray, the complex conflict context here makes the role of the Jedi (serving here both as negotiators and as "guardians of peace and justice in the galaxy") much more delicate and difficult.

And indeed, the Jedi are walking into a trap. Gunray has been advised by Darth Sidious to kill the Jedi and invade Naboo. As the invasion begins, we discover a sub-element to this conflict context: the strained relationship between the amphibian underwater Gungans, indigenous natives of the planet of Naboo, and the land-dwelling humans on the planet, descendants of off-world human colonizers. While there is no active conflict between the Gungans and the Naboo, there is a cold peace between them and they are certainly not allies.[3]

Let's pause for a moment and see where we are. So far we have: (1) a fragile governing system that includes a megacorporation alongside states within its legislative body; (2) a dispute over the legitimacy of this system playing out through an altercation over a trade route tax; and (3) a planet (the site of the altercation) that consists of an underwater native population and human colonists living in a cold peace. Phew! That's a lot for a peacekeeper to navigate! We will go more into the nature of when and how the Jedi intervene as peacekeepers in the next section, but first let's continue to track the evolution of the conflict context throughout *Attack of the Clones* and *Revenge of the Sith*.

In *Attack of the Clones*, we discover the creation of two secret armies: a clone army for the Republic on Kamino, mysteriously

---

[3] For more on the Gungans and the Naboo, see Camps and Graso, chapter 4.

ordered by deceased Jedi Master Sifo-Dyas; and a droid army for the Separatists led by Count Dooku and Nute Gunray. We also learn that the Trade Federation and two other megacorporate powers, the Commerce Guild and the Corporate Alliance, are allied with the Separatists in preparation for war. Upon discovering the droid army, the Galactic Senate votes to grant emergency powers to Chancellor Palpatine and authorizes the use of the clone army on behalf of the Galactic Republic.

Thus have we crossed a threshold in this conflict context: the Galactic Republic institutionalizes the use of armed forces (clones), which practically and formally militarizes the role of the Jedi. Practically, as we see Jedi racing at the front of long columns of clones attacking droid positions; formally, as the clones accept orders from Jedi unquestioningly and the Jedi honorifics of "Sir" and "Master" morph into "General" and "Commander."

As we begin *Revenge of the Sith*, the clone and droid armies are no longer secret or covert operations. An intergalactic civil war has officially been raging between the Republic and the Separatist Alliance for three years, with the Jedi on the front lines. But although the Jedi are "keepers of the peace, not soldiers," they are assigned to lead key military operations, such as the Council tasking Obi-Wan to hunt down and capture Separatist military leader General Grievous, and sending Yoda to defend the Wookiee planet of Kashyyyk from a droid attack.

The Jedi's role within the Republic had already been somewhat fraught and uneasy, especially as the Council became more and more political. Being coopted for military purposes only furthers the institutional corrosion of the Jedi Order. Chancellor Palpatine makes things even worse when he politically appoints Anakin as his "personal representative" to the Council without Anakin having attained the rank of Master. This complicates both Anakin's individual navigation of what it means to be a Jedi and part of the Jedi Council, as well as the Jedi Council's navigation of its own institutional identity within the Galactic Republic.

How peacekeepers intervene in conflict

How did we get here? When do Jedi peacekeepers intervene and who determines when they do? Can executive leaders unilaterally appoint "personal representatives" to peacekeeping councils? And are peacekeepers even allowed to lead forces into battle? To understand conflict intervention in the prequels and whether we can really call the Jedi peacekeepers, let's consider the following variables in each intervention: the decision-maker, the process of conflict assessment and ordering missions, the roles the Jedi filled, and the tactics they actually employed on the ground. The tables below outline these variables and whether they qualify as peacekeeping.

DECISION-MAKER	MISSION	JEDI ROLE(S)	TACTICS	PEACE-KEEPING
Chancellor Valorum	Negotiation with Trade Federation	Negotiator, ambassador	Negotiation, self-defense	Yes
Qui-Gon Jinn	Negotiation with Gungans	Negotiator	Negotiation, shuttle diplomacy	Yes
Qui-Gon Jinn	Rescue mission (Queen Amidala)	Rescuer	Defense of self and politician	No
Jedi Council	Security escort (Queen Amidala)	Private Security	Defense of self and politician	No
Jedi Council	Investigation of Darth Maul	Investigator	Inquiry, manhunt	No
Qui-Gon Jinn	Battle of Naboo	Battle support	Defense of self and politician	No

Table 1. List of Jedi interventions from Episode I

Decision-Maker	Mission	Jedi Role(s)	Tactics	Peace-keeping
Jedi Council	Security (Padmé)	Private security	Negotiation, self-defense	No
Jedi Council	Surveillance, investigation, arrest of assassin	Investigator, law enforcement	Inquiry, detainment, manhunt	No
Jedi Council	Lead clone battalion	Military leader	Engaged violence with enemy	No
Anakin	Rescue mission (Shmi)	Rescuer	Engaged violence with enemy	No
Anakin	Rescue mission (Obi-Wan)	Rescuer	Engaged violence with enemy	No
Jedi Council	Lead Jedi battalion	Military leader	Engaged violence with enemy	No
Jedi Council	Lead clone battalion	Military leader	Engaged violence with enemy	No

Table 2. List of Jedi interventions from Episode II

Decision-Maker	Mission	Jedi Role(s)	Tactics	Peace-keeping
Jedi Council	Rescue mission (Palpatine)	Rescuer	Engaged violence with enemy	No
Jedi Council	Lead clone battalion (Kashyyyk)	Military leader	Engaged violence with enemy	No
Palpatine	Anakin to spy on Council	Spy	Observation, surveillance	No

Jedi Council	Anakin to spy on Palpatine	Spy	Observation, surveillance	No
Jedi Council	Surveilliance, tracking (General Grievous)	Hitman	Manhunting	No
Mace Windu	Political arrest (Palpatine)	Law enforcement	Detainment, engaged violence	No

Table 3. List of Jedi interventions from Episode III

Now that we have listed out all the interventions taken by the Jedi in the prequels, we can evaluate them on the basis of who serves as decision-maker; what the mission is; and how the Jedi conduct themselves, in terms of the roles they assume and the tactics they use.

The Decision-Maker

Analyzing any peacekeeping mission must start off with the question of who decided to launch it and how that decision was reached. At this point, certain governance similarities and distinctions between the Republic and the UN require explanation. The two bodies are very different in their executive leadership and emergency decision-making powers. Both entities have acting executive leaders, the Supreme Chancellor and the UN Secretary General, elected by their governing bodies and with limited terms. Both roles administer large institutional bureaucracies seeking to centralize decision-making and consensus-building around peace and security across systems, with the UN Secretary General role explicitly mandated to "speak and act for peace." The UN Secretary General cannot be granted "emergency powers," but the UN does outline procedures for holding "emergency sessions," which can be requested by any UN Security Council Member or by a majority of Members of the UN.

With this foundation in place, we turn to the question: Who made the decision to send Jedi on their missions? In the prequels, there are many admirals in the starcruiser when it comes to deciding when the Jedi intervene. Sometimes the decision-maker is the Chancellor, sometimes it is the Jedi Council. Often, in moments of urgency, decisions are made on the fly by an individual Jedi.

Next is the process preceding each mission: how was the decision to launch the mission reached? To put it bluntly, it's a bit of a mess. In terms of process and procedure, the decision-making behind missions seems to be in line with Master Qui-Gon's advice to young Anakin: "Feel, don't think. Trust your instincts."

Jedi Council decision-making appears to be consensus-based: there is discussion and occasionally debate, but there is no voting mechanism or some final deciding authority; ultimately the Council reaches agreement. The Council's decision-making doesn't seem to require a full quorum of all of the Masters, however, or even for all its members to know what is going on. Decisions are often made privately and even covertly, in informal processes that sometimes involve back-channel consultations or sometimes explicitly exclude certain actors [insert angry Anakin here]. Whether the decision-maker is the Jedi Council or the Chancellor, there is little transparency and information is on a need-to-know basis. As a result, the criteria and logic for approving missions and interventions are obscure, inconsistent, and confusing—particularly to a headstrong young Jedi constantly assessing the compatibility of the directives he receives with Jedi ideals, and navigating when and how to follow instincts versus orders.

Here's a simple example. Directed by the Chancellor to kill Count Dooku upon successfully completing a rescue mission, Anakin hesitates. Upon carrying out the execution, Anakin says to Palpatine, "He was an unarmed prisoner. I shouldn't have done that. It's not the Jedi way." Palpatine responds that Dooku was "too dangerous" to be kept alive and that beheading was "only natural," framing Anakin's execution as a valid desire for revenge for Dooku cutting off his arm. Perhaps this scene does not necessarily count as an "intervention," even though it occurred during a rescue mission, but it does demonstrate the conflict between the

Jedi Code and what actions are determined to be in the interest of the Republic (which may differ depending on the decision-maker).

Looking at the chart above, it's interesting (though not that surprising) that most of the non-peacekeeping missions were ordered by the Jedi Council or initiated by individual Jedi. Operating as they do on the light side of the Force, the Jedi are not neutral parties. When they sense injustice and oppression, they feel compelled, by Code and compassion, to intervene. Accordingly, they take a side and make their stand. In this sense, they are not peacekeepers, as the term is applied in our world.

Missions

The chart lays bare the truth of Jedi activity leading up to and during the Clone Wars. Out of the nineteen Jedi missions listed, seventeen do not qualify as peacekeeping. What are they, then? Military and security missions, for the most part. Rescuing people, leading battalions, and providing battle support shift the role of the Jedi explicitly from peacekeeping to military operations in service of a state or political entity. Let's be honest: in much of their activity, the Jedi are war-makers, not peace-keepers.[4] Even missions with less of a martial tone, such as providing private security for the Chancellor or the Queen of Naboo or other political leaders, would not be classified as "peacekeeping" in our world. While UN peacekeepers are mandated to protect civilians and political processes, they do not provide private security for politicians.

Moreover, UN peacekeepers are professional neutrals. Their processes and procedures for deciding their missions are officially defined, with parameters for engagement evolving alongside the evolution of our worldly conflicts. The UN Security Council determines the deployment of peacekeeping operations. Unlike the Jedi Council, the UN Security Council is made up of member states and not a roster of individual senior peacekeepers. To justify deploying UN peacekeepers, an extensive list of criteria must

---

[4] No one articulated this better than Anakin's Padawan, Ahsoka Tano. "As a Jedi, we were trained to be keepers of the peace, not soldiers," she tells her friend, Commander Rex, in *The Clone Wars*. "But all I've been since I was a Padawan is a soldier."

be met, including consulting with relevant actors, undertaking technical field assessments, and developing formal resolutions to outline operational mandate and scope. Even after these criteria are met, there are still rules for engagement around UN peacekeeping operations. Host countries must consent to the peacekeepers being there. Peacekeepers must remain impartial and treat both sides equally. Peacekeepers are not allowed to use force, except in self-defense or defense of their ability to carry out their mandate (the original decision that gave them authority to act and defined its scope and authorized activities). Their role is to uphold rule of law and maintain order, prevent violence from getting worse and turning into war, and create space for reconstruction.[5]

Interventions: Roles and Tactics

As we've seen, most of the Jedi missions do not set them up to be effective peacekeepers. Still, it's important to examine the roles they are assigned and the tactics they employ in the field.[6]

ANAKIN: You call this a diplomatic solution?
PADMÉ: No, I call it aggressive negotiations.

Like Padmé, the most successful UN peacekeepers use soft power. They *persuade, induce,* and *coerce*—and not through violence.[ii] No blazing lightsabers on the battlefield or impromptu executions of enemy political leaders here! Picking apart the Jedi missions throughout the prequels, we see the Jedi playing nine main roles and utilizing eight types of tactics on their missions. These roles and tactics are presented in the figure on the next page, arrayed on a peacekeeping scale of peaceful, neutral, and impartial on the left; and discriminatory, partisan, and violent on the right.

---

[5] Thousands of Geonosians collectively buzzed in laughter and outrage after reading this.
[6] Or "in the swamp," "in the sand," or "in the arena," in missions to Naboo, Tatooine, and Geonosis, respectively.

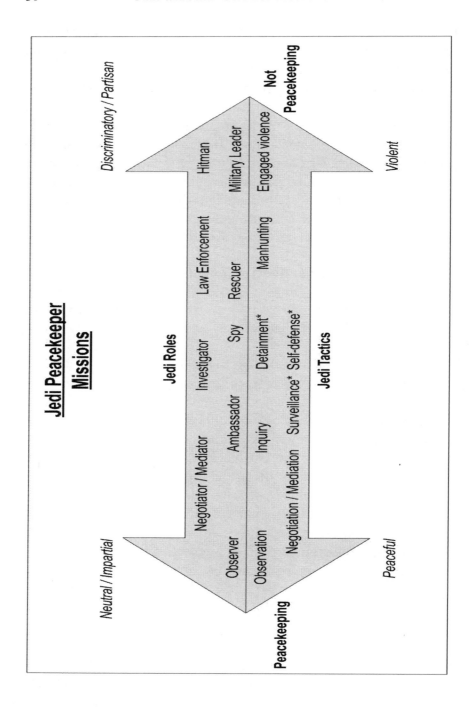

Observation, negotiation, mediation, and inquiry are the only tactics that are unequivocally within the scope of peacekeeping. Self-defense, surveillance, and detainment are conditionally permissible peacekeeping tactics, but only to prevent violence, gather intelligence, and induce cooperation. While sometimes the Jedi combine roles and tactics, combining the peaceful with the violent (such as observation and manhunting) does not transform well-intended aggression into actual peacekeeping. Thus, Obi-Wan's surveillance and investigation of a politician's potential assassin (Jango Fett) and his orders to abduct Fett for interrogation by the Jedi Council are not peacekeeping actions. Peacekeeper surveillance is for the purpose of observing conditions, patrolling, and gathering intelligence in the interests of the peacekeeping mission—not to bring assassins to justice or, as in Anakin's case, to inform competing political leaders of each other's activities.[iii]

In fact, of all the Jedi deployments throughout the prequels, only two seem to fit the peacekeeping role as viewed in our world: first, Chancellor Valorum's sending Qui-Gon and Obi-Wan to negotiate with the Trade Federation; and second, Qui-Gon's underwater efforts to persuade the Gungans to work cooperatively with the Naboo. Just about everything else the Jedi do throughout the prequels would have peacekeepers on our own planet charged with war crimes.

The very evil we have been fighting

Mace Windu:	I am going to put an end to this, once and for all!
Anakin:	You can't. He must stand trial.
Windu:	He has control of the Senate and the courts. He's too dangerous to be left alive.
Anakin:	It's not the Jedi way. He must live!

Ultimately there are many reasons why the Jedi failed and the Republic fell. Were the Jedi peacekeepers? No. Was the Galactic

Republic an actual democratic republic? Also, no. The Jedi were set up to fail within their shifting institution context. By evolving into the military arm of the Galactic Republic, Jedi security operations became part of a political campaign to maintain the sovereignty and control of a governing system over the territories within that system. The Jedi were never an objective, neutral, outside party to the Republic's conflict with the Separatists; they were participating and actively taking sides.

What we learn from the prequels is that systems and processes matter when it comes to governance and peacekeeping. Institutions must have rules and procedures around decision-making and engagement, as well as transparency around these rules and procedures. Most Jedi missions were shrouded in secrecy with no procedures around decision-making, often resulting in individual Jedi harboring internal doubts and moral conflicts around intervention (not to mention the haphazard employment of tactics on many Jedi missions). Had there been more transparency around decision-making, more explicit thresholds around intervention, and more criteria for acceptable tactics used in intervention—in other words, more clarity around the role of the Jedi peacekeeper—Palpatine might not have risen to power and the Clone Wars may never have happened.

And we would not have had Darth Vader. Anakin's turn to the dark side is the sharpest example of the damage caused by the lack of transparency, thresholds, and criteria. His turn was not inevitable. If those three elements had been in place, many of the jarring incidents that nudged him toward the dark side would never have occurred. After all, Anakin's outrage over the hypocrisy of the Jedi was justified; this is part of what makes him such a tragic and sympathetic character. In the end, the unbearable strain of striving to live as a "keeper of the peace" in the Galactic Republic—bound by the Jedi Code as well as the demands of increasingly corrupt institutions—contributed to Anakin's full embrace of the power of the dark side.

References

[i] Morjé Howard, L. (2019). *Power in peacekeeping.* Cambridge University Press.
[ii] *Id.*
[iii] *Id.*

The Gungan/Naboo Alliance: A Case Study

Jeroen Camps & Maja Graso

Merely sharing a life-giving planet has never been a sufficient reason for Earth's diverse societies to unite and commit to some common good. The geopolitical situation on Naboo (located in the Chommell sector of the Mid Rim Territories) is no different. At the start of the prequel trilogy, we are introduced to two societies—the land-dwelling Naboo and the Gungans of the undersea—who, despite spending innumerable years residing on the same planet, have never formalized diplomatic and political ties. Although the Naboo and the Gungans coexist mostly peacefully, they appear to have little to no desire to move beyond mere tolerance toward a more unified society.

At the planet core of negotiation and conflict resolution lies the notion of achieving cooperation where none currently exists. As organizational scientists, we study how individuals and collectives decide whether and how to cooperate—in other words, how they form *alliances*. Alliances allow parties to coordinate and cooperate with each other on certain matters, even when there are differences and disagreements between them on other issues. Without alliance formation, worlds (such as Naboo or Earth) would be incapable of taking collective action essential for addressing shared existential crises. Indeed, crises and threats often lead to alliances, even between those who historically have been mainly indifferent or hostile to one another. When individuals or groups confront a common enemy, they tend to unite and cooperate.[i]

We see this dynamic play out in *The Phantom Menace*. When the Trade Federation starts threatening the lives and livelihoods of both Gungans and Naboo, the two societies must decide how to respond to the threat. In this chapter, we walk through the relationship history and the key defining moments that lead to the formation of the Gungan/Naboo alliance. We also pose questions about the stability of this alliance once the threat has passed—a central concern to political scientists, organizational theorists, and anyone who seeks cooperative solutions to large-scale challenges and conflict.

Pre-alliance relationship between Gungans and Naboo: *us and them*

Historically, the relationship between the Gungans and the Naboo does not appear to have ever reached a level of open hostilities and antagonism. Both groups have coexisted separately for years with only minor strife, as remarked by Queen Amidala to the Gungans' Boss Nass: "Although we do not always agree, Your Honor, our two great societies have always lived in peace." Nonetheless, the relations they have had clearly prevented them from achieving one of the most foundational building blocks of cooperative and trusting collectives: readily acting in each other's interest and uniting for the greater good.[ii] Instead, the relationship between the two is characterized by classic *us and them* dynamics, keeping them from uniting against common enemies.

The roots of the strained relations and unresolved differences between the Gungans and the Naboo can be traced to a geographical and social divide between the surface-dwelling Naboo population and the Gungans inhabiting the planet's underwater cities and swamps. The two groups' needs to adapt to vastly different environments have led them to foster somewhat different practices and values. The Gungans developed a distinct culture marked by tribal ties, hierarchical power structures, and a general preference to remain inwardly oriented. In contrast, the Naboo enjoyed prosperity, architectural aesthetic, lush greenery, technological advancement, and easier access to trans-planetary trade and travel.[1] While each way of life was functional in their respective contexts, their geographical and cultural distance likely fostered some degree of division, misunderstanding, and prejudice.[2]

Strained or non-existent relationships pose a problem for negotiators and others who seek to form alliances. Indeed, if a negotiation partner starts by signaling dislike instead of by opening communication chains and promoting trust, it hardly sets the foundation for a pleasant negotiation or cooperation.[iii] The Gungans and the Naboo have a long history of avoiding each other, which has exacerbated not only cultural differences but also political divides between the societies. Such a situation, in the *Star Wars* galaxy as well as our own, poses difficult challenges when circumstances require societies to put aside their differences and find a common basis upon which to form an alliance.

The emergence of a common threat

The Naboo are the first to sense the threat from the Trade Federation. The threat starts subtly but becomes increasingly overt as tensions escalate and the Federation's actions grow more aggressive and menacing. Following a dispute about the taxation of trade routes in the Galactic Republic, the Federation imposes a blockade on Naboo. The Federation aims to force Naboo's rulers, led by Queen Padmé Amidala, to surrender by isolating them economically, disrupting supply chains, and creating resource shortages, economic instability, and widespread suffering. Understandably, Naboo is eager to end the blockade as soon as possible.

---

[1] Not to mention, influence. A human senator from Naboo had just been elected Chancellor of the Galactic Republic, after all.

[2] Pre-Alliance, the Naboo viewed Gungans as primitive, tribal, and uncivilized; perhaps the fact that the entire planet is called Naboo and does not carry any references to the name of the Gungans is an indicator of who is seen to be superior in this dyad. In contrast, the Gungans' inward focus likely confirmed some of the Naboo's prejudices, as the former greatly disliked outsiders and did not hide those sentiments. Gungans built their city Otoh Gunga to avoid contact with the Naboo, and they professed dislike of others. "Gungans no liken outsiders, so don't spect a warm welcome," Jar Jar Binks warns Obi-Wan and Qui-Gon before heading to Gunga City.

At first, though conflict seems imminent, both the Naboo and the Trade Federation are keen on limiting themselves to legal actions. When the Supreme Chancellor sends Qui-Gon Jinn and Obi-Wan Kenobi on a mission to find a peaceful solution, the Trade Federation sees this as a power move, favoring their opponent. Nonetheless, they remain eager to adhere to measures within legal boundaries. The Viceroy welcomes the Jedi Ambassadors with: "As you know, our blockade is *perfectly legal*" and later responds to Darth Sidious's escalating order to invade Naboo with concern: "My Lord, is that legal?"[3] Similarly, while frustrated with the Senate's seemingly endless democratic debates about resolving the conflict, Queen Amidala is also concerned about conflict escalation, which she makes clear by stating, "I will not condone a course of action that will lead us to war."

Yet the invasion of her planet is already underway. The conflict spans occupation of Naboo and political jockeying in the Galactic Senate. In both arenas, the two sides turn to measures of increasing intensity to avoid being on the losing end of the conflict. The Queen returns with her Jedi escort to Naboo, and Darth Sidious sends his apprentice Darth Maul to counter her plans. Matters escalate, and the Naboo decide to reach out to the Gungans to form an alliance against the enemy.

Although the Federation's pressures are largely directed at the Naboo and their capital city Theed, it soon becomes apparent that the Gungans will not remain unaffected by the conflict. While having no personal quarrel with the Federation themselves, Gungans risk the depletion of their vital aquatic resources, the pollution of their underwater habitats, and the disruption of their way of life. But even this threat remains insufficient to immediately foster unity between the two societies. When Qui-Gon and Obi-Wan go to Otoh Gunga with the hope of forming an alliance, both try to convince the Gungan leader Boss Nass to cooperate with the Naboo by pointing out that the Gungans themselves face a severe threat and have a common goal with the Naboo:

---

[3] Within a few seconds, the conflict escalates outside legal boundaries as Sidious responds, "I will make it legal."

> Once those droids take control of the surface, they will take control of you . . . You and the Naboo form a symbiont circle. What happens to one of you will affect the other. You must understand this.

This common-enemy/common-interest approach is known to be effective in promoting collaboration in general.[iv] However, the proposal is nevertheless met with rejection. Boss Nass does not view the droid invasion as a real threat ("Day not know of uss-en") and signals lack of trust in the Naboo ("Wesa no like da Naboo! Da Naboo tink day so smarty. Day tink day brains so big"). Apparently the emergence of a common enemy and the presence of common interests are not enough to spark a sustainable alliance.

Instead, before they can move forward together, both parties need a minimum amount of trust in one another to ensure smooth and sustainable cooperation. As mentioned before, the Gungans and the Naboo lack such trust during the initial stages of the conflict. Whether we trust others is dependent on whether we see them as *competent* (i.e., do they possess the skills and expertise required to aid us in achieving our goal), *benevolent* (i.e., do they take our needs and well-being into account), and *moral* (i.e., do they act in accordance with prevailing moral standards).[v] With these three frames in mind, we can easily see why the Gungans and Naboo have so little trust going into talks of an alliance.

The Gungans perceive the Naboo as having a history of disregarding their needs and looking down on them, which signals a lack of benevolence and thereby results in a lack of trust. It is possible that even the Jedi's own initial attitude towards the Gungan might have unintentionally fueled disrespect. Despite being enlightened Jedi, neither Qui-Gon nor Obi-Wan thinks highly of the Gungans. Their sentiments become apparent during Qui-Gon's initial interaction with Jar Jar Binks ("You almost got us killed! Are you brainless?" and "The ability to speak does not make you intelligent. Now, get out of here!") and later, when Qui-Gon mentions to Obi-Wan that he needs to go back to the city on Tatooine for some unfinished business, Obi-Wan responds ruefully: "Why do I sense we've picked up *another* pathetic lifeform?" It is unclear to what extent Gungans are aware of the Jedi's condescending attitude towards them, but it is unlikely that the Jedi's comments are helpful in creating or restoring trust.

The distrustful relationship between the two societies is also evident when the Trade Federation arrives with their droid army and the Gungans must leave their city. This turn of events makes the symbiotic relationship between the Gungans and Naboo more apparent but that alone does not lead to trust. When the leadership of both societies meet for The Summit in The Swamp, they keep a healthy distance from one another. The Queen's bodyguard, disguised as the Queen for the Queen's protection, opens by emphasizing that they come in peace. Boss Nass immediately devalues her presence, stating that he holds Naboo responsible for the invasion and its possible consequences: "Naboo biggen. Yousa bringen da Mackineeks. Yousa all bombad." At this point, forming an alliance seems impossible. With so little trust (and some measure of dislike) between them, even the threat of the Trade Federation doesn't seem like enough of a reason to cooperate.

Forming an alliance: establishing trust and ceding power

The impasse between the Gungans and the Naboo mirrors situations many of us observe in the world around us: even in the face of clearly shared common interests, a lack of trust stymies cooperation. Something needs to shake up the dynamics of the relationship for this pattern to reverse itself. This shake-up can occur in two ways. First, the shared interest may become so acute that it is *impossible* to ignore, and as we face it together, trust begins to develop. Second, we may see unexpected progress on the trust front, and even just a little forward motion in this area frees parties to reconsider their shared common interest and the value of cooperation.

We see this second form of shake-up—a truly transformative shift in the dynamic—when Queen Amidala steps out from behind her bodyguard decoy and reveals herself to the Gungans to amplify her plea for cooperation. She explains that the decoy usually is essential for her protection, but she does not want to engage in any deception with the Gungans as they talk through a possible alliance. Further, by sacrificing her own safety and willingly dropping her protection, she indicates her willingness to be vulnerable.

Being vulnerable is a strategic way to signal trust to the other negotiation party. When you make yourself vulnerable, you acknowledge that the other side possesses the power to exploit any weaknesses—while simultaneously expressing your belief that they are unlikely to do so. In the context of negotiation, a similar dynamic unfolds when we choose to disclose our interests to our counterpart, fully aware that they may use this information against us. This mutual awareness of the inherent vulnerability in sharing information contributes to the cultivation of trust between the parties. A parallel dynamic of mutual understanding similarly emerges in Padmé's revelation. In the realm of negotiation and trust dynamics, such reciprocity plays a pivotal role. By demonstrating my trust in you, I can initiate a reciprocal trust-building-and-repair process—especially when coupled with subsequent gestures, such as fostering a positive rapport, relinquishing a degree of control, and highlighting common ground. Padmé skillfully employs these tactics in the subsequent segments of her speech, and the simple act of displaying trust by making herself vulnerable is enough to disrupt the status quo and change the tone of the negotiation.

After revealing her true identity, Padmé again asks Boss Nass to reconsider the severity of the situation for both societies and the potential of cooperation: "The Trade Federation has destroyed all that we have worked so hard to build. If we do not act quickly, all will be lost forever. I ask you to help us." Padmé knows, however, that this plea won't be enough. Mutual tolerance and a shared threat alone, after all, are insufficient for building the robust trust necessary for effective negotiations, particularly when the pre-existing relationship is weak. And the Gungans' refusal to acknowledge the Federation as a direct threat gives them additional negotiation leverage and a somewhat perverse incentive to refuse to cooperate. With all this in mind, Padmé realizes that unless she changes something in the relationship's foundational power structure in the next three seconds, Boss Nass might revert to his standard response to the notion of working with the Naboo: a dismissive hand wave.

To build a sustainable alliance, both parties must acknowledge the threats *and* their interdependence in facing them; otherwise, any alliance formed will crumble at the first sign of danger. Padmé knows that a shift in trust alone won't be enough to generate an interdependent relationship. A shift in power is also needed. Her solution? Dropping to her knees, Padmé implores: "I ask you to help us. No, I *beg* you to help us. We are your humble servants. Our fate is in your hands." In falling to her knees, Padmé intentionally grants Boss Nass power over her.[4] Starting from a point of negotiation weakness, she voluntarily assumes even *greater* weakness. How is that smart?

Padmé's move turns out to be brilliant. In negotiation, it's easy to assume that the more power someone gets, the more selfish and self-interested they will behave. As it turns out, though, once a party has gained *complete* power and control over the other, they actually may become more mindful and considerate of the other party's needs.[vi] By kneeling to Boss Nass and relinquishing all power, Padmé *increases* the Gungans' receptiveness to the Naboo's needs. Her move bypasses the Gungans' initial instinct to blame the Naboo for the Trade Federation's arrival and to believe they are in no danger themselves. It prompts the Gungans to consider confronting the Trade Federation, whether to help themselves or to support the Naboo.

Indeed, after a few stressful moments of silence, Boss Nass's face is covered with amusement as he states: "Yousa no tinken yousa greater den da Gungans? Me-e-esa lika dis! Maybe wesa bein friends." And with this, the alliance between the Gungans and the Naboo becomes a reality.

---

[4] *Unlimited* power! You'd never have thought Palpatine would be envious of a Gungan, but he would have given Vader's right arm to trade places with Boss Nass at that moment.

The longevity of the alliance: possible futures

Alliances formed primarily in response to threats, of course, may not stand the test of time. Once the Trade Federation has been defeated, what will happen to the alliance between the Gungans and the Naboo? Will the Gungans and Naboo maintain their newly found alliance and use their agreement to cooperate and improve each other's quality of life? Or will the absence of the common enemy remove the very reason for their initial unity, rendering cooperation in the future less likely?

Subsequent episodes offer glimpses of new hope (and despair). In *Attack of the Clones*, Jar Jar Binks, who was initially ostracized and dismissed by his own people, has now become a representative for the Gungans working together with Padmé, who is Naboo's Senator in the Galactic Senate of the Republic. Later, when Padmé appoints Jar Jar to stand in for her in the Senate, we see evidence that she has a high degree of personal trust in Jar Jar[5] and that the relations between the two societies have reached a point where she can make this appointment without objections from her delegation and constituents. These developments indicate a certain degree of power-sharing and shared governance, which in turn could suggest a much-improved relationship between the Gungans and the Naboo.

Of course, trust is a tricky thing. It may be that the successful formation of their alliance (and Jar Jar's role in it) leads to an excessive amount of trust that ultimately backfires on a galactic scale. As Padmé's step-in Senator, after all, Jar Jar ends up getting played by Palpatine to increase Palpatine's power, setting the stage for the Clone Wars. As this unfortunate turn of events shows, even a trusting alliance does not always lead to desirable consequences.

Beyond these examples, however, it is not evident whether the Gungans and the Naboo succeed in maintaining a cooperative and respectful alliance, sharing governance fairly and equally, and representing all their diverse inhabitants after the events of the

---

[5] Of all Padmé's professional decisions, this is the most surprising. Not all diplomatic solutions are equal.

prequel trilogy.[6] We ourselves wonder whether their newly formed alliance will become an ironclad indicator of their freshly discovered collective strength and care for one another; or whether it will dissipate and see its members regressing to their pre-alliance ways.

Even if the alliance remains strong, of course, it nonetheless may be vulnerable to future challenges. Like any planet with finite resources, dependence on other societies, and vulnerability to more powerful invaders, Naboo may face catastrophic threats in the future. Climate change, erratic weather patterns, and water pollution, just to name a few examples, may threaten the livelihoods of the surface inhabitants and the well-being of the Gungans—and these harms may be experienced quite differently. Can both societies rest assured that when they bring forth a claim of imminent danger for aid, both parties will recognize it as such? Will their alliance be strong enough to prioritize each other's needs and act in each other's interest, even if it means temporarily diverting resources from their own people? Will they see each other as *us* and *them*, or will they unite under their superordinate identity[vii] and perhaps even adopt a name more representative of both societies—like Nabungan, Nagan, or Gungaboo?

We do not have answers to these questions. Still, given their unstable history before forming their alliance, and seeing the importance of fostering strong relationships in an uncertain and dangerous universe, we would be remiss not to advise both societies to reaffirm their commitment to each other and keep "bein friends."

---

[6] In *The Clone Wars* animated series, we see further activity by Jar Jar as part of the delegation representing the Naboo/Gungan shared home system, indicating some degree of ongoing alliance and shared governance. We also see further expressions of friendship between Padmé and Jar Jar. In *Revenge of the Sith*, Jar Jar and Boss Nass attend Padmé's funeral. Beyond the prequel trilogy era, however, things become unclear. In different material holding less-than-canon status, Jar Jar succeeds Padmé as Senator for Naboo, indicating that the alliance persisted, at least for a while. In canon-status material, however, there are only ambiguous hints that this occurred. An analysis of whether the alliance maintained its integrity after the immediate players moved on from their roles is justified in any event.

References

[i] Sherif, M. (1958). Superordinate goals in the reduction of intergroup conflict. *American Journal of Sociology*. 63(4).

[ii] Axelrod, R. (1986). An evolutionary approach to norms. *The American Political Science Review*. 80; Ostrom, E. (2000). Collective action and the evolution of social norms. *Journal of Economic Perspectives*. 14(3).

[iii] Lewicki, R. J. & Polin, B. (2013). The role of trust in negotiation processes. In R. Bachmann & A. Zaheer (Eds.), *Handbook of advances in trust research*. Edward Elgar Publishing.

[iv] Fisher, R. & Ury, W. (2011). *Getting to yes: Negotiating agreement without giving in* (3rd ed.). Penguin Books.

[v] Mayer, R. C., Davis, J. H. & Schoorman, F. D. (1995). An integrative model of organizational trust. *Academy of Management Review*. 20(3).

[vi] Rees, M. R., Tenbrunsel, A. E. & Bazerman, M. H. (2019). Bounded ethicality and ethical fading in negotiations: Understanding unintended unethical behavior. *Academy of Management Perspectives*. 33(1).

[vii] Brewer, M. B. & Gardner, W. (1996). Who is this "we"? Levels of collective identity and self representations. *Journal of Personality and Social Psychology*. 71(1).

How Mediation Might Have Saved the Galaxy

Amber Hill Anderson

Imagine your ship is being boarded by two ambassadors from the Supreme Chancellor. These ambassadors claim to want to negotiate, but they are notoriously good fighters and come armed with lightsabers. How conciliatory do you feel? How confident are you about advocating your position? Do you really think that these ambassadors are showing up for peaceful discussion, or are they really just trying to force a settlement?

The Jedi embody many different roles throughout the prequel trilogy, and these roles vary considerably in purposes and methods. Just in *The Phantom Menace* alone, the Jedi are described as or assumed to be ambassadors, spies, negotiators, arbitrators, bodyguards, mercenaries, police, peacekeepers, soldiers, sages, teachers, and recruiters. While these roles are not all mutually exclusive, the breadth of responsibilities that these functions serve blurs the lines between diplomatic (peacemaking) and forceful (policing or militaristic) approaches.[1] The conflicting roles overextend the Jedi and sow confusion and distrust for those around them, undermining the Jedi's aspirations for peace and stability in the galaxy.

A more effective approach in pursuit of peace would have been for the Jedi to consider assuming the role of *mediator*. Mediators are neutral third parties who facilitate conversations between individuals or groups in conflict to help them find areas of agreement.

---

[1] For more on the Jedi as "keepers of the peace," see Mayville, chapter 3.

Mediators cannot play multiple roles within a conflict or take sides; they must stay neutral and refrain from inserting their own substantive goals or agenda into the dispute resolution process. How, then, can they help conflicting parties? By facilitating the mediation process, in which parties communicate with each other to try to find agreements. In mediation, the decision-making power is in the hands of the parties, who exercise agency and self-determination in defining and resolving their conflict. Indeed, parties in mediation consent to participating and may leave the process at any point. Mediators do not impose a settlement or decide in favor of one party. If there is any outcome to the mediation process, it is an agreement upon which parties mutually and voluntarily agree.[2]

It may seem somewhat counterintuitive that one could work for peace by remaining impartial. But when it comes to dealing with conflict, we usually need more than just fighters and advocates. We need those who can guide participants through a fair and balanced resolution process while themselves remaining neutral. We do not see these kinds of individuals in *Star Wars*; rather, the narrative arcs of the saga build toward epic battles between good and evil. The good side often wins, thankfully, but even when it does, who knows how long these victories will last? In *Star Wars*, victory is not the end of conflict; usually it just sets up the beginning of the next round.

Can we aspire for more? Might a different form of peace, brought about by a different method of conflict resolution, prove more significant and enduring?

The prequel trilogy provides a cautionary tale in this regard. The Jedi win nearly every battle that takes place, and yet they lose the hearts and minds of the galactic community, as well as so much more. Had the Jedi avoided taking a sharp stance on the controversial issues that threatened to tear the Republic apart, instead taking the role of a neutral and adopting mediation practices, they

---

[2] For more on the possibilities of mediation in *Star Wars*, see Reynolds, chapter 12, in *Star Wars and Conflict Resolution: There Are Alternatives to Fighting* (Ebner & Reynolds eds., 2022).

may have emerged as more effective guardians and preservers of long-term peace in the galaxy.³

Neutrals... not partisan fighters

At the start of *The Phantom Menace*, Qui-Gon and Obi-Wan arrive on the ship of the Trade Federation as ambassadors on behalf of the Supreme Chancellor. They are purportedly there to negotiate—but of course any negotiation is doomed to fail, due to the secrecy of their dispatchment, their obvious allegiance to the Republic, the presence of weapons, and the lack of common ground for all involved parties. The Trade Federation does not want to settle under the Chancellor's terms, and thus not only do they not welcome the Jedi, they attack them.

One obvious reason the Trade Federation attacks is that they consider the Republic to be their opponents in the trade dispute. The Jedi may show up as negotiators or "ambassadors" of the Republic, but they are armed for wampa and ready to fight. Indeed, the Jedi often show almost no restraint when it comes to using violence to achieve their ends. Certainly their violence is more justifiable when they are defending themselves, such as when their ship is blown up by the Trade Federation and they are attacked by poison gas and droidekas. Using their weapons and the Force to escape danger is reasonable for the purpose of survival. Once the Jedi return to safety, of course, any attempt to switch back to the role of diplomat is tainted. The Jedi's violent actions on the ship align them with one side over the other and bring into question their motives for returning with Queen Amidala to Naboo when she loses her patience with the Galactic Senate. Are the Jedi simply continuing their diplomatic mission, or are they seeking revenge against the Trade Federation?⁴

---

³ This chapter analyzes the Jedi's actions as seen in the prequel trilogy. In the novels we sometimes encounter Jedi taking on the mantle of mediator. Notable examples are the roles played by Jedi in Alan Dean Foster's *The Approaching Storm* (2002) and Timothy Zahn's *Outbound Flight* (2006).

⁴ "I can only protect you. I can't fight a war for you," Qui-Gon is careful to clarify before they land on Naboo. It's good he got this out of the way ahead of time, given that he spends the rest of the movie fighting a war for her.

Mediators, by contrast, would not be involved in the use of violence. Mediators prevent violence by promoting open dialogue and exchange. With the Trade Federation, Obi-Wan and Qui-Gon may have been more successful if they assumed the role of neutral mediators seeking to improve communication, develop strategies, organize resources, and facilitate better understanding. The fact that the Jedi are not the leaders of any planet positions them well to serve as effective neutrals, since they are not beholden to serve the interest of one planet over another. Working as mediators and taking a neutral stance toward the dispute, they may have been able to uncover the true motives and interests of the Trade Federation, which in turn may have made an agreement with Queen Amidala and the Naboo easier to find.

Indeed, taking the time to listen and explore the positions and interests of the Trade Federation may even have allowed the Jedi to uncover the influence of Darth Sidious. Since the context of the Trade Federation is assumed and poorly understood, Qui-Gon does not provide them with an alternative path beyond invasion. He fails to understand and consider the motives of the Trade Federation beyond those of greed. Since he assumes that the blockade is about greed, rather than being the directive of some other powerful political player (here, Darth Sidious), he fails to establish a workable mediation table between the two parties right from the beginning.[5] The Jedi also lose the opportunity of addressing the conflict when it is ripe for de-escalation. When they board the Trade Federation's ship, no obvious war has yet begun and the parties are not yet fully entrenched in their oppositional positions. Mediation is more effective earlier in conflicts to intervene with parties, redirect building tension, and explore peaceful resolution. Yet Qui-Gon and Obi-Wan choose to disengage and leave the ship rather than persist in finding a path to communicate.[6] (To be fair, they had droidekas to deal with.)

---

[5] Recall Padmé in *Revenge of the Sith*: "This war represents a failure to listen."

[6] Sure, the Trade Federation was jamming communications, but isn't that what a determined pair of Jedi mediators would strive to overcome? Imagine Obi-Wan raising an eyebrow and telling a harried Governor Bibble: "Communication disruptions are our *speciality*."

Unfortunately, from this point forward, the Jedi do not attempt anything like mediation. Instead, they take the position of one side, vilify the actions and presumed motives of the other side, and turn to violence. The Jedi may have wisdom and insights to share with the parties in the galaxy, yet they are not often listened to as they themselves do not listen. Considering the Jedi emphasize that everyone should be patient and stretch out with their feelings, they would do well to consider their own advice. The deliberate approach involved in becoming attuned to the Force and appreciating the energy (positive and negative) that connects all living things would serve them well in helping parties work through disagreements. A calm demeanor, patience, and understanding of interpersonal dynamics are key tools for mediators in our own galaxy. Imagine how powerful these attributes would be if reinforced by the Force! The Force could have been used to help set up the parties for success at a mediation table—but the Jedi would have to remain neutral for this to happen.

Consent ... not coerced participation

Perhaps the Jedi's biggest misstep is when they attempt to make peace despite the lack of consent and buy-in from all parties to have them serve as peacemakers. As mediators know, a neutral process guide cannot effectively serve at the other end of a weapon. All participants in mediation must agree upon the neutral before proceeding. Consent is one of the hallmarks of mediation, and agreeing upon the neutral mediator is one of the first exercises of consent in mediation.

The Trade Federation do not consent to Qui-Gon and Obi-Wan serving as mediators. They make clear their low levels of trust by attacking the Jedi instead of sitting down with them to explain their demands of the Naboo. Then, once the lightsabers come out, the Jedi shift into new roles (soldiers), making it impossible for them to mediate an outcome.

If, instead of blowing things up, the Jedi had presented themselves as mediators needing consent from the Trade Federation to proceed, they could have discussed the reasons why mediation might be an effective approach for resolving the dispute. One of these reasons is confidentiality. In our galaxy, mediation processes enjoy strong confidentiality protections. Mediators do not share the information parties share in mediation with anybody external to the conflict.[7] Moreover, if one party shares something in confidence with the mediator, the mediator will never share this information with the other party without permission.

Confidentiality makes it possible to speak candidly, without fear of reprisal or retaliation. The Trade Federation may have an interest in speaking confidentiality with a mediator and/or other parties (and in keeping these conversations off Lord Sidious's radar), yet that possibility is never raised. Under the protection of confidentiality, the Trade Federation may have been more open and honest with Queen Amidala about their motives, and both sides could have explored areas of agreement to dovetail their interests. However, because Qui-Gon and Obi-Wan do not have a chance to take the time to explain the benefits of a confidential mediation, everyone resorts to posturing and violence.

Self-determination . . . not forced agreement

Queen Amidala initially assumes that the presence of the Jedi will lead to a peaceful negotiated agreement. When the Jedi engage in fighting, they set Amidala up for failure as she still hopes for diplomatic solutions despite everyone else moving to aggressive means. The Jedi never bring the parties to the table, instead getting themselves further entrenched in the conflict by becoming Amidala's bodyguards. In the meantime, the Trade Federation drafts an agreement that is lopsidedly favorable to their own interests. The terms of the agreement are never negotiated between the parties, much less mediated by the Jedi, and the situation quickly devolves into blockade and attack.

As described above, the Jedi's involvement on the Trade Federation's ship only intensifies the conflict. Had they served instead as mediators, they could have brought Amidala and the

---

[7] The exception to confidentiality is threat of imminent harm against oneself, others, and especially Padawans and children.

Trade Federation together to discuss areas of common interest before jointly drafting an agreement. Self-determination in mediation refers to the ability of all parties to freely participate in defining the problem, identifying possible responses, and crafting an agreement. Self-determination is closely linked to consent because both concepts require the parties to exercise free choice and agency in the substance and process of dispute resolution. Even when parties do not reach agreement, the exercise of looking for common ground can be fruitful and enlightening for everyone involved.

Another way of thinking about self-determination in mediation is through the lens of party empowerment. Mediators guide parties through a mediation process that helps the parties identify their own priorities and interests before figuring out how to fashion a joint agreement. With this in mind, were the Jedi to embrace the role of mediator, they would have to reconsider their inclination toward mind tricks and manipulations.[8] Skillful mediators clarify the positions and interests of parties to help them reach self-determined solutions. No mind tricks are used, and parties tend to be much more satisfied when they determine their own outcomes. In addition, parties are more likely to follow agreements that they themselves have created. With this in mind, were mediation to become a more common dispute resolution process in the *Star Wars* universe, the "Agreement to Mediate"[9] often signed between parties and mediators before the process begins would need to include a clause that prohibits the mediator or any party from using Jedi mind tricks. Using the Force in this way would undermine consent and self-determination.

Qui-Gon . . . possible mediator material?

In *The Phantom Menace*, we see no evidence that the Jedi are effective diplomats or negotiators, on their own behalf or in the service

---

[8] For more on manipulation and backlash, see Maravilla, chapter 15, in *Star Wars and Conflict Resolution: There Are Alternatives to Fighting* (Ebner & Reynolds eds., 2022).

[9] In our galaxy, mediation agreements lay out the rules of the game for the mediation process and are completed by parties and mediators before the process begins. Although the terms can vary, most agreements include clauses about issues discussed above such as confidentiality and the voluntary nature of the process.

of the Republic. Importantly, they lack key skills that mediators cannot function without. They are poor listeners and, when they hear something that they don't like, tend to use the Force to get their way. The Jedi of the prequels are often arrogant, deceptive, and condescending. They are frequently oblivious or indifferent to the interests of others.

Qui-Gon provides an excellent example of these deficiencies. Blithely assuming that he has earned Queen Amidala's trust, he ignores Padmé's (ironically, Amidala's) wishes. When Padmé tries to contribute to planning their moves on Tatooine, Qui-Gon's poor listening skills and disregard for Padmé's concerns lead to high-stakes, unilateral decisions on his part, such as wagering with Watto for Anakin's freedom. (Luckily that bet pays off—though, of course, more than luck was involved.) Additionally, Qui-Gon is dishonest about what he is doing with Anakin's blood, telling Anakin that he is checking for infections but actually looking for midi-chlorians, to see if Anakin should be trained as a Jedi. It is not clear if Qui-Gon informed Anakin's mother, Shmi, of the test in advance, to give her the opportunity to object. He only presents her with the bottom line afterward: Anakin has Jedi potential. At this stage, she does not raise an overt objection, of course, but how can she, considering the power and information imbalance between herself and the Jedi? Finally, Qui-Gon does not make more than a passing effort to free Shmi when he makes the wager with Watto. Perhaps Qui-Gon believes on some level that Shmi's continued servitude will make it easier to indoctrinate Anakin into the Jedi ways (no attachment and all that). Given that Qui-Gon wants to take Anakin as an apprentice, leaving Shmi behind may serve his interest. Concealing, obfuscating, and manipulating to promote one's own self-interests are not character traits of a mediator.

At the same time, Qui-Gon shows some personal qualities that suggest he has potential as a mediator. Despite his early dismissive treatment of Jar Jar,[10] he does listen when Jar Jar tells him about

---

[10] Dismissing Jar Jar with "The ability to speak does not make you intelligent" is Jedi Master-level condescension.

Gunga City and is able to convince Jar Jar to take him and Obi-Wan there, not through mind tricks but by appealing to Jar Jar's interests.[11] Additionally, Qui-Gon is considerably more open to different perspectives and possibilities than many of the other Jedi in the prequels, often questioning received wisdom and making sure he understands the basis for assumptions. When he pushes back on the Jedi's reluctance to train Anakin because of Anakin's age, for example, he exhibits one of the most important characteristics of a mediator: the ability to ask why. Finally, although Qui-Gon can be gruff at times, he generally has a patient and gentle manner that would work well in a mediation setting. The ability to treat all people (and creatures, and droids) with respect is foundational to the practice of mediation, and Qui-Gon often exhibits genuine respect for others.

How might the story have changed, had Qui-Gon built on this promising foundation and leaned into mediation more? If only someone had told Qui-Gon not to get cocky, kid, as he made up rules on the fly for dealing with others and problems. Imagine that Qui-Gon had thoughtfully and intentionally assumed the role of a mediator from the outset, including an appreciation for the values of mediation around party consent and self-determination. A mutually agreeable and peaceful solution might have been found between the Trade Federation and Queen Amidala. The invasion and war that claimed so many lives on Naboo could have been avoided. In short, many of the challenges that Qui-Gon encounters in *The Phantom Menace* would have benefited from a mediation approach. He could have spared himself all that time in the swamps of Naboo and the sands of Tatooine, and along the way, perhaps spared the galaxy from civil war. The Force was with him, but he missed his chance.

---

[11] Admittedly, he hammered on Jar Jar's interest of avoiding a thousand terrible things heading his way, and he teamed up with Obi-Wan for a bad cop / bad cop routine to persuade Jar Jar. Still, Qui-Gon was able to identify an interest of Jar Jar and use it in negotiation, so perhaps there's hope for him.

To be clear, serving in a neutral capacity is not easy, and not every conflict is right for mediation. Sometimes parties make decisions that the mediator finds problematic, as a matter of the mediator's own values or sense of justice. Sometimes parties are coming from such disparate positions of power that the prospect of true self-determination seems impossibly difficult to achieve. Had the Jedi seriously considered serving as mediators in the Trade Federation conflict, they may have reasonably concluded that a mediated agreement between Queen Amidala and the Trade Federation would not be fair due to the power imbalance and the Queen's avowed propensity to avoid war. But we see no evidence that the Jedi ever considered taking a mediation-minded approach to the conflict at all.

Peace made at the end of any energized particle weapon is likely to be fragile or to fail. A stable peace could have been better facilitated by the Jedi had they (or even a subset of their Order) served as mediators, rather than in the myriad of conflicting roles they embodied. Remember, the Jedi were uniquely poised to play the focused role of a neutral given they are not representatives of any one planet. Their connection to the Force and methodical approaches positioned them well to learn and adapt the role of a mediator. Anybody thinking of setting up a New Jedi Order, or a New New Jedi Order, would do well to give this some thought.

ROGUE ONE
There's a problem on the horizon

Rebellions Are Built on Hope ... but a Little Kairos Can't Hurt

Kimberly Y. W. Holst

A blind man walks through the streets of a bustling city. He encounters a group of soldiers leading prisoners away from the city square, and the soldiers begin firing their blasters at him. Bystanders and prisoners alike watch helplessly as the scene plays out, certain that the blind man is doomed. Yet he dodges each blast and leaves the battle unscathed.

Out of context, this scenario sounds like nothing more than an unbelievable stroke of luck. But let's put the scene in context. In Jedha City, Chirrut Îmwe, a blind man, walks toward a group of stormtroopers leading Jyn Erso and Cassian Andor to prison. Drawing on his finely tuned senses, the skills of another nearby guardian, and his faith in the Force, Chirrut states, "I am one with the Force, and the Force is with me." He then walks calmly into the blaster fire and, with an assist from Baze Malbus, successfully defeats the horde of stormtroopers.

How did Chirrut do it? It wasn't only the Force, and it wasn't simply luck. By recognizing the perfect moment to draw on the Force and engage his opponents, Chirrut used *Kairos* to avoid harm and free Jyn and Cassian.

I don't need luck

Kairos is not luck, or rather, it's not merely luck. Kairos is a Greek word meaning *the opportune moment*. At first glance, the combination of timing and opportunity may look like luck, as with Chirrut in the city square. Upon closer examination, however, this encounter and many other apparently lucky moments are actually *Kairic moments*, where parties use knowledge, observation, and flexibility to recognize and act at just the right time.

In this chapter, we examine two aspects of Kairos. First, we consider the skills that allow us to recognize and take advantage of Kairic moments. Throughout history, Kairos has been referred to as an opening, a shot, or an alignment of circumstances where an actor can successfully accomplish her goal.[i] But merely taking an opening or a shot when it presents itself is not enough to be Kairic. The actor must also be prepared. She needs to have been practicing her aim with a blaster or mastering her control of the Force if she wants to make the best use of that moment. In this way, Kairos is properly understood as the combination of timing and preparation that allows the moment to be ripe for the actor's taking.[1] What's more, skillful preparation may even make it possible to manufacture Kairos in some situations. By putting actions in motion so that an opportunity is more likely to arise in the future when the actor has the information, skills, and other tools at the ready, the actor has positioned herself to capitalize on a Kairic moment.[ii]

Second, we consider the persuasive dimension of Kairos.[iii] Negotiators and others can use Kairos as a tool to make an appeal or create space for negotiated agreement. Not only can a negotiator be on the lookout for his own Kairic moments, but he can also be looking for Kairic moments that may appeal to the opposing party and, ideally, use those Kairic moments to convince the other party to choose the course of action that the negotiator desires.

Kairos is an important tool in the negotiator's toolkit. In any conflict, it is important to be on the lookout for Kairic opportunities. There is no doubt that careful planning and the ability to build trust are important parts of any negotiation process; equally

---

[1] An example from the original trilogy: After Luke finally manages to deflect not one but three laser bolts fired at him by the training remote, Han waves it off as luck. "In my experience, there's no such thing as luck," Obi-Wan—who has prepared his entire life for whatever may come—gently teaches.

important, however, is the recognition that unexpected opportunities may arise during the negotiation and a negotiator primed to identify Kairos may be more likely to identify and benefit from such opportunities. By being open and flexible when presented with Kairic moments, a negotiator can make the most of unexpected developments in a negotiation.

You have to start somewhere . . .

. . . so let's start with preparation. Preparation is key to a successful negotiation. A negotiator's preparation may include conducting thorough research, imagining possible outcomes in light of her interests and her opponent's interests, and determining the outer limits of an acceptable proposal. She may also think in advance of how she will approach the negotiation, including anticipating and planning for difficult tactics or hardball maneuvers.[2] Without preparation, negotiators cannot make or evaluate proposals that address all the relevant interests on the table within the context of the available resources and opportunities. They need to prepare so that they aren't flying blind into bargaining.

When it comes to Kairos, preparation can help negotiators identify Kairic moments by enabling negotiators to anticipate the motivations of their counterparts so that they may take advantage of openings in the discussion where certain proposals or arguments may be particularly convincing. Moreover, it's easier for prepared negotiators to adapt their negotiation strategies to unexpected developments, which may allow them to see and capitalize upon Kairic moments. Negotiators must be careful, however, not to prepare so rigidly that they cannot respond to developments not accounted for in planning. Preparation is wasted if negotiators fail to recognize Kairos and miss the opportunity to act on well-prepared efforts. To capitalize on Kairos, one must negotiate in the moment *and* have prepared to negotiate well in advance of that moment.

---

[2] For more on hardball tactics in conflict and negotiation, see Maravilla, chapter 15, in *Star Wars and Conflict Resolution: There Are Alternatives to Fighting* (Ebner & Reynolds eds., 2022).

For an example of how preparation makes seizing opportune moments possible, recall the opening scene of *Rogue One*. Director Krennic identifies and acts on a Kairic moment when he demands that Galen Erso return to the Empire and complete work on the Death Star:

GALEN: What do you want?
KRENNIC: The work has stalled. I need you to come back.
GALEN: I won't do it, Krennic.
KRENNIC: We were on the verge of greatness.

Krennic has done his homework. When he seeks out Galen, he does so knowing that Galen will do anything to keep his wife and daughter safe. Krennic has researched Galen's current circumstances, assessed the likely values that Galen holds, and identified the potential benefits and detriments to himself and to Galen. Krennic also knows that the Death Star needs to be constructed immediately, as the growing rebel alliance will not be quieted without a great show of force. Although the Death Star can be built without Galen, it will take longer and likely will not achieve its deadly potential if Galen is not leading the design and construction. All this together forms Krennic's Kairic moment—he needs Galen in order to build the Death Star *now*, and he knows that Galen feels vulnerable *now*, with his family in immediate danger. Krennic capitalizes on this moment to take Galen back to the Empire.

Of course, the situation devolves when Lyra shows up and shoots Krennic. Krennic adapts to the situation, however, turning it into an opportunity to rid Galen of familial distractions and take him back to Project Stardust, all at once. Krennic identifies his Kairic moment and continues to bolster it through *ongoing flexibility*, a trait that is sort of a Kairic superpower. We'll discuss this trait below. But first, let's consider another aspect of Kairos: namely, the value for negotiators of spotting Kairic moments that will help the other side. Perhaps surprisingly, identifying your opponent's Kairic moment can be just as helpful in negotiation as having one yourself.

"Congratulations, you are being rescued."

Recognizing one's own Kairos is important, but it's just one piece of the puzzle. A successful negotiator also needs to be on the lookout for the opponent's Kairic moments. In this way, Kairos serves as a persuasive tool for the negotiator who recognizes the opponent's Kairic moment and uses it to induce a favorable resolution. A child hoping to watch the Podraces in the afternoon may attempt to create a Kairic moment by checking the security on the vaporator systems around the farm in the morning. When it's time to head to the stadium, he can point out that the chores have been completed and preempt his parents' argument that he needs to stay and help on the farm. But when his parents don't agree and mention that they need some items from the market, the child can capitalize upon his parents' Kairic moment and point out that he can pick up those items on his way back from the Podraces—persuading his parents that letting him go to the village will serve their interests as well.

Pointing out a Kairic moment to an opponent may not always be as simple as it sounds. For an opponent to accept an assertation that this is her Kairic moment, there must be some level of trust or credibility between the parties—it's rarely enough to tell a party that these are not the droids they're looking for and hope they believe you. If trust or credibility is lacking, a party may not be willing to recognize the other's assertion of a Kairic moment.

An example of a party failing to pick up on a Kairic moment suggested by a non-trusted, non-credible party occurs when the Alliance refuses to listen to Jyn Erso's arguments that the Alliance should attack the Empire's new Death Star before it can be used to destroy any planets. Even after hearing Jyn's initial plea, it is apparent that the leaders of the Alliance disagree about whether to stand and fight the Empire or to retreat and regroup:

PAMLO:	We must scatter the fleet. We have no recourse but to surrender.
BAIL ORGANA:	Are we really talking about disbanding something that we've worked so hard to create?
RADDUS:	We can't just give in!
VASPAR:	We joined an alliance, not a suicide pact.
ORGANA:	We've only now managed to gather our forces.

As these scattered viewpoints suggest, the Alliance is a disorganized band of malcontents. But Jyn offers the Alliance a clear strategic objective and a glimmer of hope. Gathering her courage, she patiently continues to explain to this group of strangers that her father built a weakness in the Death Star. All they need to do is go to Scarif, locate the Death Star plans, find the weakness, figure out how to exploit it, and destroy the Death Star.

Admiral Raddus recognizes the opportunity that Jyn is presenting: "If she's telling the truth, we need to act now." Emboldened, Jyn stresses again that "[t]he time to fight is now" and "[r]ebellions are built on hope." Unfortunately, the Council is not moved and declines to act on Jyn's information. Although it turns out that Jyn is correct in asserting that this is the Kairic moment to act, the Alliance leaders do not trust her. Her plan does not address the disparate viewpoints and concerns presented at the meeting. Moreover, Jyn is an unknown quantity with no established credibility—and the Council is understandably skeptical of the daughter of the man who helped build the Death Star. She can show them no proof that the weakness exists, and even if it does exist, she cannot assure them that they will be able to exploit this weakness. All these factors prevent the Alliance from recognizing its own Kairic moment.

As a result, Jyn and Cassian go rogue and seek to capture the plans on their own. The partnership between Jyn and Cassian provides a useful contrasting example of how a trusting relationship can make it easier for one person to help another find Kairos. In the past, Cassian had serious doubts about Jyn and her father; but at this point in the story, he now believes what she is saying and wants her to lead the mission. His band of saboteurs, assassins, and spies follow suit when they see the deep trust between Cassian and Jyn—and they too develop their own faith in Jyn and her plan as they listen to her speak. In this way, trust allows for shared recognition of Kairos. Cassian and the others not only see the opportune moment, they convince Jyn that the moment is *hers* for the taking, even without the support of the Alliance. This turn of events leads to the successful, but nonetheless devastating, Battle of Scarif.

If only the Alliance had seized Kairos sooner and followed Jyn in her efforts—might Scarif have avoided destruction? Would Jyn end up leading the Alliance in future efforts to overthrow the Empire? The Alliance's failure to believe Jyn's appeal means that we'll never know. And yet, Cassian's transformative recognition of Jyn's own opportune moment ultimately gives the Rebel Alliance what it most desperately needs. If rebellions are built on hope, the Alliance's new hope is built on Kairos.

Your behavior, Jyn Erso, is continually unexpected

Entering a negotiation with a plan is a smart approach and an important step in the preparation process. Failing to create a plan is like Chirrut walking into the mass of stormtroopers without having honed his Force-enabled fighting skills or making sure that Baze was nearby to assist. However, even the best laid plans can be thrown off course in a flash for any number of reasons: the opposing party presents new information, the opposing party acts illogically or in a manner inconsistent with expectations, the opposing party refuses to negotiate within agreed upon boundaries (or, indeed, at all), outside information or parties cause the negotiation to veer off course, or some other unexpected circumstance. In fact, if there is anything you should assume about negotiation, it is that *this is not going to go the way you think*. And so, part of your planning must take that into account. Plan for flexibility, and you're primed to recognize Kairos, either for yourself or for your opponent.

Flexibility is an important trait to have in any negotiation, but it is particularly important when it comes to Kairos. The ability to pivot and move quickly in order to act on an opportunity is essential to successfully capturing Kairos or convincing an opponent to act on a Kairic moment. Such flexibility requires the negotiator to remain fully present in the moment during a negotiation. Instead of relying on assumptions, flexible negotiators must actively listen, pay attention to cues presented by the opponent, ask questions that clarify context and broaden understanding, and be ready to act when new information suggests a Kairic moment that the negotiator had not been anticipating.

Jyn and Cassian demonstrate just this sort of flexibility and adaptability during the Battle of Scarif. By preparing themselves to maximize opportunities, they primed themselves to identify Kairic moments and adapt to make the most of those moments. As a result, they readily adapt to a change of strategy in order to achieve the objective of stealing the Death Star plans. Initially, they plan to use a stolen Imperial shuttle to infiltrate the Imperial base on Scarif. Their goal is to locate the plans for the Death Star and skedaddle back to Yavin 4. The Rebel Alliance may not have sanctioned the mission, but Jyn and Cassian reason that once the Alliance has the plans in hand, they will locate the weakness Galen built into the design, exploit that weakness, and destroy the Death Star.

As the battle unfolds, unexpected challenges arise. The crew members encounter heavy resistance from Imperial forces. The situation becomes dire, and it is clear that the original plan is unlikely to work. They won't be able to retrieve the plans and escape. The Rebel fleet has arrived, however, and so Jyn and Cassian adapt their plan. Instead of retrieving the plans and escaping, they decide to directly transmit the plans to the Rebel fleet above Scarif. This change in plans requires them to reach the top of the communication tower, establish a direct data link with the Rebel flagship *Profundity*, and transmit the plans to the ship.

For this plan to work, Jyn and Cassian must fight and climb their way to the top of a tower. The remaining members of their team must make contact with the Rebel fleet and instruct them to destroy the shield gate—without getting vanquished by the Imperial fleet in the meantime—so that Jyn and Cassian can transmit the Death Star data to them. Through a series of actions too complex (and thrilling) to describe here, each team is successful. They overcome each obstacle they encounter with determination, courage, and flexibility. The tower is climbed, the data link is connected, the plans are obtained, the communications array is aligned, the fighters are held off, the shield gate is destroyed, and the data is transmitted and received. Each piece, in a dazzling display of ongoing Kairos, falls into place just in time.

While Jyn and Cassian had a plan when they started the mission, they paid attention to the developing situation and pivoted when needed. Importantly, they planned for flexibility and adaptability at the outset of the mission—priming themselves for Kairos. As Jyn tells the crew, they need to act chance by chance until they win . . . or until the chances are gone. Their adaptability allowed them to act on each Kairic moment as it came along. By acting in the moment and being flexible with their plans, Jyn and Cassian were able to obtain and transmit the Death Star's plans before Scarif was destroyed.

The same flexibility is apparent in Admiral Raddus's management of the situation high above Scarif. He seems to have launched with no more of a plan beyond wanting to support Rogue One's mission. In a series of in-the-moment pivots, he does just that. Finding the right moment in the right point of space to punch a disabled Imperial Star Destroyer through the shield gate is just one example of his skillful identification and utilization of Kairic moments. The admiral's flexibility wins the day for the rebellion, allowing them to receive the data they so desperately need. Even Darth Vader's relentless pursuit of the downloaded data from the *Profundity's* tip to its tail could not overcome the crew's flexibility and courage, and Vader is foiled—well, temporarily at least—by the *Tantive IV's* last-ditch, last-moment launch from the flagship's docking bay.

What is that they've sent us? Hope

Using Kairos in a negotiation can lead to successful outcomes and a strengthened alliance between parties who have identified an opportune moment for resolving their conflict. Remember that employing Kairos in a negotiation requires the negotiator to focus on three key items: preparation, trust, and flexibility.

First, Kairos is more than just an opportune moment. To be successful in opportune moments, you must be prepared. Before the negotiation, prepare with Kairos in mind by conducting thorough research, finding ways to create opportunities, creating a flexible plan, and understanding the interests of all parties affected by the negotiation. If you were negotiating the purchase of a home, for example, you'd thoroughly research the neighborhood, think about different options to finance the purchase, identify areas of improvement and unique benefits of the home, and seek to understand specific interests of the seller. By thoroughly preparing for the negotiation, you prime yourself to identify opportunities that may arise. For example, if you learn that the sellers have already vacated the property and each day it remains on their hands is costing them money, you can use that information to get them to lower their asking price in return for a speedy closing of the deal. This is an example of Kairos aided by thorough preparation.

Second, use Kairos as leverage—but don't be a used landspeeder salesman about it. It is important to be sincere and build trust. Trust and credibility are important aspects of successfully convincing an opponent that this is their Kairic moment. When you have built a relationship based on trust, suggesting a resolution that is beneficial to the opponent will seem sincere and may be more likely to lead to agreement. If the information you present during the negotiation turns out to be credible, for example, your counterpart is more likely to trust you and agree that the suggested moment is an opportune one.

Third, be flexible and present in the negotiation. Actively listen to your counterpart, ask questions to help identify new information, notice when changing circumstances or information generate Kairic moments, and be ready to pivot to seize those moments or convince your opponent to seize them. You can never be certain what will happen in a negotiation. Unexpected information or behavior are challenges that cannot be fully anticipated or planned for. Rather than letting unexpected moments frustrate the negotiation process, pay attention as they happen. Those unexpected moments may present the Kairos you've been looking for.

References

[i] Rountree, C. (2020). Kairos and American legal practice. *Nevada Law Journal*. 20.

[ii] *Id*.

[iii] Berger, L. (2015). Creating Kairos at the Supreme Court: Shelby County, Citizens United, Hobby Lobby, and the judicial construction of right moments. *Journal of Appellate Practice & Process*. 16.

7

The Empire Is a Terrible Place to Work (But So Is the Alliance)

Amanda Reinke, Paul Story & John Martin

The Empire is obviously a terrible place to work. Between compelled employment, killing workers' family members, and the potential of being Force choked by your supervisor, it's clear that fear is the main motivator for job performance. Imperial supervisors rely on carrots (reward) and sticks (punishment)—well, mostly sticks—and these rarely lead to excellent performance. How many employees does Vader need to choke to figure this out, anyway?

Surely the Alliance is better when it comes to working conditions and job satisfaction. But if you take a closer look—and this chapter will do just that—you find the Alliance also has workplace challenges, including distrust of outsiders, disagreement among leadership, and lack of employee buy-in.

In the *Star Wars* saga, workplace power struggles push forward the plot in ways that often resonate with our own experiences as employees and supervisors.[1] By analyzing workplace interactions in the story, we gain insight into real-life issues affecting most if not all of us. What can we learn about conflict dynamics from workplace culture, for example? Conversely, what aspects of workplace culture encourage or discourage destructive internal conflict? What are the potential impacts of different management styles on

---

[1] For more on how you can obtain comparable two-way insights by focusing on the dynamics of workplace meetings, see Allen, Castro & Eden, chapter 18, in *Star Wars and Conflict Resolution: There Are Alternatives to Fighting* (Ebner & Reynolds eds., 2022).

employees, and how can supervisors use this information to make themselves more effective?

In this chapter, we use *Rogue One* to explore the employee motivators used in the workplaces of the Empire and the Alliance. We examine the role of external pressures on employee performance in light side and dark side arenas, taking care to consider what roles personal value and internal motivators play. It turns out that what we discover about the relationships between employees and supervisors in a galaxy far, far away can teach us how to reduce conflict in our own workplaces.

It's (not) a peaceful life

The Empire is a shining example of negative workplace culture and the potential results of an employee-supervisor relationship built upon *junk motivation*.[i] Junk motivation is the pressure to perform by trying to live up to others' expectations, not your own. The more one is motivated to live up to external expectations because they feel like they "have to" or "ought to," the more driven they are by junk motivation. External motivators such as "sticks" (punishments, Force chokes) and "carrots" (rewards, power, fame) are common ways to set junk expectations. Sticks and carrots indicate what behaviors an employee should or should not perform and can often leave employees feeling manipulated and controlled. What would you do if you knew Vader was going to be at your annual review, ready to choke you if you don't live up to his expectations? To what lengths would you go to get that bonus and buy that sweet landspeeder you've had your eye on, or perhaps even to get a good word in with the Emperor?

At best, external motivators influence only some employees' behavior; at worst, they cause resentment among the larger pool of employees. Employee resentment, whether from being Force choked one too many times or from not being able to achieve desired rewards, can lead to anger. And just as one fighter with a sharp stick and nothing left to lose can carry the day, all it takes is one employee disgruntled enough with this treatment to bring an entire organization to its knees.

In *Rogue One*, that disgruntled employee is Galen Erso. Galen, a former Imperial engineer, is now a family man and farmer on a far-off planet. One day, Galen's old boss Krennic arrives and tries to convince Galen to work for the Empire again. Unfortunately for Krennic, Galen hated working for the Empire and offers up every excuse to avoid going back. He implies that he retired because his wife died (who hasn't used this line to get out of work before?) and he'd rather live a life of quiet peace, adding that he can no longer work because of his feeble mind (the Empire should really consider offering family and mental health leave). Krennic knows that Galen is lying, and in an effort to negotiate, Krennic dangles a tempting "carrot" by offering fame and fortune for him and his family. Galen doesn't budge, so Krennic resorts to the coercive "stick," killing Galen's not-actually-dead wife and attempting to seize Galen's child, Jyn, as a bargaining chip.

This approach seems to work! Galen gives in and works for the Empire under Krennic's supervision. And, throughout the saga, the Empire repeatedly uses the same mix of carrots and sticks to recruit, retain, and motivate employees. But although Krennic's carrot-and-stick approach to recruitment works in the short term, it is not ultimately successful, as Galen betrays Krennic in the long run. Indeed, the Empire's dependence on carrots and sticks becomes the reason why the Rebels can destroy not one but three Imperial superweapons—two Death Stars and Starkiller Base.[2]

In workplaces in our own galaxy, employees often experience carrot-and-stick workplace cultures as negatively competitive and controlling, which can lead to performance problems and conflict. Employees may lash out at the organization (e.g., theft, sabotage), at their coworkers (e.g., threats, bullying, insults), or even at clients (e.g., misleading, lying). Other forms of retaliation may be more passive, including calling in sick when healthy, purposefully doing work incorrectly, leaving early, searching for other jobs during

---

[2] Consider: Did cutting off Luke's arm motivate him to accept Vader's job offer? And, when taking him upstairs to the C-suite to sweeten the deal didn't work either, how did trying to kill Luke with Force lightning in front of his own father work out for old Emperor Palpatine?

work hours, misusing company assets, browsing Wookieepedia on company time, or just doing the bare minimum. Even the employee who tries to please a demanding boss (like Matt, the radar technician, who is seriously killing it out there!) may suffer in the short and long terms. When employees fear they might lose their jobs, for example, they often spend too much time at work, which may lead to conflict at home. Moreover, constantly trying to reach that carrot or avoid that stick can leave you exhausted, burned out, and stressed, possibly causing headaches, stomach aches, ulcers, and an overall sense of malaise.

Take Galen. He hated working for the Empire so much he moves to another planet, becomes a farmer, lies about his wife's death, and claims mental insufficiency. After being coerced back to work (big stick), he works for years to plant a weakness in the Death Star in the hopes of supporting the Empire's downfall. Does that sound like someone who enjoys his job?

I deserve an audience . . .

Of course, it wasn't just one bad boss that drove Galen away. It was the entire Imperial workplace culture. After all, where do you think Krennic learned how to treat his employees? (Someone please cue up "The Imperial March.") Krennic models his approach to employee supervision after that of his own superiors, Darth Vader and Grand Moff Tarkin, who frequently use coercive power, such as fear and intimidation, to motivate employees.[3] This dark side to management leaves little room for employee freedom, self-value, and innovation, all of which typically help people see the *personal value* they bring in the workplace.

Personal value is the feeling of satisfaction that comes from completing tasks or goals that, from your perspective, are important and useful. Many supervisors do not recognize the importance of personal value for their employees. They dangle

---

[3] In Timothy Zahn's *Thrawn: Treason* (2019), Project Stardust's assistant director, Brierly Ronan, observes that Director Krennic focuses only on getting the job done, whereas the Emperor and Tarkin derive pleasure from playing their underlings against one another.

motivational carrots (pay, benefits, recognition, praise) because they believe these are what motivate their subordinates.[ii] While it is true that we all want (and need) good pay and benefits, managers often overestimate the power and importance of these factors. Employees actually rate intrinsic factors, like growth and professional development—things with personal value to them—as much more impactful and motivating. Ironically, many supervisors themselves desire personal value by way of validation from their superiors, even as they fail to see that their employees seek that same validation.

Krennic, for example, is desperate for recognition. His supervisors swing the carrots of approval and appreciation in front of him, but they never actually approve of or appreciate anything he does. Accordingly, over the course of the film, we see Krennic becoming increasingly angry and frustrated. Consider his exchange with his supervisor, Grand Moff Tarkin, after Krennic demonstrates the power of the Death Star for the first time:

> TARKIN: I believe I owe you an apology, Director Krennic. Your work exceeds all expectations.
> KRENNIC: [hopefully] And you'll tell the Emperor as much?
> TARKIN: I will tell him that his patience with your misadventures . . . has been rewarded with a weapon that will bring a swift end to the Rebellion.
> KRENNIC: And that that was only an inkling of its destructive potential.
> TARKIN: I will tell him that I will be taking control over the weapon . . . I first spoke of years ago, effective immediately.
> KRENNIC: [outraged] We stand here amidst my achievement! Not yours!

Stunned by Tarkin taking credit for his work and likely blocking his advancement, Krennic turns to Darth Vader. (You know someone is feeling pretty fed up with their workplace culture if they turn to Vader for help.)

Darth Vader, of course, does not help Krennic. When Krennic appeals to Vader, Vader simply expresses disdain for the entire Death Star project. Imagine how you would feel if you asked your boss for approval and they replied that your department should be cut. What's more, Vader appears incensed by Krennic's drive for recognition. Krennic tries to blame things going wrong on Tarkin, but Vader refuses to interfere with Tarkin's carrot approach. Instead, Vader relies on his own tried-and-true stick, the Force choke, served up with a side of snark aimed directly at Krennic's ambitions and insecurities: "Be careful not to choke on your own aspirations, Director." The unmistakable intent of this message can be heard light years away.

At this point, we would understand if Krennic were to take a page from Galen Erso's book and start over in some other line of work far away. Krennic has no apparent reason to continue his current career path and, from a mental health perspective, he must be suffering from the overall strain of extreme responsibility in such a toxic workplace culture. Constantly fighting with staff and with superiors will take a toll. Anybody in Krennic's shoes would be likely to suffer deep burnout, and many would be looking for the door.

Yet he stays with the Empire. From our perspective as organizational analysts, it's interesting that the only person in the galaxy with the skills to pull Project Stardust together and deliver the Death Star is also the least interested person in the galaxy in blowing up planets. Krennic was in it for the carrots, not the mission; and even when Krennic got sticks, he continued to work hard and hope for carrots someday. Likewise, in dysfunctional workplaces in our own galaxy, carrots and sticks will keep many employees working—at least for a while. Some will stay, still believing (like Krennic) the next carrot is in their reach. Many others will respond like Galen: they will look for a way out or, even worse, for a way to destroy what their employer holds dear.

You're all rebels, aren't you?

Meanwhile, the Alliance leadership isn't doing any better (though, to be fair, no Force chokes that we know of). Throughout the original *Star Wars* trilogy, we see the Rebels as the heroes—united, hopeful, and working towards personal and collective freedom (the light). It's all very nice and has you cheering for the Rebels like an Ewok (yub nub!). But in *Rogue One* we see the difficulties of the early Rebellion, when hope is waning and unity is fraught. Like the Empire, the "employees" of the Rebellion are compelled by their own junk motivation: division, deception, subterfuge, and disagreement.

Leadership decisions in the Alliance, like the Empire, are repeatedly driven by fear. Even though the Alliance has a shared vision of an Empire-less future, complicated politics and suspicions get in the way of solidarity and trust. For example, the Alliance leadership wants Jyn's help but because she is the daughter of Galen, a known Imperial weapon developer, they abduct and threaten her (hello, coercion and hostile work environment). As another example, Saw Gerrera (a former Alliance affiliate) imprisons and tortures potential allies because he fears they are Imperial spies. In these ways, the Alliance confuses peace with terror, much like the Empire but perhaps less easy to see (those Force chokes are a bit obvious).

The Alliance leaders likely assume that even if they are a bit hypervigilant at times, their people nonetheless will remain motivated by the shared mission of toppling the Empire. In any workplace, however, identification with the organization's mission will only motivate employees so far. Employers need to supply additional positive motivators through improved workplace culture, particularly when material perks are few and far between. No matter how much you care about the cause and can't stand to see the Imperial flag flying across the galaxy, arguing with a work colleague over who gets to fly one of the new X-wings and who's stuck piloting the broken-down Y-wing will bring you down for the whole day.

When positive motivators for employee performance are absent, dark side motivators seem to take root. Unhealthy work environments may develop because of a manager's inability to lead by example or because of disgruntled employees who no longer care about their work. In the case of the Alliance, infighting and the lack of consensus among leaders lead to decisions based on fear. When deciding whether to invade Scarif and search for the Death Star plans, for example, Council members disagree about the best course of action, some claiming that "we have no course but to surrender" and scatter the fleet, others not wanting to "disband[] what we've worked so hard to create." But if they can't agree on which direction the organization should take, then why have an Alliance at all? Everybody has some degree of voice, though not everybody is listened to equally or gets a vote. People like the lowly spy, the pilot, and the kidnapped daughter of an Imperial engineer, for example, don't get to help decide the Alliance's next steps.

In organizations, frequent disagreement and a lack of meaningful voice can lead to employees becoming apathetic and disengaged. Why bother making an effort to share your perspective when it doesn't matter? In these kinds of workplaces, employees put in their hours, but their identification with the organization diminishes and their sense that they are working toward a common cause begins to fade away. Many would leave if something or someone came along, offering them something better. And some leave anyway, discovering they *do* have the luxury of deciding whether they want to care about the organization's mission.

Enter Jyn Erso. Against the backdrop of the Alliance leadership's factions, distrust, and loss of direction, her impassioned stance offers purpose, unity, mutual trust, a plan, and, importantly, hope. Up to this point, she has gained the respect (if not necessarily the affection) of a few line employees, new recruits, hangers-on, and mid-level management: Cassian Andor, Chirrut Îmwe, Baze Malbus, K-2SO, and Bodhi Rook, the pilot. She earns that respect by her actions in the trenches. They see her bravery and resilience in action, and they know that like themselves, she has paid a steep price for her (and her family's) engagement with the Rebellion. Like them she has lost everything. It is only at the Council meeting that they see she has now decided to do something about it. Jyn may have started out disengaged, but somewhere between holding her dying father and returning to base on Yavin 4 her commitment has changed, and they all see it. When Jyn defies the Alliance and heads to Scarif, many others follow, including some high-ranking Rebel leaders.

Let's examine how Jyn's approach to management—not based on carrots and sticks, not predicated on fear, not fueled by junk motivation—enables her to become an effective, successful leader.

Rebellions are built on hope

Hope is a guiding light that drives key figures in the Rebellion; it overrides fear and makes possible the subsequent Rebel triumph. In workplaces closer to home, employees also need hope—hope that their collective efforts make a meaningful difference in the marketplace and assist the enterprise in reaching its desired goals and objectives. Additionally, while hope is a powerful motivator, whether in battling the evil Empire or doing one's daily tasks at work, it is short-lived and impossible to maintain absent trust. Trust makes possible all the good stuff you find in the best workplaces: mutual respect, creative thinking, healthy communication, and constructive conflict resolution. Hope is thus fostered by trust: trust in each other and, in the *Star Wars* saga, trust in the Force. The ultimately shared vision of hope that drives the rebels to take risks and ultimately to succeed is made possible only by the hard-won trust between them.

Trust starts small. It begins with individuals keeping their word and being reliable in situations where they could have acted otherwise. On the Rebellion side, for all its shortcomings, we see many such displays of trust. Despite initially being wary of each other, Andor and Jyn rely not on threats but on trust, highlighting that "trust goes both ways" in relationships. We see many examples throughout *Rogue One* of reciprocal acts of trust-building. Jyn protects Andor with the very weapon he had given her earlier. Andor saves Jyn from the detonating grenade and the dying planet.

Jyn trusts the Rebels with her father's Death Star secret. Chirrut Îmwe, a defender (or fool, according to some) of the now-defunct Jedi temple, trusts Jyn's plan despite lacking evidence. (To him, the "path is clear"; he trusts in the Force and he must follow her, as the Force divines it.) Chirrut's faith in Jyn reinforces Andor's belief in her as well; and later, Andor disobeys the Alliance's order to kill Jyn's father. Of course, when this happens, Jyn's trust in Andor is shattered because she realizes Andor and the Alliance secretly planned to assassinate her father all along. Fortunately, Jyn and Andor are able to rebuild their trusting relationship, in large part because of the trust and goodwill they already had established.

In the workplace, a trust-rich environment facilitates the emergence and effectiveness of other positive motivators. Jyn puts no pressure, either external or internal, on others, and yet she still emerges as a leader in the Alliance. She highlights the consequences of actions and inaction, helping others see the personal value of their work without the pressure that comes from trying to live up to others' expectations. No carrots or sticks are needed. The rebels who volunteer for the mission realize they might die, but they also understand what happens if the Death Star remains fully operational. They aren't volunteering for Jyn's or the high command's approval; they are doing it for themselves.

Whether you are a rank-and-file Rebel fighter in a galaxy far, far away, or a workaday employee on planet Earth, trusting relationships and hope in a higher purpose are essential motivators in cultivating a healthy and positive workplace culture. The Rogue One crew's motivation is built on mutual trust and shared mission, reinforced by Andor and Jyn each time they speak to the team. Rogue One has hope that it can persist against the worst odds and ultimately succeed in its mission—and it does.

It's a chance for you to make a fresh start

The dynamics of Jyn and the Rogue One team—trust in each other, trust in the Force, and the high purpose of a mission and hope—are in sharp contrast with the trust-barren organizational environment of the Empire, where junk motivators of carrots and sticks shape a very different workplace culture. Additionally, as we have seen, Jyn's approach to motivating her team diverges quite sharply from some of the more fearful Alliance leaders, whose vision and judgment are limited by their own suspicious, self-protective stances.

Lack of trust does not lead to success, either for the Empire or for the Alliance. The Empire relies heavily on sticks and makes promises about carrots that never seem to materialize, while the Alliance is so worried about their enemies getting the upper hand that they often disempower the very people who could help the most. For her part, Jyn remains true to herself and focuses on partnering with people who authentically share her sense of mission and personal value. She strives to help them to find their own path; and in this way, Jyn serves as a link in the chain of unique leaders in the Republic, Rebel Alliance, and Resistance who adopted this approach. It is as if she learned from Padmé and mentored Leia.[4]

When leaders forego the coercive power of carrots and sticks but instead offer trust, hope, and personal value, their followers—as the Rogue One crew demonstrates—willingly volunteer for worthwhile work, no matter how dangerous.

References

[i] Rigby, C. S. & Ryan, R. M. (2018). Self-determination theory in human resource development: New directions and practical considerations. *Advances in Developing Human Resources*. 20(2).

[ii] Kreps, D. (2018). *The motivation toolkit: How to align your employees' interests with your own*. WW Norton & Company.

---

[4] She would also have found Hera Syndulla to be a kindred spirit . . . but, as hyper-alert viewers know, she missed meeting Hera by leaving the briefing room a couple of minutes too early.

ORIGINAL TRILOGY
You're my only hope

8

Negotiating Like a Sith

Troy Stearns

"Your weapons . . . you will not need them," Yoda counsels Luke at the entrance to the cave on Dagobah. But Luke brings his weapons anyway, and he uses them to engage with what (or whom?) he encounters.

Master Yoda's advice is reminiscent of many texts written for Padawan negotiators. These books urge readers not to view negotiation as a battle, but rather as an opportunity to think through your own needs and goals, to interact with someone with different needs and goals, and to attempt to create mutual gain through constructive communication. The systems of negotiation these books propose share one central theme: When negotiating, interact with your counterpart in a cooperative process, rather than seeking to vanquish them at every turn. By engaging in a cooperative process of understanding everyone's goals, needs, resources, preferences, and motivations, skilled negotiators can identify creative outcomes that benefit everyone involved.[1]

Sounds good? Sure. Too good to be true? Sometimes. One way or another, many negotiators treat such wisdom in just the way Luke regarded Yoda's advice, with skepticism or dismissal. They strap on their weapons on their way to the negotiation table and, again like Luke, find themselves using these weapons throughout the negotiation. These negotiators clearly adhere to a differ-

---

[1] For more on interest-based negotiation, see Austin, chapter 11, in *Star Wars and Conflict Resolution: There Are Alternatives to Fighting* (Ebner & Reynolds eds., 2022).

ent philosophy of negotiation—negotiation as competition. In the competitive negotiation "arena," you must focus on achieving your own goals, no matter the price to your counterpart. At the end of the process, one of you will win and the other will lose. Which one would you rather be?[2]

Put another way, we often hear that cooperative processes ideally lead to *win/win outcomes*, solutions in which both parties gain or "win" by achieving their goals. Competitive processes, on the other hand, are more likely to result in *win/lose outcomes*, where one party (the winner) achieves their goals at the expense of the other party (the loser).

The cooperative approach might sound "nice" and the competitive approach might sound "aggressive" when contrasted in this way. Might we assume, therefore, that nice Jedi and Rebels negotiate cooperatively, leaving the competitive approach for the aggressive Empire? Nope. In practice—in *Star Wars* and in our own world—nice people sometimes negotiate competitively. Dark side, light side; Jedi, Sith; Rebels, Imperials; all engage in competitive negotiation at times. Just look at the original trilogy, where nearly all the negotiations are competitive in nature.

With this in mind, in this chapter we set aside the cooperative approach to negotiation and take a deep dive into competitive "win/lose" negotiation. We'll then go beyond everyday competitive negotiation (which you or I or an Ewok might employ) and focus on the ultra-competitive approach used exclusively by the Sith. For the Sith, competitive win/lose negotiation works until it doesn't, at which point they switch into an ultra-competitive mode where they concentrate solely on their opponents losing—even if this leads to *lose/lose outcomes* for everyone involved.

The competitive approach: "We don't have to sit here and listen to this"

We all negotiate all the time, in our personal and professional lives. While there are many ways to define negotiation, at the core

---

[2] *Han*, many of these negotiators would say fervently. *I want to be Han and not Greedo.*

of every negotiation process is one party attempting to influence another to achieve a goal. Negotiation can be as simple as a teenager asking their parents to stay at a friend's house for an extra hour, or as complex as two warring countries hammering out a peace deal. In all kinds of negotiations, participants can choose between adopting a cooperative approach or a competitive approach.

Why adopt a competitive approach? Responding competitively in negotiation is often less of a conscious choice than we realize; some of us default to competitive negotiation by virtue of our personality.[3] But even people who are not competitive by nature may behave competitively in negotiation because of the "fixed pie" mentality. When we believe that there's only a finite amount of something (the example is often a pie), we may reflexively want as much as possible (e.g., the biggest piece). But this reflexive reaction may keep us from considering whether we can trade things that are not pie, whether we even want the pie, or whether tomorrow might offer us another pie to divide. Indeed, many negotiators assume that both sides want the same thing and do not perceive any way to "expand the pie" by identifying other things they might want and could possibly offer each other. Emotions and previous history can entrench the fixed-pie mentality and cause negotiators to be inflexible and distrusting, making cooperation difficult. Finally, one party (or even both) might perceive themselves as holding so much power in the situation that they have no need to work cooperatively with the other party. Jabba rejects Luke's cooperative overtures in *Return of the Jedi* because he believes his entourage and home-field advantage give him complete control over the situation and render Luke powerless. Wanting the entire pie, Jabba chooses a competitive approach, rumbling that "there will be no bargain."

When negotiators adopt competitive approaches, they typically rely on power and coercion to get their way. Luke pulls a blaster on Jabba; Jabba pulls a rancor on Luke. Shows of power and coercion need not involve outright violence, of course; competi-

---

[3] For more on default conflict styles, see Ebner, chapter 10, in *Star Wars and Conflict Resolution: There Are Alternatives to Fighting* (Ebner & Reynolds eds., 2022).

tive negotiators often engage in less-than-violent *hardball tactics*. For example, they may take an extreme opening position, such as by asking for an exorbitant amount of money or offering to pay a ridiculously low amount.[4] Taking an extreme opening position offers the other side little incentive to work together and sends a clear message of "I'm looking out for me, not you." Such tactics may be met with meek submission and acceptance, but they are often received with outrage and competitive counteroffers. When Han demands 10,000 credits to take Luke and company to Alderaan—apparently, the value of a smuggler's ransom's worth of spice—Luke is incensed and nearly walks out, believing Han is not someone they can work with.

And herein lies one of the traps of competitive negotiation. Due to the fixed-pie mentality, competitive negotiators often equate their degree of winning to the degree of their counterpart's losing. Even when it might be best for these negotiators to define winning as gaining as much value as they can for themselves, they can't help but compare themselves to their counterparts, apparently believing that "if my counterpart isn't disappointed then I haven't won, no matter how objectively good my outcomes are." And if both negotiating parties are in this kind of competitive win/lose mindset, then we have a fight on our hands instead of a problem-solving collaboration. In such a dynamic, the potential benefits of cooperation will never be considered, and relationships will be strained or terminated. Moreover, even short-term apparent wins in competitive negotiations can quickly turn into long-term losses for competitive negotiators who are overly focused on a win/lose dynamic.

An example of the competitive approach

To illustrate this last point, let's focus on an all-or-nothing exchange between three allies, Luke Skywalker on one side and Jedi Masters Obi-Wan and Yoda on the other.

---

[4] For more on hardball tactics in conflict and negotiation, see Maravilla, chapter 15, in *Star Wars and Conflict Resolution: There Are Alternatives to Fighting* (Ebner & Reynolds eds., 2022).

Negotiating Like a Sith

In *The Empire Strikes Back*, Luke travels to Dagobah to train as a Jedi Knight under the tutelage of Yoda. While immersed in his training, Luke experiences visions of the future. The visions distract Luke from his training, as he sees Han Solo, Princess Leia, and Chewbacca in danger. Unable to ignore the visions any longer, Luke decides to leave his training to aid his friends. Yoda objects to this decision, and Force ghost Obi-Wan appears to register his disapproval as well. They both explain to Luke that he is vulnerable to the dark side if he faces Darth Vader and the Emperor before finishing his training. Luke acknowledges the danger but doesn't change his mind.

In this scene, both sides are taking a competitive approach, in the sense that they believe their own positions represent the only acceptable way forward under the circumstances. Luke suggests that Yoda and Obi-Wan are willing to throw Luke's friends' lives away, something Luke himself cannot do. Yoda and Obi-Wan argue that Luke's departure will inevitably lead to him succumbing to the dark side of the Force and basically dooming the galaxy to untold years of suffering. (Note how both parties lay a guilt trip on the other, a commonly used competitive tactic.) Both sides' perspectives coalesce into sharply opposing positions: Luke wants to leave; Obi-Wan and Yoda want him to remain.

Interestingly, while all three negotiate competitively, none of them brings out the *really* big guns. For example, Yoda never threatens Luke that if he leaves, Yoda will never again take him on as a student. Obi-Wan doesn't tell Luke the one thing that might make him pause and reconsider—the fact that Darth Vader is Luke's father. For his part, Luke doesn't lash out at Obi-Wan or Yoda by saying something like he's never coming back, and he certainly doesn't demand that Yoda accompany him to Bespin (although perhaps Yoda could have provided a demonstration of the best techniques for vanquishing Sith lords and resisting the dark side by fighting Vader himself). Instead, the scene ends with Yoda and Obi-Wan offering Luke guidance for the upcoming encounter with Vader and with Luke promising to return and complete his training once he's saved his friends.

While that final moment provides a warmer tone to their parting, ultimately this competitive negotiation around whether Luke should leave ends with a clear winner (Luke) and clear losers (Yoda and Obi-Wan).

But perhaps the outcome is not as clear as it looks. Part of the conceptual challenge of competitive negotiation is defining metrics for success. What counts as "winning" and what counts as "losing"? It is true that on the specific question of whether Luke would leave or stay, we have an answer: he left. But on the larger question of whether this was a win or a loss for Luke, Yoda, and Obi-Wan, the answer is less obvious, for at least two reasons.

First, Luke's experience on Bespin is not what he expected. He does not rescue anyone (in the end, he's the one who needs rescuing), he loses his hand and lightsaber, and he learns the very painful truth about his father. He "won" the short-term argument of whether he would leave Dagobah, but only by ignoring or discounting the valid reasons that Yoda and Obi-Wan tried to offer him. In a very real sense, he also "lost" because of his competitive approach. (He makes the best of this loss, however, by returning to Dagobah wiser, humbler, and more compassionate.)

Second, although Yoda and Obi-Wan seemingly lose the competitive argument about Luke's plan, they may not experience the situation as a loss. As it turns out, they have an *alternative*: "There is another." In negotiation, alternatives are things you can do unilaterally, without your counterpart's agreement, should the negotiation not reach a satisfactory conclusion. The better your alternatives are outside of a negotiation, the less likely you will be to agree to a mediocre outcome inside the negotiation.[5] Strong alternatives keep you from investing time, effort, and resources into a negotiation that doesn't seem to be going anywhere. On

---

[5] Consider Luke and Ben negotiating with Han in the cantina. Had they done their homework, they would have had several offers from other captains lined up, which would have given them the ability to counter Han's high opening position with something more convincing than Luke's outrage. "Why should we pay you ten thousand? That Trandoshian freighter captain over there just told us he'd take us for six thousand." And, if Han had continued to pose unreasonable positions, they would have been wise to leave the negotiation, go with the Trandoshian, and we would never even see the *Millennium Falcon*.

Dagobah, Yoda and Ben may have realized they were putting a lot of time and effort in negotiating with Luke, when they have a good alternative to training Luke—namely, enlisting Leia and training her instead.[6] By abandoning the negotiation rather than making further efforts, they avoid the relational damage that threatening Luke or manipulating him might incur. (After all, he might complain to his sister.)

Would Yoda have been so willing to give into Luke's competitive position if Luke were the absolute last hope for the galaxy? Probably not. But knowing there is yet another hope to defeat the Emperor gives Yoda the freedom to not act out of desperation, to preserve his resources, and to manage his relationship with Luke wisely. Keeping the door open offers Ben and Yoda the opportunity to "win" in the future, should Luke survive the encounter with Vader.

Taking competitive negotiation to the extreme

From this discussion, we can see that competitive negotiation involves using tactics and methods that may make it easier to get our way in the short term but could compromise relationships or lead to suboptimal decision-making down the line. That said, most competitive negotiators stay within certain behavioral and expectational norms. In bargaining a high price for providing passage to Alderaan, for example, Han negotiates competitively but does not pull a gun or demand *all* the money his potential passengers might have. The passengers, for their part, want a good rate but do not insist that Han take them to Alderaan for free.

Which brings us to the Sith. For the Sith, it's win at all costs. No tactic is too extreme, and no boundary is left uncrossed. The Sith seek to weaken the opposing party's position with threats, ultimatums, and manipulation, dominating the negotiation while being inflexible to compromise. For Sith negotiators (if they can even be called negotiators), might makes right, and compromise is

---

[6] In saying "No, there is another," Yoda seems to have overlooked that his alternative student is one of the very same people Luke is rushing off to save from grave danger. For more on developing solid alternatives, please see Reynolds & Ebner, chapter 1.

a sign of weakness. They do not seek a typical competitive outcome in which they win more and their counterpart loses more. Rather, they seek an outcome that benefits *only* themselves while leaving *nothing at all* for their counterpart.

One example of an ultra-competitive Sith negotiator is Darth Vader. Recall the deal that Vader strikes with Lando in *The Empire Strikes Back*. Vader agrees to stay out of Lando's business in exchange for Luke. Vader then proceeds to change the terms of the deal unilaterally, not once but three times, and when Lando complains, Vader cuts him off: "I am altering the deal. Pray I don't alter it any further." The unmistakable message is that Vader has all the bargaining power and would be only too happy to make the deal even worse than it has already become.[7]

Like all ultra-competitive negotiators, Vader negotiates through threats, exploiting the fear and weakness of his counterparts to extract concessions. As the scene on Bespin unfolds, Vader clearly intends to take everything he wants; perhaps, even, everything Lando can give him. If he thought one of Lando's capes would look good casually draped over shiny black armor, he undoubtedly would have taken that too. And bear in mind that even had Lando complied with all of Vader's demands, Vader would probably have left a garrison in Cloud City and levied taxes on Lando's mining operation, if only to further prove how un-beholden he is to Lando and any arrangement they may make.

But as we know, Vader takes his ultra-competitiveness too far. Lando realizes that Vader is not negotiating in good faith and, given that Lando has genuine concern for his friends and his city, he decides to work against Vader.[8] Vader "wins" the negotiation in the sense that he gets what he needs to lure Luke to Cloud City. Lando

---

[7] For additional analysis of Lando's deal with Vader, see Elfenbein & Bottom, chapter 17, in *Star Wars and Conflict Resolution: There Are Alternatives to Fighting* (Ebner & Reynolds eds., 2022).

[8] Lando was no stranger to competitive negotiations and renegotiations. Consider Lando's competitive negotiations with Tobias Beckett in *Solo* over his share in the profits from the Kessel Run. He didn't fare well against Beckett in their first negotiation and fared even worse when Beckett took advantage of an opportunity to renegotiate the deal. Even in those mutual win/lose interactions, though, neither dreamt of cutting the other out of the profits altogether.

"loses" in the sense that he is left homeless and unemployed with a Wookiee's hands around his throat and a long-time acquaintance on his way to Jabba. That said, Lando, Leia, and Chewie don't lose as much as they could have—given what Lando will become to the Rebellion, they actually gained quite a bit—and Vader, by overplaying his hand, walks away with nothing. By Sith negotiation standards, Vader lost. A "win" for the Sith would have meant Luke in carbonite, Leia and Chewie in an Imperial prison, and his future son-in-law hanging on Jabba's wall. Vader loses—and is not a happy camper about it. Perhaps the Emperor will be more forgiving . . .

One more example of the Sith approach: "You will die!"

As we've seen, the ultra-competitive Sith approach may provide immediate gains but the costs and risks are significant, in both the short and long terms. In a way, the entire *Star Wars* saga is about the folly of those who rely too much on fear and oppression to concentrate and consolidate their power.

Nowhere is this more apparent than in the climax of *Return of the Jedi*, as the Emperor and Darth Vader try to turn Luke to the dark side. Although this encounter may not look like a negotiation, make no mistake: the Emperor and Darth Vader cannot unilaterally compel Luke to join them. Luke must decide for himself whether he wants to turn to the dark side, which makes this entire back-and-forth on the second Death Star a high-stakes negotiation.

The negotiation begins with both parties taking an extreme opening position. Each negotiator wants not only to stay on their side of the Force, but to convert someone from the opposite side. The Sith ultra-competitive approach is on clear display: threats, ultimatums, baiting comments about Luke's sister, a quick lightsaber duel. Luke briefly appears to consider giving into the dark side, surging with power fueled by hate and rage, but then remembers himself, reasserts his original position, and does not budge. Eventually, it becomes obvious to the Emperor that Luke won't be turned, and he employs the ultimate competitive tactic, violence (his trademark Force lightning). With nothing left to gain, the Emperor chooses to end Luke's life (and perhaps, while he's at it, poke a sharply competitive if bony finger in Vader's eye-lens): "Now, young Skywalker . . . you will die."

Luke doesn't die, though. The small inroads he has made during the negotiation with Vader—calling him "father," appealing to his innate goodness—are enough to convince even an ultra-competitive Sith to reevaluate his approach. And while the Emperor's laser focus on winning Sith-style gives him the power to overcome Luke's resistance and nearly claim Luke's life, this focus also narrows the Emperor's vision so greatly that he cannot see other alternatives. In short, the Emperor is blinded to the possibility of Vader turning on him. Pursuing that uniquely Sith form of winning—the absolute vanquishment of your counterpart, even when you can't get what you came to the table for in the first place—costs the Emperor his faithful servant, his victory over the Jedi, and his life. Food for thought, on the long way down the shaft to the power core.[9]

Competitive negotiation is nothing new, and in the *Star Wars* original trilogy, we see heroes and villains struggling for advantage in all kinds of encounters. Sometimes competitive approaches work in their favor, as when Han Solo strikes a deal that would compensate him richly for a quick spin over to Alderaan to drop off a few passengers. Other times, engaging in competitive negotiation backfires, particularly given its effects on the future of the parties' relationship. For example, after their negotiation over freeing Han fails, Luke and Jabba are no longer on speaking terms and clearly only one of them will survive their encounter. Finally, the most intense form of competitive negotiation, practiced by the Sith, offers the most extreme versions of both possibilities and risks.

Remember that choice of a competitive approach should be the result of an intentional and strategic decision, taken when you are

---

[9] There's no way he's coming back from that one, unless somehow.

calm, at peace. Otherwise, you might find that while competitive negotiation is quick to join you in a fight, it is very much a double-bladed lightsaber.

You Can Learn the Jedi Mind Trick!

Zach Ulrich

What if I told you that you could learn techniques to subtly influence others' perceptions of you and what you're saying, similar to the Jedi mind trick? Or if I promised that you could improve your ability to interpret and predict others' thoughts and feelings, much as the Jedi do using their Force sense? Would you dismiss me as an over-the-hill swamp loon like Luke did to Yoda when they first met on Dagobah? Well, before you do that, allow me to demonstrate a negotiation and communication technique used right here in our own galaxy, *neuro-linguistic programming* (NLP). In this chapter, I will use examples from the original *Star Wars* trilogy that show striking parallels between NLP and Jedi powers. I think you'll find that using NLP to influence others in your next negotiation or conflict takes less time to learn than Han's Kessel Run and is much easier than levitating an X-wing. Ready to begin your Jedi training? Read on, and hone your NLP powers you will.

Psychologists developed NLP in the 1970s as a way of analyzing and influencing communication. Basically, researchers found that a person who pays careful attention to verbal and nonverbal cues can better understand and even influence the perceptions and thoughts of other people.[i] For example, listening for a person's "keywords"—that is, words they often use and repeat—can help us decipher and more fully appreciate that person's underlying values and motivations. Moreover, proactively *repeating back* to an individual *their own* cues can better establish that person's trust, mutual understanding, and rapport with you. This new connection between the two of you now makes the other person more likely to consider and accept viewpoints you propose or, at minimum, to engage with you more openly. In this way, NLP can serve as a powerful communication tool in negotiation and conflicts. Using NLP improves the chances that your counterparts will feel comfortable communicating their true motivations and needs and that they will find your negotiated offers appealing, which in turn improve your chances of breaking through impasses and reaching negotiated settlements.

These aren't the droids you're looking for

Jedi Knights negotiate their way through precarious conflicts all the time. Luckily for us, even as they use their formidable powers and mind tricks to influence others, Jedi Knights also provide examples of how to use NLP techniques to improve negotiation outcomes.

The most famous use of the Jedi mind trick occurs when Obi-Wan and Luke encounter stormtroopers at the Mos Eisley spaceport, so we *have* to start there. For those who somehow, inexplicably, haven't committed the scene's dialogue to memory, Obi-Wan and Luke are cruising in Luke's landspeeder when they come upon five stormtroopers searching for two droids, assuming that either the beat-up, carbon-scored little one or the tall shiny one have the Death Star plans in their memory banks. The stormtroopers ask Luke to show identification, yet it is Obi-Wan who replies, "You don't need to see his identification." And here's the moment: Remember how shocked you were the first time you saw the stormtrooper squad commander respond, "We don't need to see his identification"!? Obi-Wan then continues with: "These aren't the droids you're looking for" and "He can go about his business" and "Move along," as the hapless stormtrooper simply repeats Obi-Wan's words and finally waves the speeder through the checkpoint.

Breaking down Obi-Wan's actions in this first-ever depiction of the Jedi mind trick, we see connections between this powerful Jedi tool and the nuts and bolts of using NLP in negotiation. First,

Obi-Wan never breaks eye contact with the stormtrooper with whom he's speaking. Not once, throughout the entire exchange. In NLP, maintaining eye contact is useful in two senses. First, without eye contact with others, you lose much of your ability to convey messages nonverbally. Second, by not watching the other person's eyes, you potentially lose insight into what the other person is actually communicating, whether they know it consciously or not. Obi-Wan also uses the patented Jedi "hand wave" in this instance of the mind trick, by way of a small, subtle hand movement accompanying his first sentence and even subtler motions of his fingers the next. While I'm not recommending you go around trying the "hand wave" on your friends and loved ones, NLP practitioners know that our nonverbal communication is often more critical than the words we say. Even small gestures and nuances like eye contact and hand movements can have significant effects on the flow of communication.

And it's a good thing Obi-Wan's mind trick worked, because the consequences otherwise could have been disastrous! The stormtroopers were each packing blast rifles, and a fight with them would have pitted an untrained Luke and an out-of-practice Obi-Wan against all five troopers plus their backup. If R2-D2 were captured at this point, the plans would have been lost, the Rebel Alliance would not have known how to attack the Death Star, and *A New Hope* would have been a short movie ending on a dismal note. On top of that, who knows where Luke might have ended up . . . trained by his father instead of by Yoda, perhaps? The point is, even a seemingly minor exchange can carry with it unexpressed and even deadly conflict (the stormtroopers' weapons and armor) and the outcome of the negotiation to follow may have epic implications. Much as the Force can exert tremendous influence on how events unfold, so too can neuro-linguistic programming.

Of course, there are limits to what the Force and NLP can do. In fact, right after they get through the checkpoint, Luke comments, "I can't understand how we got by those troops. I thought we were dead," to which Obi-Wan responds: "The Force can have a strong influence on the weak-minded." The effectiveness of the mind trick, we learn, depends not only on the skill of the Jedi channeling the Force but also on the mind strength of their counterpart. Similarly, NLP relies both on user skill and on qualities of the person being influenced.

Another instance of the mind trick worth discussing takes place in *Return of the Jedi*, where Luke—now at least partially trained as a Jedi and talking a good game—uses the mind trick on Bib Fortuna, majordomo of Jabba's Palace on Tatooine. Luke seeks to gain admittance and rescue Han Solo, who is hanging on Jabba's wall, frozen in carbonite. Luke uses the hand wave and tells Bib, "You will take me to Jabba now . . . You serve your master well . . . And you will be rewarded." Bib, apparently quite weak-minded and certainly not aware of any actual or imminent conflict between Luke and his master, allows Luke to proceed.

Just as with Obi-Wan at the checkpoint, here too Luke's most overt hand wave comes at the beginning of the exchange. This suggests that the hand wave—that is, the nonverbal element of the mind trick—can be an important part of the initial phase of "implanting thoughts" or altering the other's thinking patterns. This early move seems to serve as a hook with lasting effect. You can gently reinforce it in an ongoing manner as Obi-Wan did at the checkpoint, but even if you don't (as Luke didn't, given that Bib Fortuna had turned his back on him) the hook stays in place. NLP works similarly; using nonverbal communication to build rapport and comfort with another person in the beginning of a negotiation causes you to be perceived as more trustworthy and convincing afterward, even if you focus less on nonverbal communication later.

A new element of the mind trick evident in this scene is using verbal reinforcements to maintain the connection even when you've lost eye contact and have no audience for your hand wave. As Bib Fortuna walks with Luke, Luke continues to engage verbally, keeping their connection solid even as he strengthens it by appealing to what he can surmise of Bib's motivations. He infers Bib's motivations from the context of Bib's position at Jabba's Palace, assuming that Bib wants to be seen as serving his master faithfully and would enjoy being personally rewarded. Luke not only uses his Force powers to influence Bib directly but also influences his thinking by explicitly referring to things Bib values. So too, with NLP, it is critical to identify "core values" of those with whom you are negotiating, consider how those values influence their decision-making, and communicate with them correspondingly.[1]

I feel the good in you

We've looked at two examples of the mind trick, but what about the Force sense, or the ability of Force users to feel another's thoughts? Don't you worry yourself, my Padawan, because that's what we're discussing next! An early demonstration of the Force sense in the original trilogy is Yoda telling the ghost of Obi-Wan that he senses "much anger" in Luke. Until now, Luke—who has just found Yoda on Dagobah and hopes to train as a Jedi—has given no outward indication of the anger Yoda senses.[2] Yoda, therefore, must be able somehow to intuitively sense Luke's inner anger. As a result of this Force sense, Yoda initially prefers to not train Luke, fearing this anger may be used to draw Luke to the dark side as it did his father.

When it comes to the Force sense, the movies are not clear as to whether elements of people's actual communication (verbal or nonverbal) help Jedi sense their thoughts and feelings, or whether the Jedi sense everything by tapping into a connection we non-Jedi cannot fathom. Regardless, Yoda shows his wisdom by considering what he senses in Luke only within the broader context of Obi-Wan's counsel (namely, to train Luke) and Yoda's own instincts. He does not base his entire decision on a Force snapshot of Luke's inner emotions. And this is precisely how NLP teaches

---

[1] Another example, this one from the sequel trilogy: In *The Force Awakens*, the importance of eye contact is evident when Rey's first attempt to use the mind trick on a stormtrooper guard standing behind her only incenses him. She makes eye contact and tries again: "You will remove these restraints and leave this cell with the door open." This time, he accedes to her wishes. On his way out, he obeys her follow-on command ". . . and you'll drop your weapon." Although they are no longer maintaining eye contact, she still influences him. He drops his weapon as he is fulfilling her order to leave the cell.

[2] Frustration and impatience, yes. But not the deep anger Yoda refers to here.

us to interpret the cues of others. We non-Jedi might not gather all the information the Force can provide, but we can gain a wealth of understanding by being attentive to our counterparts' verbal and nonverbal cues. As we do so, we should keep Yoda's restraint in mind; while others' cues can sometimes give us insight into what they are truly thinking and feeling, our interpretations need to be made within the broader perspective of knowing the parties to a negotiation, the situational context of the negotiation, and even what our "gut" instincts tell us. It's a good thing Yoda took this broader perspective into account, because Luke gets trained in the way of the Jedi as a result.

So far, all these examples have been of using the mind trick and Force sense for good; but what about the dark side? Recall how in *Return of the Jedi*, Darth Vader and Emperor Palpatine are strolling along the new Death Star, too cool to acknowledge the thousands of stormtroopers standing at attention, when the Emperor casually observes, "And now I sense you wish to continue your search for young Skywalker." This remark tips us off to just how powerful the Emperor's Force sense is. Vader has given no outward indication of his thoughts; indeed, his face is invisible underneath his helmet, and his bodily expressions do not seem to have shifted. Nonetheless, Palpatine has nailed it, and Vader acknowledges his desire to search for Luke. The Emperor suspects that Vader has emotional attachments to Luke, and that those attachments may in turn affect Vader's decision-making, but he still trusts Vader to proceed.[3]

In this battle of wits and Force abilities for Vader's soul, it's fortunate that Luke's ability to use his own Force sense is more powerful than his abilities with the Jedi mind trick. As Vader and Luke ride the elevator together to the Emperor's throne room on the second Death Star, Luke says to Vader, "Your thoughts betray you, Father. I feel the good in you, the conflict . . . You couldn't

---

[3] Later, the Emperor again senses something unsettled in Vader and asks him directly: "I wonder if your feelings on this matter are clear, Lord Vader?" When Vader assures him that they are, the Emperor once again trusts Vader to proceed. *Not the wisest of choices*, the Emperor likely pondered on his way down the shaft to the power core.

bring yourself to kill me before, and I don't believe you'll destroy me now." Wow! Luke senses not only what the Emperor previously sensed but also that Vader has *conflicting desires*. Luke clearly uses the *combination* of his Force sense *and* observable contextual clues—Vader's outward nonverbals indicating his hesitation—to determine that Vader is potentially persuadable and thus worth trying to convince. Had the Emperor sensed this complex internal conflict in Vader? Possibly not. Luke does, and he calls it out in an effort to influence Vader to make the right choice and aid him in destroying the Emperor.

Setting the Force aside, Luke's reading of his father and his efforts to influence Vader are exemplary uses of NLP principles. As discussed earlier, practicing NLP includes seeking an understanding of our counterpart's motivations and then using those motivations to influence them. Successfully understanding the motivations of others requires practitioners of NLP to both observe *and* infer, using a combination of their instinctive intuition *and* information regarding the context in which others are acting. Luke does both with Vader here, leading to Luke's determination that Vader is conflicted and may be open to persuasion.

So, you have a twin sister

Before this climactic scene in the throne room, Luke and Vader have an exchange on Endor that further illustrates NLP practices. Hoping to take the heat off his friends, Luke surrenders to the stormtrooper garrison, and Darth Vader descends to the sanctuary moon to take custody of Luke and bring him to the Emperor. When they encounter one another, we see another tool commonly used by NLP practitioners to influence others: *keywords*. Luke says to Vader, "Search your feelings, father. You can't do this. I feel the conflict within you; let go of your hate." Luke's phrasing here is important to examine. In the Jedi world, phrases like "search your feelings" and "let go of your hate" are often used. Luke's use of these phrases is specifically designed to evoke Vader's dormant mode of thinking *as a former Jedi Knight himself*. Negotiating Darth Vader's return to the light side is no small task, and Luke is using every tool at his disposal. He not only makes an argument for Vader to reconsider his actions, but phrases that argument in a way that, Luke hopes, will appeal to what remains of Vader's former Jedi identity.

As an NLP tool, using keywords helps us quickly establish the other's trust, mutual understanding, and rapport with us. To identify another person's keywords, listen closely to what they say. With practice, you'll find yourself not only hearing the information they seek to convey, but also noticing words and phrases that they use repeatedly. Often, repeated words and phrases represent things that are important, such as personal values, sense of identity, and goals. Accordingly, when people hear their keywords repeated back to them in negotiation and other important exchanges, they often cannot help but react emotionally, and often positively, even if they do not immediately vocalize their feelings. To strengthen a bond of trust and rapport with people, therefore, intentionally use their keywords and repeated phrases at negotiation moments during which you seek to have maximal impact.

This certainly works for Luke, who appeals to two of Vader's core identities using Vader's own keywords. To connect with Vader as one Jedi Knight with another, Luke uses the Jedi keywords discussed above. To form a father-son bond, Luke repeatedly calls Vader "father," echoing Vader's own use of the term ("No . . . I am your father"). Luke's usage of keywords is effective in both instances. Indeed, even though Vader rejects Luke's plea, saying "It is too late for me," he adds a surprisingly warm ". . . son" at the end. Vader takes Luke to the Emperor as ordered, but Vader's words and tone suggest that Luke has succeeded in making Vader think about their relationship and, maybe, about his time using the Force for good. Perhaps most telling of all, just after Luke is taken away, we see Vader pausing, staring into the distance, and apparently reflecting on Luke's words.

Darth Vader uses keywords, too. In the Emperor's throne room, Vader uses his Force sense to understand the power the words "friends" and "sister" have on Luke and then pushes those buttons:

> Give yourself to the dark side. It is the only way you can save your *friends*. Yes. Your thoughts betray you. Your feelings for them are strong. Especially for ... *sister*. So, you have a *twin sister*.

Vader goes on to speculate that "[i]f you will not turn to the dark side, then perhaps she will," causing Luke to shout "Never!" and attack Vader furiously, eventually knocking him down and lopping off his hand. While of course Vader's goals likely do not include losing an appendage, this is a superb example of Vader identifying influential keywords and repeating them back to Luke, resulting in Luke losing control of his emotions, acting out in anger, and taking one step closer to the dark side—which is Vader's primary goal at this point. Vader thus demonstrates the NLP model by using keywords to strike a deep, emotional chord with Luke to influence him for evil.

Your mind powers will not work on me, boy

Any discussion of the Jedi mind trick would not be complete without pointing out its ultimate limitation: that it does not work on Hutts![4] Jabba teaches Luke an important lesson that Obi-Wan somehow forgot to point out: namely, that the Jedi mind trick has a strong influence on the weak-minded but no influence at all on anybody else. Much in the same way, some people are less susceptible to NLP influence than others, and there are situations in which NLP is less likely to work. For example, individuals with antisocial or aggressive personalities tend to be less easily influenced by NLP techniques. And, in negotiation and other interactions where individuals may be wary of your intentions—as when communication is emotionally charged or involves sensitive topics—you may find your NLP tools have diminished impact.

---

[4] Or Toydarians, or Geonosians, or a whole lot of other folks, if we're considering all of *Star Wars* canon. In fact, it backfires more often than it works! Which begs the question: Which is ultimately more effective, the subtle nuance of NLP or the brute force of the mind trick? Sounds like a great essay topic for any negotiation course from here to the Jedi Temple on Coruscant.

Using the Force and NLP as influence tools can backfire in much the same ways. After Bib Fortuna proudly presents Luke to Jabba, Jabba immediately exclaims, "He's using an old Jedi mind trick!" And now Luke has two problems. First, if a person knows someone is using the Jedi mind trick to influence them, they will be guarded and less likely to be influenced; even if Jabba were *not* immune to the Jedi mind trick, his awareness of it probably reduces its chances of success. The same goes for someone forming a defensive mindset against anticipated use of NLP. Second, with both NLP and the mind trick, once your counterpart recognizes you are using a covert technique on them, they may very well perceive you as untrustworthy, resent your efforts, and make any attempts at influencing them much more difficult.

And yet Luke tries anyway. Luke attempts the mind trick on Jabba, even taking down his hood to make direct eye contact when ordering Jabba to bring him Captain Solo and Chewbacca. Jabba simply responds, "Your mind powers will not work on me, boy," and Luke is left to negotiate with a counterpart who now considers him an aggressive, manipulative opponent. Luke tries to recover, veering between threatening Jabba and enticing him with promises of reward. With every reason to distrust Luke, Jabba's only response is that "there will be no bargain, young Jedi," and we all know the rest (rancor, sarlacc, slow digestion, etc.). Although the heroes ultimately escape, Luke's reliance on the Jedi mind trick as his go-to move puts his friends' and sister's lives in greater danger than they previously had been. Another approach—whether actual negotiation or covert rescue operation—may have worked better in the first place.

Ultimately, this scene shows us how mastery of the mind trick may have kept Luke from recognizing that manipulation does not always work and that he should learn how to bargain with others as equals. Luke pays a price for his arrogance, and his experience serves as a cautionary lesson for users of NLP as well. When

NLP or the mind trick fail, subsequent bargaining becomes all the harder—so overreliance on NLP should be avoided.[5]

You must do what you think is right

Just as the Jedi can use the Force to support them in different ways throughout their negotiations, so too can you leverage neuro-linguistic programming. We have discussed how the Jedi clearly demonstrate three NLP techniques in their negotiations: deploying nonverbals strategically, identifying motivational cues, and using the other's keywords. These are but a few of the NLP tools available to those seeking to increase their persuasiveness in negotiation.

As with all powers, the Force and NLP can be used for either good or evil. With the powers of NLP in our grasp, we can choose to use its insights and techniques to build trust, to foster healthy relationships, and to guide people toward optimal negotiation outcomes—or we can use these techniques to mislead and manipulate, to behave more aggressively or dismissively in conflicts, and even to harm others. Whether in negotiation, our personal lives, or epic struggles to determine the fate of the universe, it is up to each of us to determine how to exercise the powers we wield.

References

[i] Bandler, R. & Grinder, J. (1975). *The structure of magic, vol. 1: A book about language and therapy*. Portions of Bandler and Grinder's original claims have since been studied and debated by scholars; the techniques discussed in this chapter represent a few of the NLP elements widely accepted and used today. For a step-by-step handbook, see Dotz, T., Hoobyar, T. & Sanders, S. (2013). *NLP: The essential guide to neuro-linguistic programming*. William Morrow.

[5] For more on manipulation and backlash, see Maravilla, chapter 15, in *Star Wars and Conflict Resolution: There Are Alternatives to Fighting* (Ebner & Reynolds eds., 2022).

10

Is Luke a Hero? The Consequences of Choosing Between Goals

Emily A. Cai & Deborah A. Cai

Luke Skywalker is headstrong and loyal. He saves Princess Leia from the Death Star prison. He joins the Rebellion to fight against the evil Galactic Empire. He wants more than anything to become a Jedi Knight—like the powerful and heroic Jedi he is led to believe his father was—so he can destroy the forces of evil that destroyed his father. Determined and impulsive, Luke acts on what he believes is right and fair, putting loyalty to his family and friends above all else.

We see this loyalty in action during Luke's training on Dagobah. In *The Empire Strikes Back*, after the battle on Hoth, Luke decides not to regroup with the other rebels. Instead, he goes to Dagobah with the goal of training to become a Jedi. But as soon as Luke has a vision of his friends in pain, he decides to leave his training to go rescue them. Rescuing his friends means confronting Darth Vader, which both Obi-Wan and Yoda insist Luke isn't ready for. They explain to Luke that his friends are being used as bait to lure him to the Emperor. Moreover, it is not at all certain that his friends will die. If Luke leaves without finishing his training, Yoda and Obi-Wan argue, he will be heading down the path to the dark side.

As we know, Luke rushes off anyway. In that moment, when Luke decides to leave his training as a Jedi Knight to save his friends, he seems like a valiant hero, disregarding his own safety and putting his friends above all else. In an act of heroism and daring, he defies his teachers and ignores the potential risks and dangers. What a courageous, selfless move by Luke Skywalker, Jedi-in-training, hero in the making, loyal to a fault.

But is Luke's decision heroic—or just impulsive? Loyal—or naive? Wise—or short sighted? How does Luke's noble goal of saving his friends compare with bigger goals, goals that would require him to stay on Dagobah, complete his training, and achieve mastery of the Force? What would a hero choose to do?

Goals and goal-setting in negotiation

Plagued by visions of his friends in trouble, Luke is faced with a choice: End his Jedi training to save his friends now, or stay in Dagobah to finish training with Yoda, which would increase his chances of conquering Darth Vader and the Emperor in the future. Yoda tells Luke that going to rescue Han Solo and Princess Leia is far too risky for Luke and for his friends. Despite Yoda's wisdom (and we all know what a wise creature he is), Luke decides that saving his friends is up to *him*—to Luke Skywalker alone—so he starts focusing on his goal of rescuing them, which means he must hit pause on his previous goal of training to become a Jedi.

Goals provide direction and guide people to achieve what they need to accomplish. In negotiation and conflict situations, clear goals—and the plans for how to achieve those goals—help keep people on task and avoid becoming distracted from what needs to be done. Setting objectives and establishing clear goals help ensure that the most crucial aspects of the negotiation are pursued. By examining Luke's goals and comparing his goals with those of Yoda and Obi-Wan, we gain a better picture of whether Luke is heroic or impulsive.

Types of Goals

Because of Luke's visions of his friends in trouble, he responds as someone who is in a crisis situation. Negotiators in crisis situations must be laser-focused on goals and objectives, because lives and other high-stakes considerations may be on the line. Keeping a laser focus on goals means understanding how different goals and motivations may interact in the decision-making of those involved in the crisis. Hostage negotiators, for example, use the acronym SAFE to track the goals that must be assessed and pursued to manage a hostage crisis:[i]

- *Substantive* goals are concrete and instrumental needs or wants. These goals are often measurable, such as money, time, or goods (e.g., pizza or blankets).
- *Attunement* goals focus on improving, or at least not damaging, the relationship with others in the crisis situation.
- *Face* goals have to do with making sure others feel their identity is supported and not disrespected or threatened.
- *Emotional* goals, so crucial in crisis situations, have to do with making sure the hostage taker's fear, anxiety, and sense of hopelessness are addressed; these goals are addressed early and continue to be addressed throughout a crisis negotiation.

Although Luke's situation is not a hostage situation, it bears many similarities, so the SAFE model provides a useful framework for assessing the various goals at stake in his decision whether to leave Dagobah.

In addition to types of goals, negotiation goals (of all types) can be classified as local, regional, and global.[ii] *Local* goals are immediate and specific concerns or interests, like going to Tosche Station to pick up some power converters. *Regional* goals are the goals one pursues over one negotiation session as part of a series of negotiations or the strategic goals that guide mid-range pursuits within a larger context, such as avenging the Empire's destruction of Alderaan by rescuing Princess Leia and gathering enough trained pilots to attack the Death Star. *Global* goals focus on what needs to be achieved overall. The defeat of the Empire is clearly a global goal, because it is the overarching pursuit that guides—or should guide—local and regional goals. Local and regional goals can distract from the big picture when people lose sight of the global goals, under which all other goals should fall into place.

We can use SAFE and the frame of local, regional, and global goals to understand the differences between Luke's goals and those of Yoda and Obi-Wan. For example, the primary interests of Yoda and Obi-Wan are to defeat the Empire, to save millions of innocent lives, and to restore balance to the Force. Yoda and Obi-Wan are concerned mostly with *global, substantive* goals, which require keeping an eye on the final outcome that must be achieved. In contrast, Luke's focus is quickly diverted to the local goal of saving his friends. Luke's concern for his friends is driven by goals that are both substantive (the need to rescue them) and attunement (the importance of preserving his relational connections with his friends). At this point for Luke, his relationships with Han and Leia overshadow the importance of any substantive, global goals that might be at stake.

Example: "If money is all that you love, then that's what you'll receive"

Being able to determine the deeper motivations for why a person chooses one path over another or one set of goals over another is an essential analytical skill for negotiation and conflict management. As a brief illustration, consider Han Solo's goals at the end of *A New Hope*. While the Rebel Alliance prepares to head out and take down the Death Star, Han packs up to leave with his reward money, presumably to pay off Jabba and anyone else Han owes.

In this situation, we see Han choose between his own local (immediate) substantive goals—to pay his debt and to secure his own survival—rather than the regional (mid-range) and highly crucial substantive goal of helping the Rebel Alliance take down the Empire's planet-destroying superweapon. Moreover, despite Han's decision affecting both his face goals (he comes across as a selfish jerk) and his attunement goals (Princess Leia and Luke think he's a selfish jerk), Han still pursues his own local substantive goals, at least initially. Indeed, Han spends most of the movie motivated by the promise of money to help himself. After all, his own local substantive goals are why he agrees to fly Luke and Obi-Wan to Alderaan, why he helps Luke save Princess Leia, and why he chooses not to participate in the strike against the Death Star.

And this is why it is such a surprise—and relief—when Han sacrifices his own immediate goals at the end of the film in favor of larger substantive goals. Not only does Han return to help with the Rebel's regional *substantive* goal of taking out the Death Star, but he is driven by relational *attunement* goals as well: Han shows up because his friends need help. Han arrives just in time to take out Darth Vader's wingman, ricocheting Vader out of the trench and clearing the way for Luke to take the shot that destroys the Death Star.[1]

By giving up his own immediate goals and pursuing a different set of regional relational and substantive goals, Han saves Luke and facilitates the destruction of the Death Star. But his decision to forego his own immediate substantive goal is not without consequences. As a result of Han's decision to return, he does not pay off his debt to Jabba, which leads to a bounty being placed on his head, his capture in Cloud City, and his body being frozen in carbonite and shipped back to Tatooine. Han lands in trouble for being unable to place his own substantive local goals in the context of the Alliance's substantive global goals. Perhaps if Luke and Leia had been able to effectively negotiate with Han, an appropriate strategic goal could have been set where Han was able to aid the Alliance as well as pay off his debts.

Evaluating Luke's goals

At first, when Luke decides to leave Dagobah to save his friends, he may appear heroic, as when Han chooses to return in *A New Hope*. Luke's decision shows that he prioritizes his friends over his own self-interest of becoming a Jedi Knight. In this way, Luke's goal of saving his friends looks like an *attunement* goal, driven by his relational concern for the well-being of his friends.

---

[1] Of course, Han still needs to protect his identity, his *face*. He therefore justifies his return by staying true to his selfish, money-focused identity: "I wasn't going to let you get all the credit and take all the reward!"

Goals, however, are often multidimensional. To fully map out all the possible goals being pursued in this situation, we would need something like the Rebel's holographic display used for planning attacks on Death Stars. Our choices are often motivated by more than one goal, and our goals sometimes overlap and even conflict with one another. Yoda and Obi-Wan point out that the *substantive* goal of defeating the Empire—a common goal that they all share—is in tension with Luke's *attunement* goal of saving his friends:

OBI-WAN: Patience!
LUKE: And sacrifice Han and Leia?
YODA: If you honor what they fight for . . . yes.

A closer look at Luke's choice to leave Dagobah suggests his decision is perhaps driven more by *face*—or identity—goals than by *attunement* goals. Although Luke is training to become a Jedi, his self-perception as a hero is, at least in his mind, called into question. Recall that his experience in Dagobah has already threatened his identity. Yoda initially refuses to train Luke, even though Luke protests that he is ready to become a Jedi. But when Yoda finally agrees to train him, it turns out that Luke is not particularly good at learning to use the Force. He lacks concentration and control. He cannot lift his ship out of the swamp. He fails in the cave. On Dagobah, Luke's identity takes hits like womp rats from a T-16.

With this in mind, the opportunity to restore his identity as a hero may be a significant part of what drives Luke's decision here. In other words, it is not only substantive and relational goals that are competing for Luke's attention. Because of his failures on Dagobah, Luke may also feel the need to rescue his friends to reestablish his identity as a hero, as someone who does the right and good thing, who places his loyalty to his friends above all else, and who can pull off a difficult rescue.

Additionally, alongside substantive, attunement, and identity goals are Luke's *emotional* goals, which affect his judgment and choices about what to do. Feelings can cloud our judgment, and in crisis situations, emotions can often thwart the ability to accomplish long-term, substantive goals that need to be achieved. When emotions are strong, negotiations often take much longer, because emotions must be calmed before people in conflict can reason clearly.[2] People in crisis often need to have their emotional concerns addressed before more substantive goals can be discussed.[3]

In this situation, Luke's emotions are running rampant. He fears for his friends; he is frustrated over his own failures during training; and—let's face it—he is probably pretty lonely from hanging out on a swamp planet with grumpy Yoda and Force ghost Obi-Wan. Luke is so consumed by the emotional tumult arising from his need to fulfill his immediate goal of preventing his friends from being tortured and possibly killed that he cannot see the larger consequences of his actions. It is within this complex emotional state that Luke faces his choice of remaining on Dagobah to complete his training or leaving to save his friends.

Emotional goals can often eclipse everything else. While on Dagobah, Luke's intense desire to accomplish his immediate goals without seeing the bigger picture is what leads him to act out of anger (when he lashes out at Yoda), fear (when he leaves to save his friends), and aggression (when he takes his weapons into the cave). In each case, Luke's emotions lead to failure. He is explicitly told by Yoda and Obi-Wan that he should not leave, that he will not be able to defeat Vader, and that he is dangerously close to heading down the path to the dark side. As Yoda points out, "Anger, fear, aggression; the dark side of the Force are they."

In Luke's case, disaggregating his emotional goals from global, substantive goals is especially difficult because Luke's emotional goals are tied to his own moral code and sense of right and wrong. For Luke, saving his friends is simply the right and good thing to

---

[2] On the other hand, when we are calm, at peace, passive, feelings and emotions can enhance our decision-making. See Colatrella, chapter 13.

[3] Remember how Anakin Skywalker turned to the dark side because he was alienated from the Jedi Order and he wanted to prevent Padmé from dying? Had Obi-Wan shared this history with Luke, Luke may have realized how he was being drawn into Anakin's Triad of Poor Decision-Making: emotional distress, extreme loyalty to friends, and certainty that he knows best.

do; letting them die is the wrong and bad thing to do. Recall that it was in Luke's absence, when he first encounters Ben Kenobi, that his aunt and uncle were killed. He may still feel tremendous guilt over their deaths, and this guilt and grief could be shaping his goals, leading him to act impulsively to avoid feeling even guiltier for the demise of his friends.

Finally, let's consider the local, regional, and global aspects of Luke's decision-making process. Whether it is his pursuit of an attunement goal or face goal, or whether it is his need to alleviate or even run from his emotions that sends Luke off to pursue the substantive goal of helping his friends, all of Luke's goals can be considered local goals. Luke chooses a whole set of short-term goals, wrapped up in an adventure of going to save his friends, over the long-term need for him to learn how to control the Force. Yoda clearly states the consequences of leaving to rescue Han and Leia: "If you leave now, help them you could" (local goal) "but you would destroy all for which they have fought and suffered" (global goal).

We see again and again that when Luke focuses on achieving his immediate local goals, that is also when he gives in to his emotions of anger, fear, and aggression. When he thinks a then-unknown Yoda is wasting his time and interfering in his path to becoming a Jedi, Luke becomes irritated and impatient. When he is unable to lift his ship out of the swamp with the Force, he becomes frustrated and dejected. When he enters the cave, his first instinct is to rely on his weapons to face his fear. And now, he decides to leave Dagobah to save his friends because he is afraid they may die. In short, Luke lets his emotions get the better of him, and those emotions cause him to be short-sighted and miss the more substantive global goals that need to be pursued—namely, becoming a Jedi Knight and helping the Rebellion destroy the Empire. Instead, his actions are repeatedly determined by his immediate goals and his darker emotions.

The bigger picture = the Force

In *The Empire Strikes Back*, Luke prioritizes immediate goals over global goals, which affects his ability to use the Force. He consistently fails in his training because he is unable to believe in the larger power and possibilities of the Force. Luke can move small stones around, but he can't lift his ship out of the swamp. He can feel the Force, but he can't control it. Yoda tries to connect Luke to a larger view of the Force, but to no avail:

> My ally is the Force. And a powerful ally it is. Life creates it, makes it grow. Its energy surrounds us and binds us. Luminous beings are we, not this crude matter. You must feel the Force around you, here between you and me, the tree, the rock, everywhere. Yes, even between the land and the ship.

Luke cannot comprehend this view: "You want the impossible."

At times, seeing the bigger picture can be as unclear as understanding how the Force works. Yet, whereas Luke's inability to see the bigger picture is the reason why he often fails, Yoda's ability to see the bigger picture is how he lifts the ship out of the swamp. In other words, Yoda can wield the Force because he knows what the Force can achieve. Luke fails to comprehend this, even after staring at his X-wing floating to dry(ish) land, which sets him up for the sharpest lesson any Jedi has ever been taught:

LUKE: I don't believe it!
YODA: That is why you fail.

Just like using the Force, greater goals serve to guide and direct us as we simultaneously pursue our other immediate and regional goals. In that sense, Luke's choice to end his Jedi training and rush off to save his friends is like his failure at the cave.[4]

---

[4] Yoda continues to chastise Luke on this point to his dying day and beyond. Did Luke ever learn the lessons his teachers tried to instill in him? For one take on Luke's process of coming to terms with all he has learned, see Hayes, chapter 14.

The consequences of Luke's choices

In choosing to satisfy his immediate emotional, attunement, and face goals, Luke puts both himself and the safety of his friends in danger. Moreover, he nearly compromises the ultimate global goal of defeating Darth Vader and the Emperor by putting himself at risk of turning to the dark side. No surprise, then, that Yoda is despondent after Luke leaves, saying to Obi-Wan: "Told you I did, reckless is he. Now, matters are worse."

By the time Luke arrives in Cloud City, Han Solo has already been frozen in carbonite and is on his way to Jabba the Hutt. Lando Calrissian helps Princess Leia and the others escape Cloud City on the *Millenium Falcon*. Luke—as predicted—loses the duel against Darth Vader and, in an ironic twist, ends up having to be rescued by Leia, whom he initially set out to save. In the end, Luke's arrival does not have an impact on his friends' fates other than to put their ultimate global goals in danger.

Further, because of Luke's decisions, Yoda is unable to see Luke as a hero or as the hope that Obi-Wan claimed Luke would be. By the time Luke returns to Dagobah, in *Return of the Jedi*, Yoda is dying: "Unfortunate that you rushed to face [Darth Vader], that incomplete was your training, that not ready for the burden were you." This is one of the consequences that comes from Luke's short-term, emotionally driven goals of trying to rescue Han and Leia. Luke was impulsive, not careful; emotional, not rational. And by leaving Dagobah the first time, he sought goals that were short-term rather than long-term, which put his own ability to be a force for good in the fight against the Empire at risk.

There is another . . . takeaway worth considering. Yoda and Obi-Wan hear and surely empathize with Luke's concerns to save his friends. They likely understand that Luke may be seeking to redeem himself, given all the identity hits he has repeatedly suffered during his training with Yoda. But instead of listening to Luke and addressing his emotional state of fear and anger and frustration, Yoda criticizes Luke further before listing out all the reasons Luke must not leave. Perhaps if Yoda and Obi-Wan had taken a more nuanced approach by engaging with Luke, carefully listening to and addressing Luke's underlying emotions and concerns—as any good crisis negotiator would do—they could have helped Luke decide based on long-term substantive goals.

Furthermore, had they engaged in such a meaningful conversation with Luke, Yoda and Obi-Wan may have been inspired to examine their own assumptions about whether Darth Vader had any salvageable good left in him. This type of examination could have led them to advise Luke differently about how to approach Vader. It is possible that Luke may still have decided to go to Cloud City, but he may have been in a much different and more constructive mindset when he left. Perhaps Luke would have surprised Vader, finding the right moment to say to him: "No, I am your son." Perhaps Vader would have turned back to the light sooner, had he encountered Luke in a more well-prepared and empathetic headspace.

But then we would have had only two movies instead of three.

References

[i] Rogan, R. G. & Hammer, M. R. (1995). Assessing message affect in crisis negotiations: An exploratory study. *Human Communications Research.* 21(4).

[ii] Wilson, S. R. & Putnam, L. L. (1990). Interaction goals in negotiation. *Annals of the International Communication Association.* 13(1).

11

Chewie Deserved a Medal: Implicit Bias in a Galaxy Nearby

Josefina M. Rendón

At the end of *A New Hope*, the Rebel Alliance celebrates their victory over the evil Empire. It is a scene of pure joy—cheers, smiles, fanfare—that all of us happily remember. Perhaps you feel the soundtrack flowing through you right now as you recall the moment when, in front of the assembled multitude of Rebel Alliance soldiers and personnel, Princess Leia rewards Han Solo and Luke Skywalker for their bravery with medals for each of them.

Standing in front of Luke and Han, a little off to the side, is Chewbacca. While he marches down the ceremonial aisle behind his companions and celebrates their award, he does not receive a medal. How odd! Hadn't Chewie been just as courageous and heroic as his friends Han and Luke? Once you notice this, you can never unnotice it; and from this moment on, the uplifting awards scene always sounds a discordant note. As it turns out, the Rebel Alliance, a seemingly benevolent organization, treats its heroes unequally. This is not to say, of course, that anyone intended to insult Chewie (this would not be a wise move, of course, given his ability to rip arms out of sockets). Certainly the ranks of the rebels are filled with non-human soldiers and leaders who, like Chewie, are powerful and respected within the community. Moreover, this is not to say that Chewie even wanted a medal or that he never received his own medal or celebration sometime later. My point here is simply to observe that during the celebration on Yavin 4, Chewie did not get a medal along with Luke and Han, and Luke and Han (as well as Leia) did not seem to be aware of the omission.

The awards scene, as is true of so many scenes in the *Star Wars* saga, presents an opportunity to reflect on human nature, which includes our assumptions, our blind spots, and our biases. Biases, both explicit and implicit, may affect perceptions and judgments, which in turn may lead to or exacerbate conflict. Developing greater awareness of our biases can help us connect and empathize with others more authentically. When we are aware of our biases, we become more capable of challenging ourselves to do more to avoid offending or harming others. Additionally, when we do offend or harm someone through intentional or even unintentional bias, improved awareness of our own biases will help us resolve the conflict more effectively.

Explicit bias: "We don't serve their kind here"

Everyone has biases. Some of these biases are *explicit*, meaning they are consciously and openly held. Explicit bias takes the form of discrimination and negative treatment of others based on categories such as race, ethnicity, age, gender, sexual orientation, disabilities, and national origin. Other biases are *implicit*, in that they operate at an automatic level and emerge as stereotypes or assumptions. Implicit biases lie deep in our unconscious and can affect how we treat and relate to others. More on implicit biases in a moment.

When most people think about bias and discrimination, they are usually thinking about explicit bias. Many years ago and in a galaxy nearby, there was in humankind a period (Obi-Wan might call it the dark times) when it was acceptable to engage in discriminatory and biased treatment of others. While the worst of those practices—actual enslavement of others of a different race—is largely abolished, other unjust practices, such as discriminatory labor conditions, still exist. Moreover, explicit bias in the form of people's bigoted views and opinions remain widespread and even protected under free-speech laws in many places. That said, many outward behaviors manifesting explicit bias have been curtailed both by public law and by private policies adopted within organizations.

Is there explicit bias in *Star Wars*? In the original trilogy, you don't see much racial prejudice as such. The main character of color, Lando Calrissian, is clearly treated as an equal, scorned like any other turncoat and embraced like any other friend. Princess Leia is a leader in the Alliance and does not appear to be laboring under sexist tropes at work or in her personal life. And Yoda, though more than 800 years old, has not been put out to pasture by ageist coworkers. Indeed, his wisdom and skill are sought by Obi-Wan and Luke.

However, we do see one form of explicit bias in *A New Hope*: bias of humans and other organic beings against droids. As sophisticated and intelligent as droids may be, they are nonetheless property and do not enjoy, say, the rights of a free citizen. Moreover, discrimination against droids is open and obvious. As Luke enters the Mos Eisley cantina with R2-D2 and C-3PO, for example, the bartender rebukes him: "We don't serve their kind here." It would be hard to show bias more explicitly than that, but just to make it perfectly clear, the bartender growls: "Your droids. They'll have to wait outside. We don't want them here." The other patrons in the cantina represent a diverse spectrum of alien life, so the issue isn't that the bar is closed to everyone except humans. Organic beings are apparently fine. The clear message from this scene is that droids are second-class citizens in organic society.[1]

Implicit bias: "We don't want any trouble"

Many of us feel that the days of stereotyping and bias are largely in the past, and we ourselves certainly don't condone unjust discrimination. In fact, we may actually feel insulted if told that we discriminate against or are biased towards others, because we our-

---

[1] Of course, we learn more about the context of droids/non-droids as the prequels and other canon material play out; there is important backstory to this policy that could provide either an explanation of the root of this discrimination or an alternative explanation for the droid ban at the cantina. Here, we address the scene as it was originally seen by viewers.

selves reject explicit bias as a philosophical, political, and personal matter.

But remember that explicit bias is just part of the story. Deep beneath the faceplates of our own conscious thoughts and behavior, in the most unconscious and unintentional manner, we may still think of others as lesser than ourselves or assume negative characteristics about them. Ironically, the more committed we are to rejecting explicit bias, the harder it may be for us to recognize that we have hidden biases deep inside our own operating systems. Over the past few decades, a growing body of research has shown that all people, even people rejecting bias in all its explicit forms, unconsciously harbor a range of *implicit* biases. Implicit biases are automatic stereotyping assumptions related to various categories of difference, such as race, ethnicity, gender, age, weight, and so on.

Let's briefly focus on how implicit bias may have functioned alongside explicit bias in the cantina, playing out how the bartender's *explicit bias* against droids may also be reflected and/or reinforced in the other patrons' *implicit bias* against droids.

We'll begin by considering Luke's response to the bartender. Luke is clearly not an organic-supremacist, and he treats his droids with respect. In fact, he appears surprised by the bartender's demand. Yet he doesn't dispute it. Luke could have expressed his disapproval of the bartender's exclusion of C-3PO and R2-D2. He could have left the cantina in protest. He could have tried to negotiate the situation with the bartender. He did not do any of these things. Why didn't Luke intercede on behalf of the droids? One reason may be that he holds an assumption—likely unconscious—that droids are not entitled to the same access as organic beings, and this assumption made the bartender's demand seem reasonable.

Indeed, all the other patrons of the cantina appear to hold this assumption as well. Many look Luke's way when the bartender accosts him, but none intervene. The customers are a diverse group of organics, and although they don't form a mob with torches and gaffi sticks and attack the droids, they certainly do not attempt to help the droids either. Rather, they quickly lose interest once they understand the reason for the bartender's shout. Even those customers who likely understand binary fluently and may have just come from a long day of working shoulder to shoulder (or whatever) with droids appear to accept that droids are excludable from organic watering holes.

Even C-3PO, the target of the bartender's ire, does not challenge either the bartender or Luke. In fact, he doesn't seem upset at all. When Luke tells him to wait by the speeder, C-3PO responds: "I heartily agree with you sir."[2] Go about your business; move along, move along.

Why did everyone, including C-3PO, accept the droids' exclusion so easily? Certainly there are practical and non-biased reasons that everyone behaved as they did. For one, Luke is searching for a pilot to take them to Alderaan. Achieving this goal means accepting the bartender's decision to exclude C-3PO and R2-D2 or risk getting kicked out of the cantina where the best pilots hang out. By complying, Luke is able to continue pursuing his goal and also spare himself from getting sunburned. For their part, the folks in the cantina may have simply wanted to avoid getting into conflict with the bartender or the newcomers, which may explain their lack of involvement. Finally, C-3PO may not have wanted to be in the cantina in the first place. It's not as if he needs a drink. And the cantina surely looks like a sketchy and threatening place, especially to a creature as high-strung as C-3PO. Getting booted gives the droid a ready excuse to seek out a safe hiding spot.

Even so, notice that Luke's body language shows little if any unhappiness, outrage, or discomfort in response to the bartender's demand. Instead, he quickly asks C-3PO to leave. Luke may be a friend to droids, but his easy acceptance of the difference in treatment in the cantina nonetheless may reflect hidden, implicit bias that droids are not entitled to the same treatment as organic beings. And even if Luke normally does not harbor bias against

---

[2] As the saga continues, we see more rights awareness among droids. Imagine how L3-37, Lando Calrissian's co-pilot and navigator in *Solo*, would have responded to the bartender.

droids, the stress and uncertainty of the moment may have made him more prone to biased behavior or tolerating biased behavior in the cantina.

How implicit bias persists: "It's such a long way from here"

By definition, implicit bias is not easy to see—it's implicit, after all. It's not intentional and it often happens unconsciously. Additionally, those affected by the bias may not provide feedback that would spotlight possible bias in action. Indeed, C-3PO and Chewbacca do not appear bothered by getting banished from the cantina or not receiving a medal. Their non-reactions illuminate three reasons why implicit bias is so difficult to identify and eradicate.

First, the victim and the offender sometimes do not even notice the manifestation of the bias and its potential adverse impact. In the cantina, Luke is likely unaware of any implicit bias motivating his behavior. C-3PO joining in agreement indicates that he doesn't perceive any bias in Luke's actions or see those actions as a slight. Chewie is part of the procession with his friends but receives no medal for his valiant service. Everybody accepts Chewie's treatment as one notch below human, and he himself doesn't seem to think anything is wrong. Our assumptions are much harder to notice in the absence of external cues that something is amiss.

Second, over time, we sometimes internalize widespread biases against us and begin to believe them. "I heartily agree with you" might hint that C-3PO *already* feels lesser than organics. In fact, throughout most of the series, C-3PO treats humans in such a way that indicates he implicitly believes (or has been programmed to believe)[i] that he is in fact of lower status than them. Just try to get him to stop calling you "Sir" or "Master." Luke couldn't.

Third, even those who are victims of implicit bias have their own set of implicit biases about others. Surprisingly, though apparently seeing himself as less than human, C-3PO also demonstrates some possible implicit bias against his friend and companion R2-D2. For example, soon after C-3PO and R2-D2 are expelled from the cantina, C-3PO says to his companion: "I would much rather have gone with Master Luke than stay here with you. I don't know what all this trouble is about, but I'm sure it must be your fault." The movies don't explain why C-3PO holds himself above R2, and it certainly may have just been a personality quirk or a feature of their relationship. It may also have been that because C-3PO can communicate beyond binary and is humanoid himself, C-3PO may think of himself as closer to human—the higher form of being—than R2, a beeping mechanic who speaks mostly with other machines.

Indeed, part of implicit bias is making us feel more connected to some people than others and accordingly treating them better, for no other reason than unconscious assumptions that we hold around certain attributes. When you meet a new group of people, for example, you may immediately identify or bond more with one or two of them simply because they happen to be from the same town as you, or look like your mother or another member of your family, or are about your same age, or have the same profession as yours. Discriminatory treatment sometimes manifests as positive or preferential treatment, after all. And although this is not necessarily bad in all situations, it can become problematic and even unjust depending on the context. A human resources manager who unconsciously prefers hiring people that remind him of himself may exclude qualified candidates and not end up with the best person for the position.

This discussion has only just scratched the surface of organic-droid, human-Wookiee, and droid-droid relations in *Star Wars*. But this scratch provides multiple examples and insights that we can reflect upon when considering our own stories of bias and how bias, whether explicit or implicit, whether toward others or toward ourselves, may affect us and those around us.

Bias and conflict: "Luke, we're gonna have company!"

There is conflict everywhere, both present and imminent. And it's not just conflict with our enemies. Just ask any married couple in our own galaxy or that galaxy far, far away. Han and Leia, for example, can attest to the fact that we often find ourselves in conflict with those we love the most. Conflict is part of our human nature and it is certainly part of *Star Wars*. Whether with enemies or loved ones, conflict can result in hurt feelings, the end of relationships, missed opportunities, destructive behaviors, and even violence.

For generations, explicit bias has been a cause of conflict. Simply put, a society that is not fair or equal is bound to experience more conflict, and the story of *Star Wars*—oppressed people rebelling against a despotic empire—demonstrates this dynamic in dramatic fashion. The same holds true for implicit bias, only in less obvious, conscious ways. Imagine yourself as Chewie, slighted after having been so courageous; as C-3PO, having your friend agree that you should be thrown out of a bar just for being yourself; as R2-D2, accused of causing a problem that was obviously not your fault at all. Would you have taken these actions peacefully, as these characters did? How about some of your friends? Would they accept this biased behavior against them?

I am certain that most of us would not have reacted as gracefully or as obliviously as Chewie, C-3PO, and R2 did. Instead, many of us would have seen such actions as thoughtless or harmful and would have reacted accordingly, perhaps to the point that our sharp response would have added fuel to the fire and escalated the conflict further. Not only can implicit bias cause stress and conflict, but it can also happen as a reaction to conflict or stress. Perhaps this is one way to interpret how C-3PO insults and blames R2-D2 after they were thrown out of the cantina. Which brings us to another important question to reflect on: Is it possible that you may have unconsciously treated others in the same way as some of our favorite *Star Wars* characters treated their own friends?

In short, bias towards others, whether explicit or implicit, may cause conflict as well as be caused by it. Striving to eliminate implicit bias is therefore not just an academic exercise. We cannot have a fair, equal, and peaceful society so long as people are harboring preconceptions based on differences of race, class, gender, and so on. In short, our galaxy would be much better if we could reduce both the amount of bias in our society and the conflict it causes.

I can't even see—how am I supposed to fight?

Explicit bias is noticeable, but implicit bias is unconscious and automatic. This makes implicit bias especially challenging to address. Like Luke, we may feel like we're wearing a helmet with the blast shield lowered, making it impossible to get a sense of what is around us. Experts recommend the following strategies to identify and reduce implicit bias in your thinking and actions.

Develop greater self-awareness. A wise Jedi from our world, Jennifer Eberhardt, has written that "[c]onfronting implicit bias requires that we look in the mirror. To understand the influence of implicit bias requires us to stare into our own eyes . . . to face how readily stereotypes and unconscious associations can shape our reality."[ii] To learn more about your own implicit assumptions, take an implicit bias test—many are available online, and the results may surprise you. It may be somewhat unpleasant to uncover biases that you did not know you had, but ultimately developing greater awareness about your own implicit biases will spare you, people you care about, and any number of strangers far more unpleasantness in the future. The more aware we are of our own tendencies, after all, the more careful we can become in treating others as we wish to be treated.

Practice empathy. "Stretch out with your feelings," advises Obi-Wan when Luke is struggling with the training remote. We should always wear our "feelings" lenses to better see how our words and actions affect others. If Leia would have imagined the medals situation from Chewie's perspective, would she have acted differently? Question how your own actions or words might affect you if they were directed at you by someone else.

Respect others as a default. It sounds quaint, but you should be kind and polite to everyone, especially those you do not know or who are dissimilar to you. This may be more challenging than it sounds. When Luke first encounters Yoda on Dagobah, he makes assumptions that appear to be based on the setting, Yoda's stature and age, and Luke's own imaginings about what a great Jedi warrior is supposed to look like. Luke quickly learns that he needs to update his mental maps, and we too would do well to follow his example. Additionally, take care to express politeness as authentically as possible, without being condescending. Finally, and perhaps obviously, avoid making jokes about anything related to someone's ethnicity, sexuality, disability, weight, or other such characteristics.

Give the benefit of the doubt. If you believe someone's bias is directed at you and you want to make them aware of their transgression, do not react with an aggressive response. Assume they mean well and be gentle in calling their attention to the impact of their words or actions. Giving the benefit of the doubt can help the other learn more quickly, without escalating conflict. Leia's efforts to free the trussed-up Luke and Han in the Ewok village—"but these are my friends"—was a gentle attempt at trying to disrupt the Ewoks' assumptions and redirect their actions. (This didn't work, as you may recall—but violence, coercion, moral judgment, and negativity were not needed to turn the tide of the situation.) Remember that implicit bias is unconscious. A comment or action that has a negative impact on you does not always equate to negative intention on the part of the speaker or actor. To help people who mean well become more aware of their implicit biases, be supportive and empathetic—not critical.

Show leadership. Take implicit bias training and encourage others to do the same. If you are in a position of authority or influence within your organization, be it a corporation, learning institution, governmental body, or any other institution, look for ways to become instrumental in bringing awareness and education to the organization and its members regarding implicit bias and discrimination.

My sincere hope is that the entire *Star Wars* fandom rallies around this cause and marches for Chewie. (When Maz Kanata gives

Han's medal to Chewie in *The Rise of Skywalker*, that is a welcome development. But Chewie still deserves his own medal.) And after that? Consider marching for the overlooked droids who arguably deserve those very same medals. Many fans have pointed out that Chewbacca was overlooked in the awards ceremony; fewer have mentioned that R2-D2 literally went through everything Luke did in *A New Hope* and beyond, even suffering a laser bolt to the dome during the trench run on the Death Star. Let's think about recognizing the little droid's contributions as well!

In both our galaxy and that one far, far away, the path to eradicating bias is long and arduous, but certainly worth following.

References

[i] Broussard, M. (2019). *Artificial unintelligence: How computers misunderstand the world*. MIT Press.

[ii] Eberhardt, J. L. (2019). *Biased: Uncovering the hidden prejudice that shapes what we see, think, and do*. Penguin Books.

Join Us or Die: Absolutism in Conflict

Alon Burstein

Luke Skywalker challenged everyone. He defied his aunt and uncle by refusing to be a farmer; he pushed back on Han's conviction that attacking the Death Star was futile; he questioned Yoda's pride in his cooking; and he upended C-3PO's belief that the droid couldn't levitate when the heroes needed a miracle.[1]

Luke also challenged one the deepest-held beliefs in the galaxy, shared by Jedi and Sith alike: "only a Sith deals in absolutes." This belief in the Sith's absolutism, first articulated by Obi-Wan in *Revenge of the Sith*, is the backbone for most of the Jedi-Sith conflict throughout the original trilogy and beyond. "Sith absolutism" refers to the notion that there are only two kinds of people in the galaxy: those who have embraced the dark side and those who have not yet embraced it but may do so later. Noticeably absent is a third category, those who turn away from the dark side and rejoin the light side. Apparently, it's a one-way path to the dark side, and once you pass the point of no return, forever will the dark side dominate your destiny—the key word being *forever*.

By contrast, although Jedi training demands devotion to the light side, the Jedi also recognize (almost obsessively) that commitment to the light side is reversible. The danger of someone falling, being tempted, or even unwittingly turning to the dark

---

[1] I could go on. Luke created a significant tactical challenge for the entire Rebel Alliance by shutting down his targeting computer during the trench run on the Death Star, helpfully explaining "Nothing, I'm all right," to people who expected to be scattered in Alderaan fashion at any moment. You get my point.

side always looms. The Sith have no such fear, instead remaining secure in their assumption that a commitment to the dark side is absolute and there is not even the slightest chance that someone will turn to the light side.[2] In fact, if there is one thing the Jedi and Sith seem to agree on, it is that servants of the dark side never find their way back to the light.

When it comes to conflict, having a reputation as "absolutist" offers some advantages. In my own field of research, I study extremist groups who use political violence and terrorism to advance their cause. Extremist groups driven primarily by religious motivations often appear to be far more devoted to their cause and more relentless than their secular counterparts—in other words, they appear to be absolutist. In these conflicts, secular counterparts may assume that there is no point in challenging anyone so uncompromisingly and absolutely devoted to their own cause. Being perceived as unrestrained, therefore, may provide religious extremists some measure of benefit or advantage in conflict. A seemingly absolutist belief in your cause creates the perception that you will go to great lengths and use every means necessary to achieve your goal.

But absolutism has conflict downsides too. As Luke himself pointes out to Emperor Palpatine in *Return of the Jedi*, overconfidence in your position can lead you to underestimate your enemy and blind you to biases and flaws in your plans. By leading you to ignore the very real possibility that you might not succeed in a negotiation or a conflict, absolutism may cause you to refrain from making a backup plan.[3] Indeed, if either side had taken Luke's

---

[2] In the sequel trilogy, Kylo Ren confesses to Darth Vader's helmet—somehow, it returned—that he once again feels the call to the light, and he asks granddaddy's assistance in resisting it. In the expanded universe, there are some stories (now considered non-canon) of Sith embracing the light side. For this chapter, though, I'm examining the no-backsies Sith absolutism as portrayed in the original trilogy.

[3] Well, except for the obvious one, which is to kill your counterpart and then see what happens. That doesn't really apply to all conflict situations, although, to their credit, the Dark Lords of the Sith do their best to push the envelope throughout the original trilogy, killing their counterparts during diplomatic encounters, workplace performance reviews, and failed corporate headhunting. For more on how these elements of Sith thinking and action affect the way in which they negotiate, see Stearns, chapter 8.

challenges to Sith absolutism seriously, events might have turned out very differently.

Once you start down the dark path . . .

Imagine you are engaged in conflict. This could be a dispute with a friend or a family member, or perhaps even involvement in a broader social disturbance or even a war. As you prepare to interact with the other side, you are told that they can tap into all their emotions, be reactionary and extremist, and use any and all means at their disposal to defeat you. You, however, are not allowed to act in that same way.[4] Understandably, you might have a bad feeling about your odds of successfully navigating that asteroid field, and you may want to know why this imbalance exists. Why must one side follow the rules when the other side doesn't have to? When Luke asks Yoda to help him understand this imbalance in the context of the light side and the dark side, Yoda immediately shuts him down—"there is no why"—and instructs Luke to clear his mind of any notion of questioning this state of affairs.

Clearly the last surviving Jedi,[5] Obi-Wan and Yoda, fully accept the notion of Sith absolutism. Despite being completely devoted to the Jedi way of life, they do not believe the Jedi have the power or the ability to bring someone back from the dark side. In fact, Sith absolutism seems to be the first lesson they feel the need to impart to next-gen Jedi, as evidenced in the first scene of Luke's training on Dagobah. Luke is giving it his all, swinging from vines, doing flips, and bearing 900 years of Jedi wisdom and snark on his back, and it still seems as if learning how to use the light side isn't in the curriculum at all. Yoda's main lesson is all about the all-consuming power of the dark side:

> A Jedi's strength flows from the Force. But beware of the dark side—anger, fear, aggression—the dark

---

[4] Any parent of a toddler, from Tatooine to Tunisia, is familiar with this match-up.

[5] I know, Ahsoka. And I know, she's (maybe) not a Jedi. And yes, Ezra Bridger and Grogu and Baylan Skoll and others. Let's just stick with the story we knew in 1977-1983, ok?

side of the Force are they. Easily they flow, quick to join you in a fight. If once you start down the dark path, forever will it dominate your destiny, consume you it will! As it did Obi-Wan's apprentice.

Luke has a hard time accepting such an absolutist view. Disregarding Yoda's advice, he takes his weapons with him when entering the cave to confront the dark side. Yoda later dubs this incident Luke's "failure in the cave," when Obi-Wan foresees that Luke will be tempted by the dark side if he goes to confront Vader in Cloud City. Yoda appears to be suggesting that by taking his weapons and aggressively decapitating his own Vader image, Luke used the Force for attack rather than knowledge and defense, proving himself dangerously susceptible to the dark side.

And yet, despite all these doomsday predictions, Luke manages not to succumb to the dark side on Bespin, even when he is at his most vulnerable. Indeed, as Luke grows stronger with the Force, his challenges to the notion of Sith absolutism grow as well. By *Return of the Jedi*, Luke is openly questioning the notion that Darth Vader is a lost cause. To Obi-Wan and Yoda, Anakin is dead. The moment he turned to the dark side he ceased to be Anakin Skywalker and became Darth Vader. They reject Luke's argument that there is still good in him, and when Luke explains that he cannot kill his own father, Obi-Wan sadly concludes that "the Emperor has already won." Here we see the powerful advantage of being perceived as absolutist: your rival underestimates their own position by deeming their own conviction contingent and swayable, while yours is complete and absolute. Accordingly, they believe themselves constrained in conflict while you, "consumed" by your cause, will do anything to win.

What would have been different for the Jedi had they not taken this absolutist view of the Sith? For starters, Obi-Wan might not have lied to Luke. In *A New Hope*, when Luke asked how his father died, Obi-Wan could have explained the complexities of the Force and the dangers of following the dark side, using Luke's father as an example and cautionary tale that would be helpful for Luke's decision-making later in practice. Moreover, Yoda might have given answers that would have not only prevented Luke's "failure" in the cave but also helped him to manage his competing emotions. As a more emotionally literate Jedi-trainee, Luke might not have made the "unfortunate" decision of rushing to face Vader.

He is more machine now than man, twisted and evil

The most significant impact of the Jedi reconsidering their absolutist view of the Sith, however, would have likely been in the meeting between Obi-Wan and Darth Vader in *A New Hope*. This was a momentous reunion, twenty years since their duel on Mustafar in *Revenge of the Sith* and ten years since they fought in the *Kenobi* series. Vader senses the presence of his former Master and insists on facing him alone. He declares that the "circle is now complete" because "when I left you, I was but the learner, now I am the Master." Obi-Wan's answer? "Only a master of evil, Darth!"[6] As this choice of words demonstrates, Obi-Wan sees the Sith as absolutists. Vader is *only* a master of evil, incapable of change or redemption.

What if Obi-Wan had taken a different stance? Imagine that he had assumed that all falls from grace can be halted by skillfully reversing stabilizers and that all people can potentially be swayed by insightful, skilled negotiation. When Luke makes this very assumption as he engages with Vader in *Return of the Jedi*, for example, we see that Vader is susceptible to emotional, logical, and relational appeals, even from an estranged son with whom Vader had, let's face it, a contentious relationship at best.[7] Obi-Wan, by contrast, was like a father/brother to Anakin and taught him everything he knew, cleaning up his messes and keeping track of the number of times they saved each other's lives. His mere presence on the Death Star clearly sends tremors through Vader's armor and cyber-nervous system. Given their formerly close relationship,

---

[6] As a snappy comeback, it's not Obi-Wan's best. At the risk of being caught using the same line twice, he could have said "Oh, I don't think so." Even "Hello there" would have had more zing.

[7] And, as long as we've mentioned the Battle of Yavin, remember that was the first time that the two shared a trench and Vader did his best to treat Luke like Porkins.

perhaps Obi-Wan could have achieved far more than Luke, and so much earlier in the saga, had he taken a different approach.

If, for example, Obi-Wan had recognized the self-defeating ramifications of perceiving your adversary as more absolutist than you, he could have engaged with Vader rather than labeling him "evil." He could have tapped into Vader's former Jedi identity, reminding Vader of the values of his old fraternity.[8] He might have told Vader he was proud of how powerful he had become, even as he was dismayed by what Vader had done to himself, others, and the galaxy at large. He might have told him that Yoda still believes in him. He could have spoken of their shared interest in protecting Luke. He could have pointed out the glass ceiling Vader has hit in the Sith hierarchy, suggested possibly teaming up against the Emperor, or asked Vader what else he might be interested in obtaining other than Obi-Wan's cloak on the floor.

We will never know if such an approach would have worked, but if it had, the galactic conflict might have been shortened by years. The millions of lives lost at Yavin, Hoth, and both Death Stars would have been avoided, and the brutal exploitation of people and planets for resources to fuel the Empire[9] might have ceased. From this certain point of view, the Jedi—because they could not give up their belief in Sith absolutism—doomed the galaxy to needless years of suffering and war.

If he could be turned, he would become a powerful ally

Of course, the Jedi aren't wrong about the Sith being absolutists. The Sith embrace absolutism, well, absolutely. In a memorable scene from *The Empire Strikes Back*, Darth Vader declares to the

---

[8] One method Obi-Wan might have applied to work around Vader's cognitive filters to evoke such positive emotions is neurolinguistic programing (NLP), the closest thing to a Jedi mind trick that our galaxy has to offer. To learn how you can use NLP to turn your friends and family away from the dark side, see Ulrich, chapter 9.

[9] Flash to *Andor*, which showed an Empire-wide judicial system that was actually an enslavement pipeline, to *Rogue One*, which showed the Empire brutalizing its own scientists and engineers, and back to *Return of the Jedi*, in which Moff Jerjerrod committed to double the efforts of his workers in order to complete the second Death Star on schedule, even though they were already laboring as hard as they possibly could and despite Jerjerrod's own assessment that meeting the deadline was impossible.

Emperor that Luke will "join us or die." This unassailable self-assurance echoes throughout the movies. But just as Luke challenges the Jedi's belief in Sith absolutism, Luke also challenges the Sith's own absolutist stance, stating repeatedly that he will not turn to the dark side *and* that Vader can still return to the light. Like the Jedi, the Sith reject Luke's challenge, quite literally laughing (well, cackling) in Luke's face.

As with the Jedi, Luke's challenge to Sith absolutism sharpens as he matures. In *The Empire Strikes Back*, Luke appears to believe that the Sith are indeed absolutists. When Luke and Darth Vader meet at Cloud City, Luke does not say a word before engaging Vader in combat, and the only time Luke says anything of substance (beyond a little smack-talk of his own, like "you'll find I'm full of surprises") is when he has no choice, after losing his hand along with his lightsaber. By *Return of the Jedi*, however, Luke is ready to engage in actual discussion and negotiation. He now refuses to accept the Sith's absolutist self-perception, instead drawing both Vader and the Emperor into meaningful exchanges meant to undermine their assumptions and self-assurance.

When Vader arrives on Endor to take Luke into custody and deliver him to the Emperor, for example, Luke says that Vader used to be Anakin Skywalker, his father. Vader reacts somewhat defensively, revealing a crack in his absolutist façade. Poking Luke in the chest with a (blessedly unlit) lightsaber, he asserts: "That name no longer has any meaning for me." Showing remarkable mastery of the skills of listening to your counterpart in negotiation and attending to their verbal and nonverbal cues, Luke picks up on this response. Pushing further along that same pathway, he shares his own sense of Vader's conflict and evokes memories of Vader's forgotten life. Visibly cornered for a moment, Vader redirects the conversation to Luke's lightsaber. Importantly, Vader never disagrees with Luke in this scene about his conflicting emotions. Instead, Vader appears resigned to accept his own absolutist reality, responding gently to Luke's entreaties to return to the light side: "It is too late for me, son."

However, Vader's Sith conditioning eventually kicks in and he is soon spouting the absolutist party line about having gone down a one-way path with no escape, even if the path leads to him killing his own son. This scene depicts one of the inherent dangers of absolutism. Unrelenting devotion to a cause binds you to a very specific position, and your ability to consider alternatives that may serve your interests far better is inherently curtailed.[10]

Only your hatred can destroy me

Arriving at the second Death Star, Luke encounters the Emperor, who encourages Luke to give in to his anger and "strike me down with all of your hatred, and your journey towards the dark side will be complete!" Note that this was not in fact the case. Luke does initiate violence in this exchange, slashing at the Emperor and then engaging in a lightsaber duel with Vader. But even during these altercations—in which Luke does get upset, especially when Vader mentions Leia—Luke challenges the Sith's absolutist ideal by turning off his lightsaber and recentering himself each time he realizes how far down the path he has gone. The Emperor's decision to hit Luke with Force lightning may simply be an attempt to preserve Sith absolutism by destroying the evidence that the pull of the dark side is not as inexorable as advertised.[11]

As discussed above, the entire conflict between Jedi and Sith would have been remarkably different had the Sith been less absolutist in general, or if either group had engaged with Luke's challenges specifically. Had the absolute confidence and self-assurance in the one-way path of the dark side been taken down a notch, the Emperor might have been inclined to put more trust in his own instincts the first time he sensed something was off with

---

[10] Returning to our own galaxy for a moment, similar drawbacks of absolutism are observable in religiously motivated violent groups as well. Such groups may end up being bound by the rules of their own religion, which may make it impossible to achieve their goals. For example, both the Taliban and Hamas have stated that although they may be able to achieve more of their goals using different tactics or rhetoric, they nonetheless feel bound to religious-absolutist principles that cannot be set aside.

[11] This scene is mirrored in the Emperor's seduction of Ezra Bridger and his ultimate failure to turn him to the dark side in the last episode of season 4 of *Rebels*.

Vader. When Vader reports to the Emperor that Luke has arrived at Endor, for example, the Emperor appears unsettled that Vader felt Luke's presence yet the Emperor had not, and he suggests with some suspicion that Vader's feelings may be complex. But then the Emperor accepts Vader's simple reassurance that his feelings are clear and immediately returns to his plan to send Vader—the very Vader he has just doubted—to fetch his son. Here we see a self-defeating element of Sith absolutism: the Emperor is unable to fathom that Vader may be experiencing paternal emotions or wavering in his devotion to the dark side. Had the Emperor trusted his initial suspicions rather than adhering to his absolutism, he might have dodged a dive down a long shaft.

Other examples of misjudgment resulting from absolutism appear throughout their interactions. Vader does not consider the possibility that Luke will choose death on Bespin (or convoluted survival), instead believing that he will come with him as "it is the only way." Neither Vader nor the Emperor give even the slightest thought to Luke's repeated argument that Vader is conflicted and still has good in him. Consider his constant messages to Vader, on Endor and in the throne room: "I know there is good in you, the Emperor hasn't driven it from you fully"; "I feel the conflict within you let go of your hate!"; "Your thoughts betray you father, I feel the good in you, the conflict . . . You couldn't bring yourself to kill me before and I don't believe you'll destroy me now"; "You failed, Your Highness. I am a Jedi, like my father before me!" Luke is showing all his cards, but the Emperor cannot see them. His judgment, instincts, and emotional reading are completely clouded by his absolutist conviction that there is no such thing as returning from the dark side. Until someone does.

Many of the truths we cling to depend greatly on our own point of view

The Jedi and the Sith disagree. They disagree over everything from the nature of the Force, the proper regime type in the galaxy, the very meaning of the concept "good," and the best color for lightsabers. The one thing they do agree on, however, is that the Sith—

the more aggressive, angry, hate-filled, and "negative" side—are absolutist in conflict. While a Jedi is open to different points of view and thus can be tempted by the dark side, the Sith are fixated on a one-way path with no turning back.

This depiction suggests that absolutism in conflict is always bad. But absolutism is not inherently "evil," it is simply an all-encompassing conviction in the truth of your perspective. A party to conflict could be absolutist about *any* position they hold, and this absolutism may lead to substantial advantages. As discussed above, the Jedi respect the Sith's conviction, fully accepting that they may lose followers to the dark side without being able to convert anyone back to the light side. The Sith thus gain advantage from how their absolutism impacts the Jedi mindset. Beyond that, they use their absolutism offensively, as when the Emperor wields his confidence to draw Luke into his influence; and defensively, as when a struggling Vader reconnects to the dark side simply due to his conviction that he "must."

Simultaneously, however, absolutism has its weaknesses. As we see in *Return of the Jedi*, absolutism breeds blind spots: your extreme conviction prevents you from seeing your own weaknesses, identifying fractures in your ranks, or recognizing that you face a more belligerent or powerful rival.[12] Ultimately, Luke's "absolute" conviction that absolutism is but a phantom menace is proven accurate.

In our own world, we are quick to label others (or even ourselves) as absolutist in different ways as conflict escalates between us. We often dismiss the notion that our opponents' stance can be swayed and that we ourselves should be open to hearing other points of view. Such absolutism may prevent us from reaching sensible resolutions to conflict. Perhaps it's time to listen to Luke—impatient, unready, and challenging as he may be.

---

[12] As Qui-Gon eloquently states in *The Phantom Menace*, there is always a bigger fish, but an absolutist framework makes it harder to see.

SEQUEL TRILOGY
The greatest teacher, failure is

13

The Intuitive Force and the Wisdom of Feelings

Michael T. Colatrella Jr.

We know that the Force, the energy that surrounds and binds all living things in the *Star Wars* universe, is a source of potentially immense power. Using the Force, a Jedi Knight can levitate star fighters, displace boulders, and even astroproject onto another planet.

But one of the Force's most powerful uses throughout the *Star Wars* saga involves something more internal. Through the Force, the Jedi gain heightened awareness of their own feelings and the feelings of others. This awareness is as important, perhaps even more so, as controlling people and making things float. Without awareness of feelings—without sensitivity and attunement to the emotions at stake in a situation—relationships may degrade, conflicts may fester, and negotiations may stall. Moreover, the ability to make wise decisions suffers when the decision-maker does not take the emotional landscape of a situation into account.

Consider, for example, a basic difference in decision-making style between C-3PO, the beloved, if often frazzled, golden humanoid droid, and Rey, the Jakku scavenger and budding Jedi. C-3PO is a mostly rational decision-maker. He is fond of calculating the odds to guide his life choices and telling them to others to guide theirs. His recommendations are informed primarily by data and logic. And yet C-3PO is not exactly famous for wise decisions.

In contrast, Rey uses both facts and feelings to make choices. Early in *The Force Awakens*, for example, Rey is finishing a meal in the desert in the shadow of a fallen AT-AT walker's foot pad, when she hears the distressed beeps and whistles of a droid. She senses something is wrong and immediately rises, grasping her staff. Over the next dune, she sees that Teedo the parts seller has captured a droid. Without hesitation, apparently on gut instinct alone, Rey negotiates the droid's release in a forceful fashion and Teedo retreats into the desert. In this way, Rey meets BB-8, a droid that will play a pivotal role in her life and the sequel trilogy more broadly. This is one of the first decisions that we see Rey make, and its speed and confidence are fueled by intuition and emotion.

In this chapter, I will use additional examples from the sequel trilogy to demonstrate how factual knowledge and intuitive knowledge are complementary components of that most important ability of a Jedi Knight—wisdom in decision-making.

I've got a bad feeling about this

In *Star Wars*, whenever a character says they have a bad feeling about this, they're usually proven right. But in Western culture, knowledge and wisdom (and, consequently, good decision-making) are deemed to be products of rational, logical reasoning and analysis, not feelings. Emotions, as a source of knowledge, play a subservient role to reasoning; in fact, emotions often are considered an obstacle to making good life choices. This Western cultural sentiment is captured in the Oscar Wilde quip that "the advantage of emotions is that they lead us astray." Yet the important decisions we make in negotiation and conflict situations, such as whether and how to settle a dispute, cannot successfully be made with cold logic. The same goes for a multitude of life choices, including choices made in negotiation and in conflict situations.

For example, let's examine the complex decision-making around negotiating job offers. The employer has to consider the immediate value the candidate may bring to their business along with the candidate's experience, potential, the amount of training and guidance they will need, opportunities they may have with other employers, and many other considerations. The candidate must compare the potential benefits of the new job to their current job or other life circumstances, job duties, opportunities for advancement, the nature of the new work environment, and many other issues. These parallel tracks of employer/candidate decision-making are further complicated given that each party has their own resources and tendencies on three important fronts: the information they possess, the information they deem relevant, and the way they process that information. Engaging in negotiation, these two tracks combine, merge, or collide, as parties share information (or do not), consider it (or discard it), and process it (jointly or separately).

While Western culture would have us assume that parties always discuss the cold hard facts and reach logical conclusions in such situations, the reality is that intuition and emotion play a key role. Employers offer jobs and candidates accept them for reasons that may include logical analysis but also draw on emotions.

We see an example in *The Force Awakens*. Han Solo offers Rey a job on the *Falcon*, to serve as his second mate. He gives Rey information on most of the elements listed above, and he assumes Rey will jump at his offer. Who wouldn't? Especially a scavenger girl from Jakku? The details are enticing: keeping up with Chewie and Han, low pay, and a boss who promises he won't be nice to her. It looks like the perfect job for someone with Rey's interests and qualifications. Yet she turns down the offer. Even though this is exactly the kind of job Rey wants, she is bound to Jakku by emotional ties: loyalty, desire to belong and be loved, and fear of missing out. Her parents will come back for her one day, she believes, and if she leaves, they will never be able to find her. So long as these emotion-based assumptions dominate her decision-making, she'll never take a job that pulls her away from Jakku.

Thus do emotions affect choices in negotiation—and they also play a role in how people make decisions in interpersonal conflict. What information should they share? How much responsibility should they take for the conflict? And, perhaps most consequentially, should they even attempt to resolve the conflict or should they give up on the relationship? In these encounters, as in decision-making around job offers and other life choices, understanding the role emotions and intuition play in decision-making is useful.

As a quick example, consider Rey's encounter on Kijimi with Zorii Bliss, Poe's former friend-slash-spice-running partner-slash-romantic interest. Zorii is mad enough at Poe to want to see all of their brains in the snow. She only holds back because she recognizes Rey as the one the First Order is searching for and figures she'd be better served by turning Rey in for a bounty. The conflict escalates into violence, ending with Zorii's blaster aimed at Rey's face and Rey's lightsaber at Zorii's throat. Yet each of them holds back from killing the other. "We could really use your help," Rey says. Her lightsaber doesn't waver as she adds "please." "Not that you care," Zorii responds, her finger still on the trigger, "but I think you're okay." Rey replies, "I care," extinguishing her lightsaber and extending her hand to Zorii.

Think of all of the complexities that went into those choices, on both sides. Zorii was influenced by her desire for revenge, her need to protect her crew, the valuable bounty waiting for whomever brings Rey and her friends in, her capacity to keep on fighting, and the harm facing her from that beam of light humming uncomfortably close to her throat. Rey had to consider her friends' safety, the laser dueling pistol aimed at her eye, Zorii's aggression, and the price the galaxy will pay if she fails in her mission. So much to calculate on both sides, yet in the end, the conflict de-escalates only due to both characters' on-the-spot intuition that the other was dependable, could be helpful, was not a bad person, and above all should not be killed.

Your antenna is bent

In our galaxy, neuroscience helps explain why it is better to approach complex decision-making more like a Jedi than a droid. The *somatic marker theory*, formulated by UCLA neurobiologist Antonio Damasio, posits that emotions not only are a desirable element of good decision-making but are an essential aspect of it.[i] Damasio explains that every experience we have is laden with emotions—good, bad, or indifferent. Our minds record the emotional aspects of these situations by "marking" the physical feelings we experienced as the situations transpired. These might be the rapid heartbeat of the fear or anxiety we felt, the exultant feeling of joy, or the nausea accompanying a feeling of disgust. As we encounter decision points further along life's path—what to eat for breakfast, what work project to complete first, where to go on vacation—our brain compares these circumstances to similar experiences and decisions from our past, applying both the factual information as well as emotional information through the somatic markers from previous experiences. It is this combination of factual and emotional information regarding past experiences that allows us to make wiser choices in the present moment. If you rely only on reason in decision-making, notes Damasio, "it's not going to work."

That rationality alone does not produce good decisions is illustrated in Damasio's treatment of a patient that he calls Elliot. Elliot had been a highly successful businessman in his thirties with a wife and family. After he had a large benign brain tumor removed that was causing life-threatening pressure on his frontal brain lobes, he became by all accounts a changed person. When Damasio first met Elliot, Elliot was jobless, broke, nearly homeless, and divorced twice. Other doctors could find nothing wrong with him to explain his inability to function in the world. Indeed, Damasio's first series of standard neurological tests showed no psychological, physiological, or neurological abnormalities. Tests revealed Elliot to be of superior intelligence, with good short-and long-term memory, the ability to concentrate appropriately, and without any diagnosable personality dysfunction. Yet, after doctors removed his brain tumor, Elliot could no longer keep a job, make sound life choices, or maintain good relationships at work or at home.

Pioneering new neurological testing, Damasio demonstrated that Elliot's tumor and subsequent removal had severed important neurological pathways that enabled Elliot to access crucial emotional memory to make decisions. While Elliot's intelligence, logical analysis, and factual memory were as functional as C-3PO's, the emotional information was absent from his decision-making function. Without this emotional impetus, Elliot would need to be prodded to get up for work. Once at work, he could not prioritize tasks appropriately. To him, one task seemed as important (or unimportant) as another. This was because there was no emotional charge connected with any of it. He would sometimes get bogged down in factual details such that he would be paralyzed with indecision. Sound familiar? He also was prone to making catastrophic business choices that ultimately caused his financial ruin. Emotional memory—feelings—it turned out, is required to successfully function in the world. Damasio's theory posits that somatic markers improve decision-making, and their absence severely and catastrophically diminishes decision-making.

This brings us back to our comparison between C-3PO and Rey. Rey is the person you want to make decisions in a crisis. She uses both rationality and emotional memory to guide her actions. Her gut feeling is as important as the rationality underlying any decision, maybe even more so. Conversely, C-3PO, and I say this with all affection, is usually a hot mess in a crisis, offering nothing but facts, odds, and, of course, a healthy dose of humor.[1]

Thinking through sensations: "I feel it"

When we first encounter Rey, we find a scavenger who salvages parts from ships lying partially exposed in desert sand like fossils. Her work is not only arduous but dangerous as well. She climbs impossibly high, twisted infrastructures and must leap between dangling cables hundreds of feet in the air to access spaceship bits and bobs not yet plundered. Prying loose consoles and converters, she scrapes out her sustenance. Rey conveys her collected space-

---

[1] C-3PO does experience fear, which carries through to new situations and affects his behavior. But the droid often attempts to make decisions using only protocol and numbers. Just think back to *The Last Jedi:* The entire Resistance is trapped in a cavern, Luke Skywalker projects himself halfway across the galaxy to fight Kylo Ren in order to buy time for the rebels, and all C-3PO can contribute to the situation is informing anyone who would listen that the odds of finding an unmapped hidden exit are 15,428 to 1.

ship scrap to town on a land-schlepper and trades them for food, hoping to obtain enough to go through the whole thing again the next day.

Rey's routine is disrupted when she rescues BB-8, a spherical astromech droid who, unbeknownst to Rey, carries a crucial part of the map that leads to the location of Luke Skywalker. Both the Resistance and the First Order are looking for BB-8 to complete the map. The Resistance hopes to enlist Skywalker's help in rekindling the Jedi Order to aid in defeating the First Order, the despotic governmental successor to the Empire. If the First Order obtains the map before the Resistance does, they will kill Skywalker to prevent Jedi support to the Resistance.

The day after rescuing BB-8, Rey brings the droid along as she attempts to trade more salvaged ship parts for food. Upon seeing BB-8, Unkar Plutt, the Jakku scrap trader, offers Rey sixty food portions for the droid. This is an Emperor's ransom to a poor scavenger who lives hand to mouth! You can see Rey is tempted to take such an unprecedented offer of security. Rationality alone would dictate that she take the offer. But an expression of resolve flashes across her face, a feeling that this would be a bad choice, despite its obvious benefits. Based on this feeling, she refuses to sell, a decision that prevents the First Order from obtaining the map to Skywalker and thus gives the universe a chance to escape despotic rule. Through use of feelings, Rey has learned one of the most important negotiation lessons: sometimes the best deal in a negotiation is no deal.

In our galaxy, Rey's wise decision to not trade BB-8 for food, supported by feeling instead of pure rationality, finds support in the work of John Coates. Before Coates undertook his research of human decision-making, he was a Wall Street trader. As a trader, he noticed an odd trend. The stock trades that he planned out rigorously and rationally often made no money, while the trades that "felt good" usually made money. Rationality played a part in these money-making trades, but so did feelings. He noticed this trend in his fellow traders too. The most successful traders were not necessarily the ones with prestigious academic degrees or sparkling intellects. They were traders who heeded "gut feelings" about trades. Fascinated by these informal observations, he spent the next decade studying the role that gut feelings play in good decision-making and risk-taking.

Coates's later research supported his earlier observations that gut feelings count for a lot—not only in successful trading, but in human decision-making more broadly. Coates calls these gut feelings *introception*. Introception is the body's awareness of its inner state:

> We have senses like vision, hearing and smell that point outward to the external world; but it turns out we also have... sense organs that point inward, perceiving internal organs such as the heart, lungs, liver, etc. ... [I]t is this diffuse information, flowing from all regions of the body, that gives us the sense of how we feel.[ii]

Coates found that the traders with the highest degree of introception made the most money and lasted the longest in their jobs. It turns out that our brains process enormous amounts of unconscious information, and that information is so varied and complex that it is communicated to us through our feelings. Good judgment, therefore, requires us to listen closely to these feelings.

One of the qualities of a Jedi, or anyone strong with the Force, is that they rely heavily on introception in guiding their actions. Consider Luke's first training session with Rey, in which he has her sit, breathe, and "reach out." The first time, she stretches her hand out, causing Luke to eye-roll into the next galaxy. Once chastised, Rey understands. She centers herself and reaches out with her *feelings*. That centering process involves an unspoken phase of connecting with her feelings, hooking herself into introception before reaching out.

Beings who are not Force sensitive are perhaps less capable of introception. "All of us experience these signals," Coates explains, "but some of us feel them more keenly than others." To demonstrate varying degrees of introception between individuals, Coates conducted experiments where he connected people to a heart monitor and asked them to tell him when their hearts beat. Some people could report with terrific accuracy the beating of their heart, while others had no idea when and how quickly it was beating.²

Intuition: The light is always there

As we know, Rey has stayed on Jakku for years because she believes that her parents will someday return for her. But Rey ends up leaving Jakku at the beginning of *The Force Awakens* to escape the First Order, arriving on the planet Takodana in a castle-like watering hole owned by the ancient and wily Maz Kanata. Rey is at a crossroads, having to decide whether to join the Resistance's search for Luke Skywalker or to return to Jakku to continue waiting for her parents. Maz says, kindly:

> I am no Jedi, but I know the Force . . . Close your eyes. Feel it. The light, it has always been there. It will guide you.

Maz is advising Rey to trust her intuition as to what is true and what to do next. Following this advice, Rey listens to her intuition and joins the search for Skywalker.

We can define intuition as an insight or knowledge "involving emotionally charged, rapid, unconscious processes."[iii] Most of us have experienced guidance through intuition in our lives to a lessor or greater extent. Like feelings, intuition is a source of knowledge seemingly detached from cold logic because *how* we obtained the knowledge is often unconscious or not evident. Put another way, intuition helps us make good decisions without conscious analytical thought.

---

² It is possible to improve this kind of introception and cultivate a deeper awareness of the signals your body is sending you. You can, for example, have a friend take your pulse and see if you can sense your heartbeats. Or use your favorite exercise monitoring device to track your heart. Better yet, begin a meditation practice, which is an excellent way to become more in touch with the sensations and information your body and unconscious mind are sending you.

Although many of us would acknowledge the importance intuition plays in guiding our lives, until recently there was very little formal scientific study of it. That is, until Dr. Joel Petersen at his Future Minds Lab at the University of New South Wales conducted a series of simple but ingenious experiments to show that information obtained by our unconscious mind improves our conscious decisions.[iv]

The experiments required participants to predict the apparently random movement of a dot across a computer screen. Unbeknownst to the participants, while observing the dot's movement, the experimenters flashed subliminal images. This technique is known as continuous flash suppression. The brain unconsciously registers the images, but the images are flashed so quickly that the conscious brain is unaware of them. In Petersen's experiment, some images were "positive" images, such as of babies and puppies. Some images were of "negative" images, such as snakes and guns. The experimenters flashed positive subliminal images when the dot would move in one direction and negative subliminal images when the dot would move in a different direction.

Petersen and his colleagues found that groups that had the benefit of the unconscious information were more "accurate and confident" in their predictions of the dot's movement. Moreover, as the task became more complex, participants relied even more on the unconscious information and their response times got faster. These recent findings are evidence of the unconscious mind improving conscious choices.

We see the same dynamic in *Star Wars*, where the Force acts as a source of knowledge and wisdom, particularly with respect to feelings and intuitions. One of my favorite aspects of the sequel trilogy is the story arc of Finn, the former stormtrooper. We have come to expect that the Jedi and the Sith are the only ones to use the Force for knowledge and guidance. We are unsurprised, for example, when Kylo Ren immediately knows who helped Poe Dameron, the captured Resistance pilot, escape: "The one from the village, the stormtrooper." And then, in *The Rise of Skywalker*, we see that same stormtrooper (non-Jedi Finn) also relying on intuition as sure knowledge. At one point, Finn says of his joining the Resistance: "the Force brought me here." And most tellingly and crucially, during the battle on Exegol, it is Finn who knows which Sith ship out of thousands is guiding the deadly fleet and must be destroyed: "It's that one," says Finn. "I feel it." And it is.

Once you go looking for non-Jedi use of intuition, it's everywhere—as Finn himself discovers when encountering Jannah, another former stormtrooper whose entire company followed their intuition in deciding not to open fire on civilians, putting aside their training and sense of self-preservation. Clearly, intuition is one part of the Force available to us all.

Conclusion: Bring back the balance

Like all great fantasy and science fiction stories, *Star Wars* illustrates essential truths about human nature, including the power of the human mind to know truths and facts—to make sensible and wise decisions—through feelings, bodily sensations, and intuition. As poet and philosopher Ralph Waldo Emerson famously wrote: "(the) wise Seer within me never errs. / I never taught it what it teaches me; / I only follow, when I act aright." Compare these lines to Yoda's statement to Luke after the sacred Jedi texts are destroyed: "Wisdom they held, but that library contained nothing that the girl Rey does not already possess." For both Emerson and Yoda, wisdom about the outside world is intrinsically connected to emotions, feelings, and intuition.

One doesn't have to be a Jedi to harness the intuitive power of the Force. To do so, first recognize that emotions, gut feelings, and intuition provide essential information that will render you more accurate and confident in decision-making. Second, when confronted with important or difficult decisions, proactively search your feelings and gut reactions about the various choices. Which feel good? Which make you feel uncomfortable? Kylo Ren feels the awakening Force within Rey just as he feels his father's presence on Starkiller Base and his mother's presence aboard the Resistance ship he is targeting for attack. Certainly, some of this awareness of feelings is an outcome of his Force sensitivity, and this awareness improves his decision-making (even if we ourselves would disagree strongly with some of those decisions). The rest of us? We all have an inner awareness of our own emotions and intuitions, to some degree, and some of us to a considerable degree. Something inside us has always been there, but having read this chapter, now it's awake. Search your feelings; you already know the truth.

References

[i] Damasio, A. (1994). *Descartes' error: emotion, reason, and the human brain.* Penguin Books.

[ii] Coates, J. (2012). *The hour between dog and wolf: how risk taking transforms us, body and mind.* Penguin Books.

[iii] Lufityanto, G., Donkin, C. & Pearson, J. (2016). Measuring intuition: Nonconscious emotional information boosts decision accuracy and confidence. *Psychological Science.* 27(5).

[iv] Paul, A. M. (2021). *The extended mind: the power of thinking outside the brain.* HMH Books.

14

Why the Uneti Tree Had to Burn: Luke Skywalker Gets to Yes with Himself

Sherrill W. Hayes

If the Skywalker family is famous anything other than their skills with a lightsaber, it is their battles with their own inner conflicts. Yet some fans were surprised and even dismayed when, in *The Last Jedi*, they encountered an unhappy, unhelpful, self-pitying, and cynical Luke Skywalker.[1] Here was a dispirited man struggling with his mistakes, confronting a difficult legacy, and negotiating his role in the universe. Ultimately he finds his way back to the Force and to himself, but it isn't easy. Luke's journey in the sequels serves as an example of how to reestablish a sense of self and purpose in a difficult, conflict-ridden world, especially when a person has found that the story—including the very role they played in the key conflicts of their time—did not quite turn out the way they thought it would.

"We need Luke Skywalker."

The sequel trilogy opens with a mystery: "Where is Luke Skywalker?" In *The Force Awakens*, we learn that Luke Skywalker is missing and the Resistance has been desperately searching for him. Eventually the Resistance, led by General Organa and helped by Han Solo, discovers that Luke is hiding on an island in the distant system of Ahch-To, home to one of the original Jedi temples.

---

[1] This portrayal of Luke is highly controversial within the *Star Wars* fandom; the nastiness of the online rhetoric surrounding it merits its own conflict analysis.

In the movie's closing scene, Rey, a scavenger girl from Jakku (aka "nowhere"), tracks Luke down and apprehensively holds out his lightsaber as a gesture of invitation to return to the Resistance. Roll credits, and the audience is left to ponder this scene for a few years, perhaps imagining Luke's triumphant return.

Imagine (or remember!) our shock in the opening scene of the next film, when Luke takes the lightsaber and dismissively tosses it over his shoulder. What has happened to Luke? The person Rey meets on Ahch-To is not the same triumphant, smiling young man who hugs his friends and communes with Force ghosts at the end of *Return of the Jedi*. That Luke was a confident champion, practically the last man standing on (before escaping) the second Death Star. By contrast, the person who tosses the proffered lightsaber aside is angry, defiant, reclusive, even smarmy. And bitter. So, so bitter.

After so many years of Luke blaming Darth Vader, and then the Empire and its Emperor, for everything that was rotten with the galaxy, it was certainly surprising to learn that the target of Luke's current acrimony is none other than the Jedi Order—himself included. Luke is determined that the Jedi's role and stature in galactic history should end, and he will ensure they end by enforcing his hermitage and refusing to intervene. Which includes refusing to train future interventionist Jedi. Despite Rey's pleading, Luke is steadfast: "I will never train another generation of Jedi." While Luke relents after seeing some of Rey's Force abilities, he withdraws again when he sees a connection forming between Rey and Kylo Ren, Luke's fallen apprentice. Rey leaves Ahch-To believing Luke is a lost cause.

The depths of Luke's disillusionment with the Jedi become clear when he attempts to burn down the Uneti tree, a library of the original copies of sacred Jedi texts. Yoda's Force ghost arrives just in time to tell him just how far he has strayed from his path, reminding him to confront, learn from, and teach his mistakes. Indeed, from the cave on Dagobah, to his fleeting attempt to kill young Ben Solo before he becomes Kylo Ren, and ultimately in rejecting a chance to connect with Rey to train a new generation of Jedi, Luke's journey has been marked by significant failures.

At this moment, Luke realizes he has fallen down a reactor shaft of despair and regret. It would be easy to brush away the annoying little Force ghost with his sharp insights and even sharper (and inexplicably tangible) stick, and just fall all the way to the core. But Luke chooses to redeem himself, in an epic return that is no less remarkable than Darth Vader's or Kylo Ren's ultimate turn back to the light. At the end of *The Last Jedi*, when all hope is lost and the Resistance seems doomed to fail, a stronger, gentler, less gray-bearded Luke emerges from the shadows of an old Rebel bunker on Crait to comfort his sister General Leia. Afterward, Luke's Force projection faces down Kylo Ren and the whole First Order with only a laser sword, buying the Resistance time to escape. In Luke's final scene, we see a person accepting his place in the universe and becoming one with the Force.

"And this is the lesson."

What can we learn about ourselves from Luke's journey? Given the Skywalkers' propensity for internal conflict, it is only natural to apply frameworks for understanding conflict and negotiating its resolution to understand Luke's transformations. Once you do, it is as clear as the island air that in each, he *negotiated with himself* over who he would become.

Let's lay a little groundwork. In 1981, Roger Fisher and William Ury released the blockbuster *Getting to Yes*,[i] one of the truly sacred texts for negotiators, mediators, and other conflict professionals in our galaxy. Then, in 2015, William Ury published his own prequel, *Getting to Yes with Yourself*.[ii] Ury's principal message in this book is that success or failure in negotiation is rarely due to other parties. Rather, negotiation outcomes hinge far more on the internal struggles of the negotiator, not unlike how a Skywalker resolving internal struggles has the potential to save the galaxy. Ury emphasizes the value of embracing personal truths, accepting past mistakes, and striving for self-acceptance.

Analyzing Luke's journey in *The Last Jedi* through the framework provided in Ury's book opens new windows for better understanding Angry, Bitter Luke as well as Redeemed, At-Peace Luke, as he moves past self-judgment to self-acceptance, embraces the power of self-reflection, and harnesses empathy through self-understanding. It also illustrates a few key lessons that can help us better understand how to say "yes" to ourselves when we would rather find our own private island and disconnect from the Force.

"Leia blamed Snoke, but it was me. I failed."

Who doesn't dream of a comeback, right? Not Luke. Perhaps he had too much on his plate? Nope; as Rey tells him, "I've seen your daily routine; you are not busy." Indeed, Luke rejects Rey's approach not because he wants to spend more time spearfishing and squeezing blue milk from thala-sirens, but because his experience training Ben Solo led him to an inner "no" rather than an inner "yes." Luke's cold stare at Rey, flippant toss of the lightsaber, and refusal to train her are rooted in the fear and blame he has felt since the moment he ignited his lightsaber and fleetingly considered killing Ben Solo in his sleep.

Luke's near-fatal encounter with Ben is described three times in the movie: first by Luke, then by Ben, and finally, by Luke again. Our grasp of the story evolves as we are exposed to these layered viewpoints. In the final telling, which Luke only shares when cornered by Rey with his own lightsaber levelled at his head, Luke bares all, including the deep sense of his personal responsibility that had been missing from his earlier account:

> [Ben] would bring destruction, and pain, and death, and an end to everything I love because of what he would become. And for the briefest moment of pure instinct, I thought I could stop it.

At that moment, Luke ignited his lightsaber out of fear (you can almost hear Sidious cackling "good, good"); however, the light side of the Force took hold of his conscience and Luke pulled back.

Luke reflects that the instinct "passed like a fleeting shadow and I was left with shame, and with consequence." If the encounter had been visible only to Luke, he might have simply wallowed in self-blame. Unfortunately, Ben woke up and saw not an internally conflicted mentor, but an angry assassin. This is the moment where the two men's stories of what happened diverge, which is typical when people are recounting a conflict situation. In Luke's story, he was on the defensive, struggling with inner conflict. In Kylo's version, Luke was trying to strike him, necessitating a parrying blow.

In telling and retelling the story, Luke becomes trapped in destructive *self-judgment* rather than adopting the more constructive stance of *self-understanding*. Ury points out that "[o]ur natural tendency is to judge ourselves critically and to ignore or reject parts of ourselves. If we look too closely, we may feel . . . like running away" (19). Running away to Ahch-To, Luke obsessively replays the shameful moment of considering killing Ben Solo, viewing himself through Ben's (misunderstanding) eyes. By remembering this moment from Ben's perspective rather than his own, Luke loses sight of the reasonable and understandable concerns and fears that brought him to that point in the first place.

To address the tendency to focus only on the negative, Ury suggests *going to the balcony*, or stepping out of ourselves and our perceived role in this conflict to view ourselves and those we are in conflict with from a higher vantage point, much like we might observe actors in a play. From this place, we can watch events unfold with a sense of calm and self-control. After sequestering himself on Ahch-To, Luke remains as far from the balcony as one can get, anchored in a stance of self-judgment and recrimination. Consider his comment to Rey, where he blames himself for the emergence of the First Order: "Leia blamed Snoke, but it was me. I failed. Because I was Luke Skywalker. Jedi Master. A legend." Luke is unable to see himself more clearly until he recounts his experiences to Rey (she was not part of the conflict with Kylo at Luke's Jedi Temple, so when Luke sees himself through her eyes, it's like going to the balcony) and accepts further insights from Force ghost Yoda. Once Luke can view the complexities surrounding his choices and actions in that moment as well as those of others, he can begin the process of self-acceptance for his actions and choices.

"I need someone to show me my place in all this."

The act of seeing yourself from the balcony—particularly, the more scruffy-looking you are—can be a powerful initiator of the process of self-reflection. Once on the balcony, though, figuring out how to interpret what you see without fear or self-judgment is challenging. Being self-reflective while retaining a realistic and positive view of ourselves is tricky, and we often need reminders to be compassionate. Consider how often you remind loved ones to be self-forgiving or self-accepting, while forgetting to remind yourself of the same thing! In Luke's case, both Rey and Yoda help unravel the view Luke has developed of himself in isolation on Ahch-To, making it possible for Luke to find appropriate new frames through which to understand the tragedy of his Temple's collapse and his role in Ben Solo's turn to the dark side . . . as well as his own role in the turmoil currently engulfing the galaxy.

Luke sees his failure with Ben Solo as an extension of the legacy of the Jedi, who have (in Luke's view) failed the galaxy in the past and doubtlessly will fail the galaxy in the present. This view deepens Luke's resolve to isolate himself and bring an end to the Jedi Order. Moreover, Luke sees his personal failures as stemming from Jedi training and philosophy, providing further justification for why it all must end. Ury points out that "[h]olding on to the past is not only self-destructive because it distracts us from reaching mutually satisfying agreement, but it also takes away from our joy and even harms our health" (99). Luke's insistence on the Jedi's past being both present and prologue in his own life is harming his ability to deal with himself and effectively train Rey.

A different perspective on the legacy of the Jedi occurs later in the film, in an exchange between Luke and Yoda as they stand before the flickering flames engulfing the Uneti tree. Luke protests, "I can't be what she [Rey] needs me to be." Yoda replies:

> Heeded my words not, did you? Pass on what you have learned. Strength, mastery. But weakness, folly, failure also. Yes, failure most of all. The greatest teacher failure is.

Luke's focus as a Master was on appearing strong, wise, and infallible, in the way that he thought others needed to see him: "a legend." He believes failure is evidence of a problem, whereas Yoda tries to help him understand that failure itself may be necessary for growth.

This paradox of failure highlights one of Ury's key ideas: the need to reframe our picture of ourselves when we are stuck in a negotiation.

> If we truly wish to shift from an adversarial to a cooperative approach . . . we would do well to ask ourselves . . . What is our working assumption? Can we think, act, and conduct our relationships as if the universe is essentially a friendly place and life is, in fact, on our side? (67)

As a Jedi, Luke knows this perspective because we see him teaching Rey that the Force is about connecting to all living things and that this connection to life is more powerful than the dark side. But when it comes to introspection, Luke has shut himself off from the Force. In Ury's terms, Luke has changed the frame of his working assumption regarding the galaxy: once "friendly," it is now "unfriendly." Some of Ury's words would have been helpful to Luke here, namely that "[o]ur ability to relax and let life flow depends on how solidly anchored we feel in a friendly world . . . Reframing allows us to relax and to accept life just as it is" (98).

Consider the examples of General Organa and Vice Admiral Holdo in *The Last Jedi*, and then Generals Poe and Finn in *The Rise of Skywalker*. They believed—and were proven right—that they had friends out there in the galaxy, that everywhere were people sympathetic to their cause, and if their allies couldn't pop in to give support at the Battle of Crait, they nonetheless would turn up for a potluck battle against overwhelming odds on Exegol. Likewise, as we adopt self-reflective habits and practice reframing our mistakes and fears, we can pass on what we have learned through our successes and failures, offering words of encouragement to ourselves and others. We do these things not out of hypocrisy or hubris, but out of understanding and empathy.

"You've closed yourself off from the Force."

Let's pause for a moment on the notion of empathy. Empathy is incredibly valuable, a force connecting all living things; but empathy is cognitively hard to implement and emotionally threatening to our self-image and sense of security. We learn through Rey's training that Luke has closed himself off from the Force. This is partly strategic, as a connection would potentially make it possible for Force sensitives to find him, but it is also emotionally significant. At an emotional level, Luke is so concerned about making the same mistake with Rey as he did with Ben, that he cannot allow himself to connect with Rey. Indeed, when we are in conflict, it can feel dangerously destabilizing just to look at another person's opposing point of view. And it is even more difficult to feel what it must be like to *be* them, because exercising this kind of empathy forces you to see them (as well as yourself) differently.[2]

Sometimes what's needed is for another person to give you an empathic kick in the robes. Recall Luke in full-on soapbox lecturing mode, Jedi-splaining to Rey about the failures of the Order, when she cuts him off to provide some much-needed perspective. She doesn't argue Luke's point that the Jedi were the ones who trained Darth Vader (which admittedly doesn't look good on the Order's annual activity report), but instead raises an equally valid point: "[it was] a Jedi who saved him [Darth Vader] . . . You saw there was conflict inside him. You believed that he wasn't gone. That he could be turned." In this exchange, Rey reminds Luke that he has already been successful in possibly the most difficult

---

[2] For more on empathy, see Peterson & Kaufman, chapter 14, in *Star Wars and Conflict Resolution: There Are Alternatives to Fighting* (Ebner & Reynolds eds., 2022).

negotiation of all time—getting to yes with Darth Vader—by looking beyond the surface to a deeper level of understanding and offering empathy.[3] This illustrates the first step on the path to becoming more understanding and empathetic: offering respect.

Respect doesn't mean agreeing with or condoning another's point of view. Respect operates on a different level. Ury notes that "the cheapest concession you can make, the one that costs you the least and yields the most, is to give respect . . . to give positive attention and to treat the other with the dignity with which you would like to be treated" (117). In Luke's case, he offered respect to Darth Vader as Anakin Skywalker by calling him "father," something that opened the door to an eventual deep change. In Rey's case, she offers Luke respect by acknowledging his successes and treating him like a person, rather than as a legend. Her respect for Luke helps him again see himself as a teacher. Ury writes that respect "is essentially a yes to others, not to their demands, but rather to their basic humanity" (118). Respect, in other words, is the kyber crystal of empathy.

Empathy and respect are crucially important when navigating life's difficulties. As we get wrapped up in conflicts, especially internal conflicts, our own empathic balance and capacity for respect can get out of whack, which can lead us to force things on others (the Kylo Ren Special) or to withdraw from engagement (the Island Luke Routine). These seemingly opposing approaches lead us to the same essential outcome: we make decisions unilaterally, rather than through communication, cooperation, and partnership with others. The more we lash out or the more we withdraw, the greater the risk of harming ourselves and others we claim to be protecting, and of missing out on what connection and joint work have to offer.

---

[3] In this exchange, Rey takes a page from R2-D2's playbook. Remember how Luke tells R2 that he's never coming back and nothing can change his mind? R2 responds by playing Leia's "Help me, Obi-Wan Kenobi, you're my only hope" message, reminding Luke of his reasons for getting involved in the Rebellion in the first place. Never underestimate a droid!

Conclusion: "Never be afraid of who you are."

Ury writes that the "key to finding win-win-win solutions that serve everyone is to be able to change the game from *taking* to *giving*. By taking, I mean claiming value only for yourself, whereas by giving I mean creating value for others" (144). In the end, Luke transforms himself by reorienting to the Force, the Resistance, and the larger needs of the galaxy.

Consider how through Luke's interventions on Crait he provides Leia with consolation; the Resistance with a publicly visible, just in time, Luke Skywalker Legend moment they sorely need; and everybody in the cavern with the opportunity to survive and save the galaxy. "He's stalling *so we can escape*," Poe Dameron realizes. "We are the spark that'll light the fire that'll burn the First Order down." In Luke's final moments, he gives of himself for the greater good of the galaxy. His projection onto Crait is an expression of his renewed connection with the Force and, by extension, of his renewed empathy.

Although *The Last Jedi* and *Getting to Yes with Yourself* were developed for very different purposes and audiences, seeing Luke's thoughts and actions through Ury's framework provides important insights into how our internal conflicts affect (and are affected by) how we handle conflict in the outside world. Ury's book helps us analyze one the most startling character arcs in *Star Wars*: Luke's journey from hero to hermit before transforming into the one-man army facing down the First Order on Crait. Re-engaging with his internal conflicts, Luke moves through self-judgment to self-acceptance, embraces the power of self-reflection, and re-harnesses the empathy he knew earlier in life. Having done so, he is set to engage in external conflicts with confidence, conviction, balance, and power. By following Luke's example and getting to yes with ourselves before attempting to do so with others, we can achieve Luke's results in our own lives.

References

[i] Fisher, R. & Ury, W. (1991). *Getting to yes: Negotiating agreement without giving in* (2nd ed.). Penguin Books.

[ii] Ury, W. (2015). *Getting to yes with yourself: (And other worthy opponents)*. HarperOne.

15

Making the Force Live: Sources of Negotiation Power[1]

Olivia Hernandez-Pozas & Orlando R. Kelm

The Empire has fallen, yet the galaxy is once again in grave danger, this time from the rise of the malicious First Order. As the First Order gains strength, it begins to resemble the Empire: Star Destroyers dominate systems, stormtroopers raid worlds, dark side space wizards rule from behind the scenes, and of course, there's a new superweapon—even bigger than the Death Star.

Seeing where all this is heading, Princess Leia—now General Organa, leading the Resistance against the First Order—realizes she desperately needs her brother, Luke. Reunited, Leia and Luke may be powerful enough to prevent the destruction of all they have fought to create. Luke has vanished, however, and the only clue to his whereabouts is a map in Lor San Tekka's possession on Jakku. General Organa sends the Resistance's best pilot, Poe Dameron, to retrieve the map. But the First Order intercepts Poe on Jakku, and the sinister Kylo Ren commands his forces to destroy the village, kill San Tekka, and capture Poe. Luckily, Poe's droid BB-8 escapes with the map.

One way to analyze this scene (and *Star Wars* more generally) is through the lens of power. Who has the leverage and when? How does control shift from one side to the other? Why does Finn freeze when given the order to fire on the villagers? What is the

---

[1] From George Lucas's definition of the Force, as summarized in Laurent Bouzereau's *Star Wars: The Annotated Screenplays* (1997).

significance of Kylo catching a bolt from a blaster? These questions tie back to one of the central themes of the *Star Wars* saga: namely, how a relatively weak and little-resourced splinter group manages to generate enough power to successfully challenge an oppressive and despotic empire.

In negotiation, discussions of power often focus on a negotiator's ability to achieve preferred goals or to develop an advantage in the bargaining process. But power dynamics in negotiation are not just about wielding power against the other side or resisting having power wielded against you. Negotiators also must consider how to build and increase power beyond where it stands in the current moment. *Star Wars* provides many excellent (if highly dramatic) illustrations of where power comes from and how power plays out, and we can apply these insights about power in our own everyday negotiations.[2] Moreover, the saga, and particularly the sequel trilogy, provide many examples of how parties—even weaker and less-resourced parties—generate power and leverage in negotiation and conflict situations.

In this chapter, we will consider some of the primary sources of power through examples from the Resistance and the First Order. As we walk through these examples, remember always to tread carefully when dealing with power. Just as a Jedi should only use the Force for knowledge and defense, never for attack, so too an effective negotiator must be skillful and sensitive in using power. Power in the wrong hands, or power in the right hands but used in the wrong way, can lead to needless suffering and destruction.

Forming alliances: "This is a rescue!"

The first source we can tap to build our power is forming alliances so that we may collaborate with partners. There is power to be gained by working with like-minded others.

As an example, consider Poe. When Poe is captured by the First Order in *The Force Awakens*, he tries to resist Kylo Ren's Force-enabled attempts to discover the location of the hidden map,

---

[2] For more on power dynamics in *Star Wars*, see Viscomi, chapter 1, in *Star Wars and Conflict Resolution: There Are Alternatives to Fighting* (Ebner & Reynolds eds., 2022).

but Kylo eventually discovers BB-8's existence and Poe becomes expendable. Once this happens, Poe is powerless. He has no means to negotiate with Kylo as he has nothing to offer him; he is literally captive to the will of his opponent. Perhaps the only reason Poe is still alive is because the First Order probably requires a ton of paperwork to execute someone in an orderly fashion. Things look grim, but then Poe suddenly hears a stormtrooper speaking to him in a low and fast voice: "Listen carefully and pay attention. You do exactly as I say, and I can get you out of here." Poe wonders if this guy could be part of the Resistance, but further discussion reveals that the stormtrooper mainly wants to know whether Poe can fly a TIE fighter. Poe seizes upon the opening and reassures the stormtrooper: "I can fly anything!"

Note how both men are relatively powerless at this point. The stormtrooper wants to get away from the First Order, but he is a low-ranking soldier who cannot fly a ship. Poe wants to get away from the First Order as well, but he is a prisoner with no access to a spacecraft. Together, however, they are able to generate power and achieve their individual goals. They do so by *forming an alliance* that allows them to leverage what they both bring to the table. The source of their power is their *goal interdependence*. Neither can achieve their goal without the other. Instead, Poe and the stormtrooper (later dubbed "Finn") work as a team to enact their escape plan. As a team working against the First Order, they have access to a TIE fighter and the skill to use it.

Alliances are deep sources of power in that they can make possible successful collaborations vis-à-vis a shared opponent in the short term as well as provide ongoing benefits into the future. After escaping the First Order, Poe and Fin head to Jakku in search of BB-8. Their ship is attacked, and they are forced down and separated. Finn assumes Poe has been killed, leaving Finn to fend for himself. Eventually the two reunite and resume their collaboration. In this way, their alliance, which generated the power necessary to make possible their escape, continues to serve as the foundation of a loyal relationship that helps maintain and increase their power in the struggles ahead.

Knowing your counterpart: "Your game is old"

Another source of power in negotiation is knowing your opponent. Successful negotiators, before negotiating and during the negotiation, seek to uncover the interests and concerns that may be motivating the other side to negotiate.[3] Identifying all the interests and concerns in play helps negotiators develop proposals and agreements that will work well for everyone involved. Negotiators who take the time to learn and understand where their counterparts are coming from, therefore, are often much more successful at the bargaining table.

Additionally, negotiators benefit from becoming familiar with the style and tactics of their negotiation counterparts. If you know in advance that your counterpart tends to use certain tactics in negotiation—engaging in displays of sharp emotion, for example, or maybe holding the relationship hostage— you can prepare for these tactics and better avoid being manipulated or thrown off by them.

As an example, consider what happens when Finn, Rey, and BB-8 team up with Han Solo and Chewbacca. No sooner have they begun to discuss how to return BB-8 and his invaluable data to the Resistance than their freighter is boarded by Bala-Tik and the Guavian Death Gang. Han Solo owes Bala-Tik fifty thousand credits and Bala-Tik wants his money—now! Han doesn't have the money, of course, so he starts to negotiate in his normal fashion of smooth-talking his way out of tight situations. Bala-Tik has been a victim to Han's smooth-talking style before, and he scoffs: "Your game is old . . . You've played it too many times." Of course, Bala-Tik's negotiation style is also fairly predictable, consisting mostly of aggressive force and threats of violence. As a gang leader, he deals with smugglers and thieves all the time. *Might makes right* likely has been his most successful approach to negotiations and conflict.

Knowing your counterpart's style can increase your negotiation power in part by decreasing the effectiveness of their style.

---

[3] For more on negotiation, see Austin, chapter 11, in *Star Wars and Conflict Resolution: There Are Alternatives to Fighting* (Ebner & Reynolds eds., 2022).

Both Han Solo and Bala-Tik are masters at their approaches to negotiation, but they know each other so well that their tried-and-true styles are simply less effective. In negotiation, the more we use the same competitive technique with the same negotiator, the less effective it gets.[4] Our counterparts learn, and so do we. In this instance, Bala-Tik isn't going to let Han talk his way out of this one, and Han knows that he should have prepared a backup plan to counter Bala-Tik's signature trigger-happy approach. Han probably wishes there were a table between them for a quick game of sabacc or perhaps to provide cover for drawing his blaster. But truth be told, Bala-Tik probably knows those tricks as well.

Bala-Tik derives some power in this stand-off from knowing Han's style and tactics. Han emerges victorious, nonetheless, despite having no chance of ending this negotiation in his usual method and no time to prepare a backup plan. Han's power and advantage here ultimately come from the lethally destructive rathtars he has on the ship. Perhaps Han's last-ditch backup plan always involves relying on his own luck . . . and it is a stroke of luck indeed that Rey accidentally pushes the button that releases the rathtars. Ouch.

Leveraging resources: "Can you get the droid to Leia?"

A third source of power in negotiation has to do with leveraging resources. This source of power draws on both resources that you possess and resources that you develop. Let us explain.

Following their rathtar-aided escape on the *Eravana*, our five heroes head to Takodana to meet with Maz Kanata. Han knows that there is no way that he can get the *Millennium Falcon* past the First Order, but he is pretty sure that Maz can get BB-8 and the map to the Resistance. Maz is sympathetic to Han's request and the situation they find themselves in, and she likely has the power to get the map to Leia. However, she initially withholds the resources

---

[4] Interestingly, the reverse is true for cooperative style of negotiation. The more cooperative negotiators use the same techniques with each other, the more effective they get. Just think of how hard it was for Finn to get Rey to take his hand the first time they met, and how easy this got over time.

Han requests in order to achieve two of her own goals: reengaging Han with the Resistance and returning Han back home to his life with Leia:

> You've been running away from this fight for too long. Han, nyaki nedo wa'ata. Go home.

Maz tries to recruit Finn to the fight as well, though when he vehemently objects, she uses her connections to hook him up with a job that will take him far, far away. Finally, after observing the Force call to Rey and realizing that Rey—like Han and Finn—seeks to avoid joining the fight against the First Order, she attempts to motivate her to join by offering her two things: a mission and Luke's lightsaber.

Notice how Maz is in a powerful position. She has the knowledge and capabilities to provide refuge and hiding places; to facilitate escape, passage, and employment; to introduce and connect people; to store and bequeath precious items; and to provide others with meaningful tasks. Maz holds all these resources, and these resources give her power.[5]

The idea that power comes from controlling resources is a familiar notion to many of us. Less familiar is the realization that even when we do not control resources, we can build resources in negotiation through research and situation assessment. We often hear about doing *due diligence* before engaging in a negotiation. This basically refers to doing our homework, studying the issues, learning about our counterpart, and getting all the background information that we can. Due diligence is both a way to prevent harm (by identifying risks, for example) and to generate power (by gaining information, for example).

Building power by gathering information is a key theme in the *Star Wars* saga. Much of *The Force Awakens* is about finding a droid with the missing map (BB-8) or finding the missing map within a droid (R2-D2). The movie starts off with Poe receiving

---

[5] Maz also has the two sources of power we have already discussed: alliances (as with Han) and the ability to read people (as with Rey and Finn).

the map from Lor San Tekka, who explains that "this will begin to make things right." Kylo wants the map too, so he interrogates San Tekka and then Poe. Clearly everyone perceives the map as a resource that will grant power to the possessor. Later, after the scene at Maz's establishment, Kylo captures Rey and brings her to Starkiller Base, again looking for the map. Kylo uses the Force mind probe and also berates Rey with intimidation, threats, insults, and attempts to make her feel hopeless:

> You're just a scavenger . . . Your friends are traitors, murderers, and thieves . . . You've seen the map, it's in your mind right now!

Kylo's attempts to probe Rey's mind are obviously painful, but Rey resists his attacks and responds by giving him useless information, like the technical characteristics of a droid. Then, to everyone's surprise, Rey suddenly shouts: "Get out of my head! I am not giving you anything!" She has discovered that she too is capable of the Force mind probe and, after probing for a moment, says to Kylo: "You're afraid you will never be as strong as Darth Vader." A shocked Kylo abruptly ends the interrogation and hurries to consult with Snoke. The scene shows how obtaining key information can empower a person in conflict and negotiation. Kylo extracts Rey's fears and tries to use them against her; Rey does the same to Kylo. In other words, they both attempt to gain power over the other through Force-enabled "research."

Leveraging resources in the service of negotiation power, then, means using what you have and also researching what you need. And in the process of doing the latter, you well may end up with more of the former. For Rey, the mind probe on Kylo yields more than just information about Kylo. She also learns about abilities and capabilities that she did not know she had. She discovers the intensity and range of her mental strength, and she begins to realize that she can use the Force. From this point on, Rey has newly found power. Her awakening to these abilities only strengthens her ability to draw from them.

Drawing on multiple sources of power: "Oh, the General? To me, she is royalty"

So far, we have discussed the following sources of power: forming alliances, knowing your opponent's negotiation style and tactics, and leveraging resources. Let's take a moment to consider how moving flexibly and strategically between these sources of power can serve as a power multiplier.

Leia provides an excellent example. Each of her many roles provides her with different types of power. She is a princess *and* a general *and* a senator, someone who possesses both traditional and symbolic power as well as military muscle, coercive clout, and political sway. In each of these roles, Leia is accustomed to building alliances with other powerful people and networks, in the service of shared plans and joint projects. She commands significant resources, and her alliances allow her to draw on even greater resources depending on the situation. And, as we know, Leia is much more than just a power broker. She is a friend, sister, wife, and mother—highly relational and interpersonal roles that often require alternative negotiation styles and approaches, depending on the circumstances.

All of Leia's roles involve different capabilities and expectations when it comes to exercising power and engaging in negotiation. She manages the different sources of power available to her by seamlessly moving between her different roles. Her ability to lead powerfully comes in part from her facility with shifting between sources of power as the moment demands. She can be directive, telling alliance partners and others what to do; and she can be facilitative, helping others discuss suggestions, collaborating around resource constraints and needs, and reaching joint conclusions. She summarizes and conveys decisions to those who must implement them in ways that they can understand and follow, thus continuing to build alliances and intangible resources such as trust and goodwill. She knows how to utilize everyone's skills to put the actual plan into action.

When the threat presented by Starkiller Base becomes evident in D'Qar, for example, General Organa organizes the Resistance forces, declaring that they must destroy the weapon immediately, before it can be used again. Just making a declaration, however, does not instantly send everyone hopping in the right direction. Leia coordinates closely with Admirals Statura and Ackbar, who provide recommendations on possible counterattacks. She invites the newcomer, Finn, into the high-level group because she knows he possesses inside information. Finn's own desire to help Rey leads him to offer to guide the strike force to the location on Starkiller Base from where they can destabilize the thermal oscillator. Leia oversees this planning and coordination, maintaining the bearing of a general as she moves all the pieces into place and prepares the Resistance for possible attack. Then, right before Han leaves, Leia shifts gears and says, with love and conviction: "If you see our son, bring him home."

In all these encounters, we see Leia using power stemming not only from formal hierarchies (general, senator, princess) but from interpersonal relationships as well. Leia knows her counterparts inside and out, and she can adjust her style and approach in her encounters with them accordingly.[6] From that knowledge and those adjustments, she generates power.

Remaining resilient: "My friend's got a bag full of explosives"

Finally, let us look at one last source of power: the power that comes from resilience, particularly resilience in the face of failure.

Han, Chewbacca, and Finn arrive at Starkiller Base with the goal of deactivating the shield. Truth be told, Finn doesn't know as much about Starkiller Base as he has led everyone to believe. His real motivation is rescuing Rey. Of course, Han also has a private motivation of his own, in that he wants to find Kylo (Ben) and bring him home.

Both heroes find the droids they are looking for, if not the outcomes they desire. Finn is ultimately knocked out by Kylo in the woods and Rey ends up rescuing him. Before that, Han comes

---

[6] Let's not forget her handling of Poe in *The Last Jedi*, with whom she made various stylistic choices (some stern, some gentle) in managing his temper and excesses.

face to face with Kylo, who removes his mask and asks for Han's help. Han agrees, of course, and Kylo—for whom "help" meant assistance in becoming more Vader-esque—murders him.

Failure. Shocking, unexpected, unfair, unwanted failure.[7]

If there is anything we learn from life, from *The Force Awakens*, and from negotiation, it is that sometimes things don't work out as expected. Failures happen. Roadblocks impede our advancement. Talks turn into stalemate, and agreements evaporate. One of the vital truths of negotiation is that to progress, we need to learn from our failures and mistakes. As Yoda says later in the sequels:

> Pass on what you have learned. Strength. Mastery. But weakness, folly, failure also. Yes, failure most of all. The greatest teacher failure is.

Seeing the Resistance attack falter against Starkiller Base, the group decides to return and blow up the oscillator themselves. Their resilience in coming up with new courses of action after hitting roadblocks is what ultimately brings down this system-killing weapon.

It is natural to focus on the tragedy of Han's death, with our own horror and despair reflected in Chewbacca's howling rage as he shoots and wounds Kylo. The real takeaway, though, is not that Han failed to bring his son back to Leia and the light side; it is that despite this failure, our heroes still needed to complete their mission. Chewbacca is in anguish but keeps his head in the game; as usual, he is always about the mission, never about the medals. He blows up the oscillator and arrives in the *Falcon* in the nick of time to evacuate Rey and Finn. And ultimately, although the loss of Han was tremendous, his efforts were not in vain. Kylo Ren eventually does become Ben again. In the saga, as in negotiation

---

[7] The group's primary mission was also a failure. They did manage to take out the shield, scoring bonus points for dumping Captain Phasma in the trash compactor along the way. However, even with the shield down, the Resistance assault on the oscillator was ineffective.

and life, failure in one area does not mean that all is lost in every area forevermore.

The Force Awakens beautifully illustrates many strategies for building power in negotiation: forming alliances, knowing your counterparts, leveraging resources, and remaining resilient, particularly in the wake of tragedy and failure. As we work through our own negotiations—especially when we feel like we are disadvantaged or relatively powerless—we would do well to remember the examples of Finn, Poe, Rey, and those in the Resistance. Even when all hope appears to be lost, they remain mindful of opportunities to generate and exercise power.

16

The Light Side, the Dark Side, and the Third Side

Danielle Blumenberg

No matter how many times we hear the opening score, we get excited at the sound of the iconic horns heralding the beginning of any *Star Wars* film. We know we're about to embark on an adventure of good versus evil, packed with exhilarating action. Looking past the blasters and listening past the horns, we quickly become fascinated by the characters themselves, as they deal with their own individual struggles and complexities, as well as the power and drama of their relationships. Ultimately the saga centers around the strength of the characters' interpersonal connections (not the power of their weapons) and how the development of those relationships is crucial to our protagonists overcoming adversity.

Take Rey and Kylo Ren. Uniquely connected through the Force, they may be the key that unlocks the galaxy from tyranny and oppression. But how does this pair, who start out on opposite sides, end up coming together and using their combined strength to end this destructive conflict and bring order to the universe? And how did their relationship, literally borne from conflict, become a powerful Force dyad? The First Order and the Resistance have been in an intractable conflict for a very long time, in a galaxy far, far away, yet by the end of the sequel trilogy, the conflict has been transformed. How did this happen?

Two words: the Force. *Star Wars* fans know the Force has a light side and a dark side, but few realize that the Force also has a

Third Side. It is this Third Side of the Force that enables Rey and Kylo to unite, the Resistance to prevail, and balance between light and dark to be restored.

We're going to win this war not by fighting what we hate, but saving what we love

Before we get to what we mean by the "Third Side," let's briefly explore what we know about the Force. When Luke introduces Rey to the idea of the Force during their first study session in *The Last Jedi*, he describes the Force not in terms of dark or light, but rather from the larger perspective of life in the galaxy: "the energy between all things, a tension, a balance that binds the universe together." He then guides her to recognize this nature of the Force inside herself:

LUKE: Breathe. Just breathe. Reach out with your feelings. What do you see?
REY: The Island. Life. Death and decay, that feeds new life. Warmth. Cold. Peace. Violence.
LUKE: And between it all?
REY: Balance and energy. A Force.
LUKE: And inside you?
REY: Inside me, that same Force . . .

From this dialogue we learn that the Force is inside all of us. It binds us together; in a sense, it is the water we swim in, the air we breathe, the culture we live in. The Force surrounds us, like a community or world; it can view us from the outside, from above, not tied down to our point of view yet still understanding us and our actions in context. As such, it offers a perspective that can help provide the balance between us.

When it comes to conflict, then, the Force is not partisan or aligned with any one specific position. Instead, the Force presents multiple angles or a "third side" that promotes understanding, resolution, and even transformation. In *The Third Side: Why We Fight and How We Can Stop*, conflict and negotiation expert William

Ury defines the Third Side as a way of viewing and approaching conflict not from any particular side but instead from a broad overarching perspective that includes both parties' points of view as well as the needs of the surrounding community.[i] Ury's book offers a comprehensive analysis of how shifting perspectives can transform conflict.

This chapter will examine two of Ury's central themes: first, the three major skills required to develop a Third Side mindset; and second, the ten roles that we may step into to better respond to conflict situations. As it turns out, Rey and Kylo implemented these skills and adopted many of these roles to resolve their conflict (and ultimately save the galaxy). Once familiar with these skills and roles, we can aspire to do the same with our own conflicts.

The belonging you seek is not behind you . . . it is ahead
When it comes to achieving a Third Side mindset, the first skill Ury suggests is learning to view conflict from the "balcony" as opposed to the seeing it from the "dance floor." When in conflict, our natural tendency is to see things from our own perspective, like dancers on a crowded dance floor facing only each other. We assess the situation from our own certain point of view as if there was no other, and we only see whatever is in front of our nose. But when we go to the balcony, we can see the bigger picture. Broadening our perspective lets us look at our counterpart's side of things and gives us a new look at our own, along with an expanded sense of context and how what's happening fits into the bigger picture. This new perspective can enable the discovery of common ground.

How do we get to the balcony? Sometimes someone outside the conflict can help. Mediators, for example, strive to see all dimensions of a dispute when they work with people in conflict.[1] Through listening, mediators can understand the various perspectives involved and help parties find commonalities and ways to work things out. In a nutshell, mediators and other third-side external parties have always had a seat on the balcony. Particularly

---
[1] For more on mediation and its galaxy-saving potential, see Anderson, chapter 5.

skilled third parties may even be able to help parties in conflict see things from the other's perspective; they can lift them up to the balcony, so to speak, even if only for a moment.

A far greater challenge is going up to the balcony by ourselves when *we* are the ones in conflict. Indeed, it is often hard to even consider going up there without the support of a mediator or someone else encouraging us to do so. The threat of the balcony view is the fear of what we might discover from that vantage point. Instinctively, we worry that seeing the broader picture may require us to back down or make concessions. It feels safer staying in the comfort zone of our own perspective, often leading us to make one-sided or sweeping demands.[2] Knowing more about the broader situation can certainly alter how we see the conflict and the other parties to the conflict, but this doesn't have to weaken our perspective or stance in any way. When Rey and Kylo use the Force mind probe on each other—ostensibly to gather information they can use to attack the other—they both develop insights that make them more compassionate and focused, even as they continue fighting. Their brief stints to the balcony by way of the Force highlight, for each of them, the humanity and value of the other.

Before they engage in dueling mind probes, however, neither Rey nor Kylo demonstrate any capacity to go to the balcony. In fact, *The Force Awakens* sets them solidly on the dance floor in opposition to each other. We first meet Rey on the desert planet of Jakku. Rey is a scavenger, seemingly abandoned by her parents, trying only to survive on the harsh desert planet. Although she is self-assured and self-reliant, she lacks a sense of belonging and fears leaving Jakku, as she may miss her parents' return. Through a series of events, starting with saving BB-8 from a fellow scavenger, Rey reluctantly joins the Resistance.

Elsewhere in the galaxy, Kylo Ren is apprentice to Supreme Leader Snoke, hunting for a map leading to Luke Skywalker. Snoke wants Kylo to destroy Luke, who is the last of the Jedi Order, believing that Luke's destruction will annihilate all hope in the

---

[2] For more on how one-sided "absolutism" served the Sith, see Burstein, chapter 12.

galaxy. We soon learn that before turning to the dark side, Kylo Ren was Ben Solo, the beloved son of Princess Leia and Han Solo.

As movie viewers, we can see many things from the balcony. For example, we recognize that despite their disparate backgrounds, both Rey and Kylo feel they don't belong. They both search for inclusion, understanding, and acceptance, something most of us can relate to at some point. Stuck on the dance floor, however, this isn't apparent to the two parties: Kylo Ren sees a scavenger girl preventing him from going full Vader, and Rey sees a monster who killed his own father. It takes time—and use of the Third Side skills—for them to be able to go to the balcony and see each other, and their conflict, in a different light.

They win by making you think you're alone

Ury's second Third Side skill has to do with listening—listening to truly understand all perspectives while avoiding judgment or bias. The tricky part is doing so without necessarily giving up your position.

Of course, before we can listen, we need to communicate. Parsecs apart, Rey and Kylo are out of touch, as parties in conflict often are. So, the Force plays a Third Side role of creating the connection that enables Rey and Kylo to communicate with each other from across the galaxy. This connection helps them overcome not only costly intergalactic calling charges, but also something many of us face when we're deep in conflict: an inner resistance to reaching out to the other. The Force makes this contact for Rey and Kylo; we non-Force users must take the brave step of reaching out to the other side.

Once connected, Rey and Kylo face the same challenges we all do: namely, how can we use the opportunity to speak to make the situation better, rather than lashing out? Being in contact with the other is daunting because it puts us at risk. We direct power to our deflector shields, attempting to reduce our vulnerability by using valuable moments of communication for transmitting rather than receiving. It is far easier to make demands or hurl accusations than it is to listen—to not only stop talking, but to truly hear the other's perspective, treating it as something valuable, instead of something threatening. It can be difficult to consider and attempt to understand the other's words, rather than fixate on how to reject and refute them. It's a strange paradox that going to the balcony may actually bring us closer to our dance partner. Each time Rey and Kylo communicate, they work past initial resistance to engaging and go on to discover more about the other and their differing perspectives. Naturally, they don't always like what they learn. Still, over time, it leads them to more common ground and shared understanding.

As an example of how listening can bring parties closer together, recall the moment when Rey, in the cave on Ahch-To, observes a mosaic of the Prime Jedi. The figure is holding a lightsaber and depicted as half-light and half-dark, representing the balance between the opposing sides of the Force. Rey is struggling with the duality inside herself and when she describes to Luke the darkness she feels calling to her, Luke doesn't listen well—instead, he reacts with fear and shuts her down. Afterward, when connecting with Kylo, Rey mirrors Luke's approach, casting accusations at Kylo and not seeking information. Unlike Luke, Kylo responds with curiosity. He ignores Rey's insults, instead asking questions. While their conversation ends without any breakthroughs, it clearly has an impact on Rey. The next time the Force connects them, Rey reciprocates Kylo's curiosity, asking questions and listening as she seeks to understand his past actions. When Kylo tells her about the night he destroyed Luke's training temple, he includes Rey in his story. "He sensed my power, as he senses yours, and he feared it." This resonates with Rey, and their mutual listening begins to move them past their conflict.

Why what? Say it!

During this conversation, Kylo is not only using the second skill of listening; he is also, perhaps unwittingly, using the third skill: speaking from the Third Side. Speaking from the Third Side means using words and actions that can influence and transform conflict. Asking good questions of all involved parties is a good example of speaking from the Third Side, because questions can uncover each party's interests and create opportunities for reflection.

But thoughtful questions are not the only way to speak from the Third Side. This skill also includes making different forms of statements. Along with questions, for example, you might interrupt your counterpart constructively (as opposed to impatiently). At one point during a Force connection, we see the following exchange:

REY:	Then why?
KYLO:	Why what?
REY:	[struggling to articulate what she wants to say]
KYLO:	Why what? Say it!

While Kylo's interruption sounds disruptive and aggressive, he's actually trying to be constructive by pushing Rey to formulate the question that had distressed her since Han Solo's death in the form of a query rather than an accusation. "Why did you . . . Why did you kill him?" she asks, relieved to be talking about this at last. "I don't understand." This example shows how speaking from the Third Side can take many forms; the one constant is a genuine desire to understand where the other is coming from.

Learning to speak from the Third Side requires both personal reflection (internal) and constructive dialogue between the parties (external). Rey's experience in the cave and through the Force connection provides her with opportunities for both. Seeking to move beyond her past, Rey looks for answers about her parents from the dark place beneath the island, but what she really wants is to find herself. Her underground experience with the dark side of the Force deepens Rey's understanding of herself and, unexpectedly, of Kylo. Kylo recognizes and empathizes with Rey's loneliness, compassionately responding to Rey's vulnerability, offering acceptance. Rey sees Kylo as conflicted, Darth Vader style, and responds with empathy. This moment of tenuous transformation of their conflict is embodied by their touching hands, epitomizing what Ury explains to be the goal of the Third Side: not to *resolve* conflict, as conflict is important and necessary for growth, but to *transform* it into an experience both parties can grow from.

Rey and Kylo seek to understand the extent of their own power and where they fit in. They struggle with the darkness they feel because they are forbidden to acknowledge it. Those around them don't understand that they can actively choose the light and still acknowledge the dark without acting on it. Years ago, Luke reacted out of fear when he discovered Kylo's connection to the dark side; now, he responds with a strikingly similar, hut-demolishing, fear-generated response upon discovering them touching hands.

Strengthened by her newfound feelings of acceptance, Rey is empowered to engage in productive conflict and conversation with Luke. Luke acknowledges his part in Kylo's path and describes that when he had sensed Ben's darkness, he briefly considered attacking him, resulting in deep sorrow and shame, and compelling Luke to close himself off from the Force. Rey then speaks from the Third Side by taking Luke to the balcony, showing him how two parties can see the same event very differently. Without judgment, Rey gently reminds Luke of the grace he once extended to his father, Darth Vader, who was similarly conflicted in the Force like Kylo. She then explains that Luke's primary failure was believing Ben's decision to go to the dark side was complete and absolute. While Rey doesn't convince Luke in this moment, he does start to reconsider his self-imposed exile and re-engage with the Force on behalf of the Resistance.

Rey's trajectory on the island—from learner to explorer, from isolated to connected—demonstrates her growth as she begins to embrace the Third Side. Her encounter with Luke also illustrates how it is sometimes easier for people to speak on behalf of the Third Side regarding others' conflicts than it is to apply that same perspective to their own. Now more confident in her abilities to see the broader view of conflict, Rey continues using these skills in her own conflict with Kylo.

My place in all this

Along with the three skills of seeing, listening, and speaking, Ury identifies ten roles that individuals can assume when engaging in conflict with a Third Side mindset. We can move between these ten roles in many kinds of conflicts, whether we are parties to those conflicts or not:

- *Providers*, who enable parties in conflict to meet their needs.
- *Teachers*, who give people skills to handle conflict.
- *Bridge-Builders*, who forge relationships across lines of conflict and foster genuine dialogue between parties.
- *Mediators*, who bring disputants to the table and facilitate communication between them.
- *Arbiters*, who determine disputed rights and promote justice.
- *Equalizers*, who democratize power and promote its fair sharing between parties.
- *Healers*, who repair injured relationships and encourage apology with the goal of reconciliation between conflicting parties.
- *Witnesses*, who pay attention to escalation and watch out for early warning signs.
- *Referees*, who set limits to fighting and establish rules of fair conflict.
- *Peacekeepers*, who provide protection by getting in between the parties as they fight and enforcing peace, even using force to protect the innocent and stop the aggressor.

In his book, Ury provides a comprehensive explanation of how these roles work within constructive conflict resolution. Here, let's look at some these roles with respect to Rey and Kylo's conflict. As we know, the Force was an instrumental part of their connection, so we'll start by examining the roles of the Force in the conflict. Then we'll identify which roles Rey and Kylo played, with special emphasis on how these roles helped them enact a Third Side mindset.

The Force acts as Provider by opening the door for communication between Rey and Kylo. Then, as Bridge-Builder, the Force creates the bond between Rey and Kylo that cuts across the boundary lines of their conflicts and affiliations, enabling deeper communication and trust building. We don't yet know it, but the Force has bonded them together as a Force dyad, building them the most powerful bridge of all.[3] As Mediator, the Force keeps bringing Rey and Kylo back to the table; they may not be happy to be there, but with each opportunity to engage in continued dialogue without interference of others, they discover more common ground. Throughout the sequels, the Force-created connection serves as Healer for Rey and Kylo's isolation and loneliness.[4] Certainly some of their interactions are violent, yet with each successive connection, the pair becomes a little less combative and a little more confident. They become increasingly curious as they share their individual stories with one another.

Equally important are the Third Side roles Rey and Kylo independently assume at different points in the conflict. For example, Rey's strong belief in Kylo's capacity to redeem himself, returning to the light, is a form of Bridge-Building. She plays the role of Witness when hearing of his mistreatment by Luke, and she is an Arbiter in challenging Luke to acknowledge the true version of this situation. She also Witnesses Kylo's mistreatment by Snoke. The Force may have set Rey and Kylo up as a dyad, but they both engage in Bridge-Building to give that relationship meaning. This includes their moment of touch, their continued metaphor of outreached hands, their remembering of things that are important to one another, and their inviting the other to join them on their side of the Force. Their bridge leads them to ardently believe that they will end up together on the same side of the Force. This cross-cutting tie prompts Kylo to intervene when Snoke threatens Rey,

---

[3] Ury says that "bridge-building takes place all around us, sometimes without us even perceiving it" (133). Remember how Luke describes the Force to Rey?

[4] In a very real sense, the Force is a pivotal character in its own right.

playing the role of Peacekeeper by standing up for the weaker party and killing Snoke. In turn, Rey and Kylo begin working together to defeat Snoke's guards, saving each other's lives in more acts of Bridge-Building. While Snoke claims to have initiated the Force connection between Rey and Kylo, intentionally stoking Kylo's insecurities as bait for Rey, the dyad's connection only continues to grow stronger after Snoke literally falls to pieces. Afterward, Rey and Kylo continue to play Provider roles for each other by keeping the communication channel open.

Note that each party can assume Third Side roles at different points in the conflict without having to give in to the other in any way. In other words, adopting a Third Side mindset can add depth to your conflict and durability to your relationship, but doesn't require you to concede value or issues of principle. For example, even after Rey and Kylo's momentous hand-touch, they each maintain their own version of the Force vision and believe the other's understanding is wrong. For all their Bridge-Building, they still can't get to the balcony to try and understand what they have experienced jointly; they remain solidly on the conflict dance floor. They are certain of their own points of view and positions, with Rey begging Kylo to call off the attack on the Resistance ships and Kylo pleading with Rey to join him on the dark side.[5]

In our own, far less exciting galaxy, we don't have the Force to play Third Side roles such as Provider or Bridge-Builder. But each of us can certainly remember how we've helped family members, friends, co-workers, and even strangers in their conflicts by taking on the roles of the Provider, Bridge-Builder, Mediator, or Healer. As you go through the list of ten roles, consider what roles you've played when you've stepped in to help others in conflict.

---

[5] This moment is reminiscent of two other similar dance floor moments: Anakin's pleas to Padmé after falling to the dark side and his pleas as Darth Vader to Luke to join him there. Each of those moments would have benefited from a Third Side mindset, but Anakin was too wrapped up in his own identity issues to even consider this. See Blumenberg, chapter 4, in *Star Wars and Conflict Resolution: There Are Alternatives to Fighting* (Ebner & Reynolds eds., 2022).

We had each other. That's how we won.
In the end, Rey and Kylo seize the opportunities the Force presents, albeit slowly and reluctantly. With each Force-enabled encounter, they grow in strength and begin to show humility and vulnerability to each other. They step towards the balcony in a way that builds rapport and positive momentum in their relationship, culminating in their successful joint stand against Palpatine. The resulting "triple win" is ultimately achieved as Rey makes peace with who she is, Ben (Kylo Ren) is redeemed, and Palpatine is gone (again). Together, Rey and Kylo have restored balance to the Force and brought peace to galactic society at large, no longer oppressed by the First and Final Orders.[6]

We may not be able to use the Force to lift rocks, but using the Third Side roles and tools may prevent stones from being thrown. The Force as defined by Luke exists in us and we can all use Third Side skills and step into Third Side roles to help ourselves and others constructively manage conflict.

May the Third Side of the Force be with you, always.

References

[i] Ury, W. (2000). *The third side: Why we fight and how we can stop*. Penguin Books.

---

[6] Made it this far? For a very different take on Rey and Kylo Ren's relationship from a conflict perspective, see Spradley & Spradley, chapter 8, in *Star Wars and Conflict Resolution: There Are Alternatives to Fighting* (Ebner & Reynolds eds., 2022).

17

Does Jedi Training Reduce Stress?

Jill S. Tanz & Robert R. Tanz

It's a hot day on Crait, maybe the hottest in recorded history. The white salt on the ground looks like snow, but it isn't—and somehow that only makes the air seem hotter.

And yet standing there is Luke Skywalker, lightsaber in defensive position, looking cool as a Hothsicle. The fate of everything he's ever fought for is on the line, but you wouldn't know it from his composed face, calm breathing, and steady gaze. Luke's composure is in sharp contrast to Kylo Ren, who radiates anger, frustration, and impatience. Luke emerges victorious, and his success is directly connected to maintaining his calm, focus, and deliberate approach. Kylo Ren? He loses spectacularly, undermined by his own rage.

How does Luke pull off his success in this pivotal scene in *The Last Jedi*? How does he control his reactions in this high-stress encounter? Can we non-Jedi learn from Luke to counteract stress in our own conflicts?

When the Force isn't with you

The word "stress" has various meanings, and in this chapter, we are not referring to the common "I'm so stressed" feeling that you may experience when, say, looking for parking at a sold-out *Star Wars* movie where there is no actual threat. Rather, we use "stress" to mean the physiologic changes that occur once a perceived threat triggers something called the "physiologic stress response."

Here on Earth, the physiologic stress response first developed in fish over 700,000,000 years ago. When creatures (human and others) become aware of a threat, the stress response is triggered, mobilizing the body to counteract the threat. The response is complex and affects many parts of the mind and body. Hormone production, including adrenaline and cortisol, is initiated in the brain. Adrenaline is triggered through the neural system, immediately produced in the adrenal gland, and pumped through the body via the bloodstream. The cortisol trigger travels more moderately to the adrenal gland, and cortisol slowly enters the bloodstream building up more gradually than adrenaline and taking much longer to diminish. Small amounts of cortisol improve both physical and mental performance, as when a time limit looms. But as stressors continue to trigger the stress response and the amount of cortisol builds, both physical and mental performance diminish.

You may be familiar with an adrenaline rush after experiencing a near accident on the road or after a roller coaster ride. Adrenaline's impacts are palpable: you feel your heart pounding in your chest and your palms may get sweaty. Cortisol's effects are subtler, and we are usually unaware of its presence.

How do these hormones impact our bodies? Extra energy in the form of glucose and fat become available to the muscles and brain. Heart and breathing rates increase to provide more oxygen to the muscles and brain. The brain goes on high alert to improve its function while the immune system proactively prepares to fight off infection and repair wounds. Digestion, growth, and reproductive systems slow down to preserve energy. Pupils dilate to improve vision. That moment when the *Millennium Falcon* shifts from being a lumbering freighter hauling cargo to a nimble battle craft jumping to hyperspace? That's what the physiologic stress response is supposed to do to our brain and body.

We see evidence of the physiologic stress response throughout the *Star Wars* saga. Remember the moment in *The Force Awakens* when stormtroopers land at the Niima Outpost, for example? A local points the stormtroopers toward Rey and Finn, and the troopers begin to advance in their direction. Rey and Finn feel physically threatened and run. In our terms, Finn and Rey are reacting to a "stressor"—namely, the threat that they will be shot or captured. The stress response causes the changes described above, and these changes help Rey and Finn think more clearly and run faster toward the *Falcon*, away from the physical threat presented by the stormtroopers.

But even non-physical threats can lead to the physiologic stress response. Why? Because our brains do not distinguish between physical threats and psychological or social threats. This means that our stress reaction kicks in even when we are in no physical danger. Just walking into a strange environment (like the first time Rey enters Maz's castle on Takodana), facing an unfamiliar situation (like Finn watching Maz crawl across the table toward him) or being singled out in public (like hearing Maz shout out "HAN SOLO!" as the crowd falls silent) all serve as stressors and will trigger the stress response. The stress response also is triggered when we feel judged, see a former opponent, or get into an argument with someone. Finally, even in the absence of an identifiable social or psychological threat, the stress response is triggered by experiencing our own strong emotions. Fear, anger, shame, and feeling out of control can be just as potent stressors as physical and social threats from the outside. These emotions are very common in conflict situations or even in negotiation.

Each encounter with a social threat or a strong emotion will trigger another stress response and our stress builds. When stress hormones are repeatedly triggered, adrenaline levels quickly increase, and just as quickly diminish. Cortisol, as mentioned above, takes much longer to build up and can take hours to go down. This means that if there are repeated stressors the cortisol level builds and builds . . . and lingers.

At first, the build-up is beneficial. Rey and Finn escape the stormtroopers on Jakku in part because the stress hormones help them run faster and react better as they fly and blast their way to safety. Over time, though, in unfolding situations, as more stressors pile on, the increasing cortisol level becomes problematic or even toxic. Many of the mental capacities needed in a conflict situation start to diminish. In *The Last Jedi*, Poe Dameron challenges the authority of Vice Admiral Holdo and demands to know her battle plans. Poe assumes Holdo is abandoning the *Raddus* out of cowardice. He becomes angry and throws a chair. When Holdo calmly orders guards to remove him, he feels shame and embarrassment. Each of these is a stressor that escalates cortisol levels with predictably bad results.

The dark side within

How do repeated stressors undermine our ability to negotiate and deal with conflict? Higher levels of stress hormones trigger many changes in our brains. Research shows that we perceive faces to be angrier than they really are when we are subject to high levels of stress hormones.[i] Seeing an angry face may arouse our own anger and stress hormones, and high levels of stress hormones cause us to hyperfocus and to ignore additional information that may give us the perspective we need to make better decisions.

Stress can also impact memory in a variety of ways and interfere with cognitive flexibility and decision-making. All in all, high stress hormone levels interfere with many systems that are necessary for optimal decision-making. After confronting Holdo, Poe's cortisol level may well be in the toxic range and his thoughts are straitjacketed, making it harder for him to see other explanations for Holdo's actions. He is likely misinterpreting her actions toward him as more hostile than they really are. After all, Holdo soon admits to Leia that she actually likes Poe.

What to do when the First Order threatens?

There are four common behaviors animals and humans employ when physiologically stressed: fight, flight, freeze, and "tend and befriend."

- In the *fight* response, stress triggers aggression and fighting. This can take the form of actual violent combat with an enemy, as when Finn lashes out and fights with Luke's lightsaber when he is attacked by stormtroopers on Takodana.

Often, though, the aggressive response is directed (or "displaced") at a bystander instead of at an actual enemy. For example, when Kylo Ren discovers Rey has escaped her cell on Starkiller Base, he displaces his fight response by attacking the chair where Rey had been held captive. An aggressive reaction may also be expressed as a threatening glare, a snide comment, or an insult ("traitor!" or "scavenger scum!").

- The *flight* response can involve literal running away or something more subtle, like darting eyes or fidgeting. Compare Finn running away from the stormtroopers on Niima Outpost—classic flight response—and his turning away from Captain Phasma, hyperventilating and sweating, as she's speaking to him on the *Finalizer* after the raid on Jakku. In both cases, Finn wants to get as far away as possible from the threats around him.
- A third response is to *freeze*. Some animals maximize camouflage by holding still to become less visible to predators. Humans can also freeze, becoming hypervigilant but motionless and holding their breath or breathing shallowly. This response gives time to consider options before charging ahead. When Finn receives the order to kill the villagers on Jakku, his first response is to freeze.
- Finally, scientists have identified a fourth response, *tend and befriend*; a social behavior to nurture and comfort others. Females are more likely to choose this response than males, although it can occur among males who are stressed, particularly when they are in groups where trust already exists among members. Rose Tico shows her impulse to "tend and befriend" when she prevents Finn from flying into the superlaser siege cannon on Crait, later telling Finn that they survive by "saving what we love."

Sometimes individuals seem to prefer a particular response. Poe Dameron certainly fights more often than he flees; just try to get him to call off his assault on a dreadnought. Sometimes individuals will exhibit certain stress behaviors under certain conditions. Sticking with Poe, we note that he doesn't always fight: He flees the *Finalizer* with Finn rather than lash out at the nearest stormtrooper or go after Kylo Ren. He freezes in the final battle above Exegol when he concludes (incorrectly) that no allies are coming to their aid. Finally, overwhelmed by the responsibility he bears after Leia dies, Poe's first move is to seek out Finn to be his co-general and share the stress of command—a moving illustration of tend and befriend.

Keep in mind that although fight, flight, freeze, and tend and befriend are common default responses to stressors, stress responses often reflect the totality of the circumstances, both in terms of the people involved and the situation at hand. Most people won't pursue a fight against overwhelming odds or flee into the arms of their enemies, for example. Many may initially freeze, if only to consider their options.

Escaping the dark side

In addition, differences between individuals may affect people's susceptibility to stressors:

- *Experience in similar situations.* A new recruit in the Resistance may freeze or even flee when confronted with the physical threats of battle while an experienced fighter will not.
- *Confidence in our ability to deal with the situation.* Confidence may result from good outcomes in similar past situations or may reflect an emotionally stable personality. Han Solo has talked his way out of a lot of sticky situations before and is also equipped with a ridiculously high level of self-confidence. His certainty in his ability to talk down the Guavian Death Gang and Kanjiklub on the *Eravana* is at the root of his calm demeanor and "we can work it out" attitude.
- *Resources at hand to cope with the threat.* Armed with a blaster, a Resistance fighter is much more likely to charge into

- *Sex.* High stress hormone levels also have different impacts on men than women.[ii] Men are less able to inhibit negative emotions under high stress. Their anger builds and this, in turn, produces more stress. High stress levels in women, however, increase their ability to inhibit negative emotions and they are better able to problem-solve and to make decisions. Maz Kanata shows this when she gives Poe and Finn the description and location of the Master Codebreaker in *The Last Jedi*. Even in the middle of a violent union dispute, Maz can still problem-solve.
- *Individual temperament.* We each have personality factors that contribute to how we react to a stressor. Some people are intense, hypervigilant, and have a lower threshold to stressors, while others may remain largely unfazed until faced with a higher level of stimulation. Poe's temperament most likely shields him from stressors that will impact the more hypervigilant Finn.

So, many factors affect the impact of stressors on different individuals. The stress system evolved to be responsive to a variety of different circumstances and each of us reacts differently depending on internal traits and the external situation.

Jedi control or Sith chaos

Let's examine different ways the stress response can have an impact on difficult situations and conflict. We know that the Jedi and Sith engage with their fair share of stressful encounters, and we know that they prepare for and respond to these encounters in dramatically different ways. Can we learn anything from them to improve our own functioning in stressful situations?

The Jedi are known for their serene, centering approach. Jedi training focuses on maintaining a calm mind and not letting emotions get out of control. Luke teaches Rey to breathe and reach out to feel the Force in *The Last Jedi*, just as Maz Kanata had told her to close her eyes to feel the Force in *The Force Awakens*. Rey learns to calm herself and diffuse strong emotions by concentrating on her connection to the Force. She uses this same technique when Kylo pushes her to the edge of an abyss at Starkiller Base: she closes her eyes and calms herself before resuming the fight.

The Sith take a different approach. Using the dark side requires stoking and then channeling powerful negative emotions like fear and anger. The physiologic stress response therefore provides the Sith with powerful fuel. This helps explain what appears at first glance to be Kylo's anger management problem. Whenever he is frustrated and angry about the failed outcome of some plan, he lashes out and destroys whatever is around him. In *The Last Jedi*, when Snoke sneers that Kylo is "just a child in a mask," Kylo smashes the windows and destroys his mask. Clearly Snoke's disapproval is a major stressor for Kylo, and this emotional outburst would seem to add even more stressors. Why does Kylo never try to bring this under control, we wonder. Wouldn't improved control advance his cause better in his competition with Hux and his tutelage with Snoke? We soon learn, however, that Kylo doesn't have so much an anger management problem as an anger management *system*; he intentionally creates stressors to tap into the dark side of the Force. By amping up stressors such as negative emotions (for example, those associated with the proximity or death of his estranged father) and even physical pain (remember him punching his injury during the fight with Rey on Starkiller Base), Kylo generates the power and concentration he requires to bend the Force to his will.

Thus does Jedi training counteract the stress response, while Sith training leeches from it. This contrast is never more on display in the sequels than when Kylo and Luke face each other on Crait in *The Last Jedi*. Kylo Ren is full of rage and hate, emotions that provide him certain advantages but ultimately impair his fighting abilities. Kylo is quick and strong but suffering from tunnel vision and poor decision-making.[1] He focuses all his firepower on Luke, ignoring the other Resistance fighters, and he fails to notice or question the many suspicious features of the situation— for example, why Luke remains utterly unharmed by the walkers or why the surface salt is not scratched away when Luke moves. Meanwhile, Luke is calm and able to perform at full capacity.[2] His Jedi training in concentration and channeling the Force enables him to counteract some of the negative consequences of his physiologic stress response. Luke's training combined with his experience give him confidence in his fight with Kylo. At this high stress moment, Luke manages his emotions and maintains his focus, allowing him to control his Force projection—from one planet to another—with incredible precision.

How to act like a Jedi

How can we non-Jedi utilize elements of Jedi training to counteract or at least manage the stress response more effectively? While we're all waiting for a local Jedi Academy to open, is there some way for us to get ahead of the game? Yes! Although we cannot draw on the Force, we can rely on our own abilities, our human physiology, and our amazing human brains.

Calm and Focus

Jedi training emphasizes clearing the mind to focus on one task. Luke has total mastery when teleporting his image across the galaxy and engaging Kylo Ren. Rey has this as well, as we see when she calms herself during her lightsaber battle with Kylo at Starkiller Base. But you don't need to be a Jedi to focus and calm yourself. When facing threats from every side, mere mortals can take a deep breath or two before deciding on how to go forward.

---

[1] When even General Hux's second-guessing of your decision sounds reasonable, you know your decision-making is not at its finest.

[2] Of course, as we discover later in the movie, Luke was not facing any risk of actual physical harm from Kylo since he was not physically present on Crait. Nonetheless, he was pouring all his life-force into this encounter, and the risk he faced in failing—Kylo quickly discovering he was using the Force projection to distract him—would result in the death of his sister and so many others depending on him. No lack of stressors there.

Slow, deep breathing can counteract the stress response and restore some of the function lost when cortisol builds up after repeated stressors. Like Rose Tico using her Haysian ore medallion to focus her thoughts and consider her next course of action, we can focus on a positive image or on deep breathing to counteract the stress response. When we feel threatened physically, socially, or by runaway emotions, we can take an extra breath, focus our thoughts, try to maintain or restore our balance, and then shift to considering options for our next move.

Acknowledging Our Emotions

We can help ourselves deal with high emotions by first acknowledging the emotions we are feeling. Studies conducted through scanning people's brains with MRI machines show that our amygdala and the prefrontal and parietal areas of our brains are altered when we name an emotion we are feeling, and that alteration in turn reduces our cortisol levels.[iii] Rey often tells Kylo that she can feel the conflict in him. This acknowledgement is intended to help Kylo see that he still has good in him, but it also helps him acknowledge the strong emotions he feels and may help him lower his emotional level. More directly, consider the only moment we see Kylo somewhat at peace in *The Force Awakens*, when he communes with what's left of his grandfather and names the disturbing emotion he's experiencing.[3]

Control

Jedi training certainly boosts a sense of control. It's pretty easy to feel in control when you are holding a lightsaber and have the power to manipulate people and move rocks. How can non-Jedi enhance their own sense of control? As noted above, experience with a situation is a huge help. But if we haven't dealt directly with this situation before, three strategies can help:

---

[3] His "pull to the light" is his name for a rush of emotions that might include love, empathy, missing home, concern for others, remorse at having ordered a massacre, and so on. You know, the usual mix.

- *Cast a broader net*: Upon reflection, we may realize that we have had indirect or analogous experiences that, upon translation to the current circumstances, improve our sense of control over the situation.[4]
- *Take a break*: More generally, stepping away from a volatile argument gives us time to think more clearly about our emotions, resources, options, and allies. It helps recalibrate our internal sense of control, even in situations in which we lack any applicable experience. Taking a break also allows our stress hormones to subside and our mental function to improve.
- *Go to the balcony*: While stepping away from an encounter gives us time to regain calm and control, we can take it a step further and consider what's happening from an outside perspective.[iv] Looking at the situation "from the balcony" can dissipate strong emotions and prevent impulsive behavior that may make things worse.[5]

So, when you are surrounded by threats (physical or social) or by strong emotions, take a lesson from the Jedi. Calm your mind and step aside if you can, taking the time to marshal your thoughts, your resources, and maybe even your allies. Reflect on previous experiences and imagine how an outsider might see the situation. As your sense of calm and control increases, your actions will become more intentional, mindful, and strategic. Even if you cannot control the odds, you can shift them in your favor.

Jedi training is one pathway toward successful management of the stress response, but much like the Force itself—as Luke explained

---

[4] When a roomful of trained fighter pilots clenches at the impossibility of the shot required to take down the first Death Star, Luke Skywalker applies just this method. Sure, it is his first Death Star, but the shot isn't unfamiliar to him: "I used to bullseye womp rats in my T-16 back home. They're not much bigger than two meters."

[5] For more on going to the balcony, see Blumenberg, chapter 16, and Hayes, chapter 14.

to Rey—this training does not *belong* to the Jedi. Take inspiration from the little boy with the broom, Temiri Blagg, at the end of *The Last Jedi*: we all have the potential to achieve Jedi-like results.

References

[i] van Peer, J. M., Spinhoven, P., van Dijk, J. G. & Roelofs, K. (2009). Cortisol-induced enhancement of emotional face processing in social phobia depends on symptom severity and motivational context. *Biological Psychology.* 81.

[ii] Kinner, V. L., Het, S., & Wolf, O. T. (2014). Emotion regulation: exploring the impact of stress and sex. *Frontiers in Behavioral Neuroscience.* (8).

[iii] Herwig, U., Kaffenberger, T., Lutz, J. & Brühl, A.B. (2010). Self-regulated awareness and emotion regulation. *Neuroimage.* 50(2).

[iv] Mischkowski, D., Kross, E. & Bushman, B.J. (2012). Flies on the wall are less aggressive: Self-distancing "in the heat of the moment" reduces aggressive thoughts, angry feelings and aggressive behavior. *Journal of Experimental Social Psychology.* 48(5); Ury, W. (1993). *Getting past no: Negotiating in difficult situations*. Bantam.

18

Flyboy! Traitor!
Unpacking the Poe/Holdo Conflict

Rachel Viscomi

Conflict is messy. That's why people often avoid it. But when we engage conflict skillfully, it can be an incredible source of value. After all, any time emotions rise and opinions clash, we're bound to be talking about something important. For many of us, though, it's hard to see that something through the raised voices, the frustration, and the occasional slammed door. What we need are tools to decipher what's happening in conflict and how we can get to the heart of the matter, like having our own astromech droid who can scan the Imperial network for the best route to our destination.

David Kantor's Structural Dynamics model offers one way of understanding ourselves and others and improving the way we engage in conflict.[i] In Structural Dynamics, we examine conflict through three frames—action, communication, and order. When we view conflict this way, a set of structural patterns emerges that helps us see the situation differently and move away from assigning blame and making judgments, which may escalate conflict. And the good news is that we don't even need to visit Babu Frik to access this new language. Though it may not be part of our regular programming, it's easy to learn and apply.

In this chapter, we will go through the basics of Structural Dynamics before turning to one of the most dysfunctional and complex conflicts in the sequel trilogy: the interaction between

Amilyn Holdo and Poe Dameron in *The Last Jedi*. My goal is not to change your mind about these two—whether you think Holdo is a toxic, traitorous leader or that Poe is an arrogant, insubordinate flyboy is not the point—my hope is simply that you'll walk away with a deeper understanding of why they locked into a destructive dynamic and what it might look like for either of them to get their head out of their cockpit and behave more effectively, creating better results for both of them and for the Resistance overall.

The three frames: action, communication, and order

The three frames of Structural Dynamics help us name and understand the patterns that shape our behavior and that of others, leading to better understanding of why we get stuck and how to move forward constructively.

The first of these frames is *action stances*. Any time we make a statement or ask a question, we do one of four things:

- **move**: making a suggestion or offering an idea ("Let the past die. Kill it if you have to");
- **follow**: accepting or building on a suggestion ("Copy that, Blue Leader");
- **oppose**: pointing out a challenge or a flaw with an idea ("We can't get through their security shields undetected");
- **bystand**: taking a step back to offer a neutral perspective on the broader dynamics of the interaction ("He's doing this for a reason. He's stalling so we can escape").

Healthy communication requires all of these actions, each of which can advance the conversation in a helpful way. Without moves in a conversation, we have no forward motion. Without someone to follow, we lack implementation. If no one opposes, we end up with yes people who don't raise concerns or try to find possible complications. And without someone to bystand and focus on the process of *how* we are interacting, we can fall into unhelpful patterns and fail to engage productively.

The second frame of Kantor's model is *communication*. Kantor distinguishes between three communication *domains* or primary focuses of the speaker's message. In any message we might emphasize:

- **affect**: the message directs attention to feelings and impacts on people ("In every corner of the galaxy the downtrodden and oppressed know our symbol and they put their hope in it");
- **meaning**: the message relates to the reason we're engaging in an effort ("We are what they grow beyond. That is the true burden of all masters");
- **power**: the message commands action, efficiency, and implementation ("I want every gun we have to fire on that man").

To engage constructively with others we need communication to flow through each of these domains—we need to feel connected, be inspired, and be effective. Despite that, people often have a strong default preference that leads them to communicate in one domain more than others. This can be a recipe for misunderstanding. When we are focusing on feelings while someone else is speaking to efficiency, we can get our wires crossed.[1] The more we can be aware of and speak to someone else's domain as well as our own, the more effectively we'll be able to connect.

The third key frame of Structural Dynamics is our *rules of order*. This frame focuses on the preferences each of us has for our "operating systems," or how we make decisions.

In an **open system**, decisions are made collaboratively, with input from multiple people. The scenes where Finn and Rose (and subsequently Finn, Poe, and Rose) brainstorm about a plan to disable the tracking device illustrates an open system, as each offers ideas and concerns as they together generate a plan. A **closed**

---

[1] Consider Rose Tico and Finn's conversation after she crashes into him to prevent his kamikaze run against the First Order's battering ram cannon (power domain). "Why would you stop me?" he asks. "I saved you, dummy." she replies. "That's how we're going to win. Not fighting what we hate, saving what we love" (affect domain).

system, by contrast, is top-down and hierarchical—think of Snoke disciplining Hux when he is disappointed in his performance, or Kylo Ren ordering stormtroopers to take Rey to his ship. Finally, a **random system** prioritizes autonomy and independence. People behave and make decisions independently, often without coordination. One example of this might be Luke's decision to Force project himself to face Kylo on Crait, which he undertakes without consultation with Leia or the Resistance.

Operating system preferences often develop in childhood, either as an embrace of our family's preferred operating system or as a reaction against it. As a result, many of us feel more at home in one system and may chafe against the one furthest from our preference.

Still looking to the horizon. Never here, now, hmm?

Before we move on, let's take a moment to reflect on our own default tendencies using the three frames of the Structural Dynamics model.

Action: Are you more comfortable proposing ideas (moving) or poking holes in them (opposing)? Are you typically sitting on the sidelines to observe behavior (bystanding) or stepping in to see things through (following)? See if you can spot stuck action sequences in your daily interactions. When your boss moves, does the rest of the team jump to follow as if she were Snoke, stifling unspoken concerns? Do you and your sibling find yourself playing out a move-oppose dynamic like Kylo Ren and Rey?

Communication: Do you identify more strongly with one of the communication domains, prioritizing meaning, like Yoda, or affect, like Rose? Do you find yourself talking at cross purposes with a colleague who wants to determine the next action steps (power) while you'd like to take a step back and ensure the plan you're executing still makes sense (meaning)?

Order: Are you more comfortable in a closed operating system with hierarchical roles and responsibilities like Hux or in a random system where you can exercise your best judgment like Luke? Do you prefer it when everyone agrees in advance on the meeting agenda (open system), or would you rather build it on the fly together (even more open)?

The more attuned you are to your own default tendencies, the easier it will be to course correct when you are clashing with someone else.

Breaking down the Poe/Holdo conflict

The near-mutiny from *The Last Jedi*, involving an epic throwdown between Captain Poe and Vice Admiral Holdo, is a good candidate for Structural Dynamics analysis. Let's use the three frames to get a better sense of why and how things go off the rails.

The most obvious fault line between Poe and Holdo is that they have radically different operating system preferences. From the very opening scenes of *The Last Jedi*, we see Poe's strong preference for a random operating system—one in which each person exercises their best independent judgment regardless of the existing hierarchy. Poe considers Leia his mentor and clearly values her approval, but that does not stop him from countermanding her direct order to disengage rather than destroy the dreadnought. He hears her order and proceeds to turn off his radio, explicitly deciding to disregard her input and substituting his judgment for hers. In the context of a military command structure, this is grounds for a court martial. But Poe is so convinced that it is appropriate for him to exercise his best independent judgment that he fully expects that he will be celebrated for his daring, despite the loss of life it creates. He believes that taking bold and gutsy risks, even in contravention of the command structure and without strategic coordination with one's team, is the work of heroes.

Note that this perspective makes sense for Poe. As a child of resistance fighters in the Rebel Alliance, he has grown up on stories of daring escapades in which orders are defied and glory ensues. He seems hurt and misunderstood when Leia admonishes him. He tries, unsuccessfully, to redirect her ("There were heroes on that mission"), unable to understand why she is not celebrating what he sees as a victory. This preference is reinforced when Poe announces to Threepio that he has no intention of asking Vice

Admiral Holdo for permission to execute a complex plan with Rose and Finn. He remains confident that retaining autonomy and exercising his independent judgment will result in a better outcome overall.

Vice Admiral Holdo's preference for a closed operating system is also immediately apparent. Holdo is introduced to us as a military leader whose reputation precedes her ("Battle of Chyron Belt Admiral Holdo?"), even as she might not square with the stereotype Poe has of a military leader ("Not what I expected!"). A closed operating system—of which a military command structure is a perfect exemplar—values structure and clarity. Roles and responsibilities are clear. Hierarchy dictates who does what, when, and how.

Holdo is as committed to a closed system as Poe is to a random system. She wants him to know his place. She repeatedly admonishes him to behave in line with his (new) rank—to do his duty, go to his station, and follow orders. He repeatedly disregards his duty, his station, and his orders, chafing against the constraints of a closed system. The operating system clash drives the most tension in these scenes. Each character has expectations for how the world should work that the other does not share, so each of them feels the other is behaving unreasonably.[2]

The second clash between the two is visible through the communication frame. In high stakes moments, we often default to speaking with emphasis on a particular value. Poe's primary communication domain in this context is meaning. He wants to understand what is happening and why. He is unwilling to follow orders that he doesn't agree with, so until he understands, he will continue to push back. As Holdo takes up her mantle as acting General, she begins in affect and meaning, acknowledging the sorrow of the moment and articulating the importance of preserving lives ("Four hundred of us on three ships. We're the very last of

---

[2] As a structural matter, Holdo is correct about Poe's role. His behavior is out of line. As a practical matter, her failure to recognize (as Leia does) that she can leverage his strengths more effectively by drawing him in rather than pushing him away ends up being a strategic miscalculation.

the Resistance . . . That spark, this Resistance, must survive. That is our mission").

As Holdo concludes her introduction and moves into action, she becomes laser-focused on execution and her communication domain shifts from meaning to power. Poe is desperate for more information so that he can move forward, and she (possibly for reasons of operational security, his insubordination, his subordinate rank, and her sense of time pressure) does not feel she owes him more explanation. In other words, their communication preferences are mismatched, as he keeps demanding answers and she keeps issuing orders.

This brings us to the final clash, through the frame of action stances. Given that both feel entitled to lead—Holdo, by virtue of her rank, her confidence in her strategic analysis, and her belief in the importance of a closed operating system; Poe, by virtue of his faith in himself, his sense of frustration, and his commitment to a random operating system—they both often default to *moving*. The dynamic of competing moves does not contribute to forward motion. Each person moves, without accepting input or influence from other person.

In the moments of sharpest conflict between Poe and Holdo, all three frames are in play simultaneously. Holdo makes frequent moves in closed power while Poe makes frequent moves in random meaning. He insists that he needs to understand ("I just want to know the plan"). Holdo responds from within the frame that makes sense to her ("Stick to your post and follow my orders"). Her statements focus on efficiency and clarity. She is preoccupied with action and trying to make things happen. She does not want to stop and justify her behavior to someone who, in her view, has been responsible for the loss of many resistance fighters due to his own hubris and disregard of the command structure.

At the top of a military hierarchy, moves in closed power make sense. The military structure is designed to enhance clarity and efficiency. Those at the top of the hierarchy lead; those under them follow. From Holdo's perspective, it makes sense for her to issue orders. After all, she is the acting General. The person at the top of the hierarchy is tasked with thinking strategically about the big picture. On the ground, an individual decision may seem wrong-headed, but within the larger context, may make good sense. Given that, her prerogative is to set the mission and ensure it is implemented in a way that prioritizes efficiency and direction.

As we've seen, implementation of other people's plans is not Poe's strong suit. He prizes autonomy and meaning and, more importantly, he sees himself as a leader. There's a reason he sits up a little straighter when D'Acy announces that the chain of command is clear. He suspects, wrongly, that he's about to be tapped to take charge. His blind spots prevent him from understanding why he's not yet ready for that role. Seeing himself a leader, he bristles at following.[3] He wants to be giving the orders. Poe, especially at the beginning of the film, has an underdeveloped ability to follow and similarly stunted ability to bystand. He repeatedly defaults to the move and oppose stances, even when they continually land him in hot water. Leia admonishes and demotes him, but it takes a while for him to learn to get his head out of his cockpit. From Poe's perspective, though, he's doing what heroes before him have done—he's exercising his own judgment. For all he knows, Holdo could be a double agent like Palpatine in the prequels. Given the quick nature of the change in command, he doesn't know that Holdo has Leia's vote of confidence and, given his commitment to meaning, he's a skeptic by nature. He wants to be able to make up his own mind about whether something makes sense. What he sees as Holdo's insistence on blind obedience triggers his defiance.

Hope is like the sun

There is one moment where we see a brief connection between Holdo and Poe. Notably, it's a moment where their default dynamics are disrupted. Poe moves in meaning, but also in affect. He asks Holdo to offer hope that they will make it. Rather than moving or opposing in power, Holdo chooses to bystand in meaning:

---

[3] For more on gender-based differences in negotiation and their contribution to this conflict, see Eisenberg, chapter 16, in *Star Wars and Conflict Resolution: There Are Alternatives to Fighting* (Ebner & Reynolds eds., 2022).

POE:	Tell us that we have a plan! [move in meaning] That there's hope! [move in affect]
HOLDO:	When I served under Leia, she would say hope is like the sun. If you only believe in it when you can see it . . . [bystand in meaning]
POE:	. . . you'll never make it through the night. [follow in meaning]

In this scene of brief connection, Holdo softens for a moment and is able to hear Poe's move as something deeper than insubordination. In that moment, she seems to acknowledge his desperation and fear; and although she does not go so far as to bring him into her decision-making process, she nonetheless responds in a way that engages him. She invokes Leia, offering a sense of what they all share. Instead of continuing to move in closed power, Holdo meets him in meaning, and, channeling Leia, attempts to offer a broader perspective. Immediately, the dynamic shifts. Voices soften and, for a brief moment, they seem closer together.

Of course, this moment of brief connection is quickly disrupted when Poe notices that Holdo is fueling the transports and jumps to moral conclusions about her plan and her motivations ("You're not only a coward, you're a traitor!") (move in affect). After Poe erupts in anger, the moment is gone and Holdo's response is (can you guess?) her trusty go-to of move in closed power: "Get this man off my bridge." Consider what may have happened if Holdo had stayed the course by continuing to speak to Poe in meaning and affect:

> Poe, I know you don't yet trust me, but Leia and I have served together for decades. (move in affect, move in meaning) She has taught me everything I know and I will not let her down. (move in meaning, move in affect) I want you to know that I am doing everything in my power to ensure the survival of the Resistance. (move in meaning) I am asking

> you to trust that we are on the same team and to let me do my job. (move in affect, move in meaning)

Could she have simply told him what was going on? Of course. (In that case, she might have shifted her action stance from primarily moves to primarily follows.) But let's assume that she was concerned that his inclination to shoot from the hip might mean that he'd choose to disregard orders and either act on highly sensitive information without coordination or share it with lower-level members of the Resistance without thinking through the risks.[4] If she had recognized that his commitment to a random operating system and repeated entreaties to understand the plan made it highly likely that he would not follow orders simply because they were issued but would respond well to communication in the meaning domain, she might have engaged with Poe in a non-dismissive way, acknowledging his genuine commitment to the cause, even without choosing to disclose information she preferred to keep confidential.

On Poe's part, if he had understood and acknowledged that Holdo did not owe him any answers (recognizing her seniority in a closed organizational operating system), he might have asked for them rather than demanding them. For example:

> Vice Admiral Holdo, I appreciate that your job is to set the mission and mine is to carry it out. (follow in meaning) I know you don't need to tell me the plan, but I want you to know that if you can help me understand what I'm working toward, no one on this team will work harder to ensure our success than I will. (follow, coupled with move in open meaning)

---

[4] While she might not have envisioned all the particulars, it's safe to say that Holdo would not have been surprised to learn that the impulsive Poe had shared mission-critical information with Finn (whose loyalty to Rey supersedes his loyalty to the cause) and Rose (a mechanic he'd just met) within earshot of DJ (who sold out the Resistance for personal gain).

In other words, Poe could have used a follow—acknowledging some of what she'd shared—coupled with a move, expressing his preference for communication in the meaning domain.

Where there was conflict, I now sense resolve

If you've made it this far, hopefully you are beginning to see how this model can help you diagnose why you are getting stuck and how to navigate moments of conflict more effectively. With awareness of your own tendencies regarding each frame, you can begin by working to expand your repertoire. Which action propensities, communication domains, and operating systems do you use least? Where might you begin to stretch your muscles?

When you find yourself in conflict, you might first look to see if one of the four action stances is missing in a conversation. If so, introduce it. When you feel your blood pressure rising because it feels like your concerns are being ignored, tune into the framing of their messages. Do you think you're in a conversation about whether you're both equally committed to this relationship while the other person thinks you're discussing whose turn it was to take out the trash? If so, you may have a mismatch in communication domains. What seems most important to them? Are they worried about people and feelings? Purpose and reasoning? Efficiency and action steps? Take a step back and try to see if you can address both of your areas of concern—you might begin in their frame and then move to your own.

And when you're caught in judgment and convinced their behavior is unreasonable, it's possible you have an operating system conflict on your hands. Consider a bystand move to describe what you've noticed. ("We seem to have different expectations here. My sense is that you think this should be a collective decision, whereas I understood that we would each make an independent decision. Do I have that right?") Once you agree on where the disconnect is, you can work to agree on a way forward rather than letting frustration and judgment drive the conversation. The more you cultivate these skills, the easier and more rewarding you will find it to move toward the conflict rather than avoid it.

While conflict is less likely to arise when our behavioral styles align more easily, the fact is that it often comes bearing gifts, even if we don't recognize them at first. Although Holdo is frustrated by Poe's unwillingness to simply follow orders, perhaps she also ultimately recognizes how his behavioral profile can also offer much-needed strengths—after all, having someone who is willing to take action (move) and to find flaws in a plan (oppose) can help make a plan stronger; having someone who is willing to stand up to ensure alignment around purpose (meaning domain) can help to inspire a team to work toward a common goal: and someone who is willing to take initiative and assume responsibility even when it's not technically within their position description (random operating system) can invite proactive engagement and creativity. Often the people we find most challenging are the people whose way of seeing things is the most unlike our own, and therefore, the most able to counterbalance our own tendencies, helping us to leverage the value hidden within conflict. Perhaps this is why, as Poe is being lifted away after Leia has stunned him, Holdo remarks, "That one's a troublemaker. I like him."

References

[i] Kantor, D. (2012). *Reading the room.* Jossey-Bass.

Contributors

Amber Hill Anderson, MA, works with rebels and the Empire to find solutions as the owner and mediator at Hilltop Mediation LLC. Amber also teaches conflict resolution, communication, and negotiation classes to Padawans at University College at the University of Denver. In the classroom and at the mediation table, she keeps a little optimism.

Danielle Blumenberg is owner of The Way Matters, a coaching and consulting company that works with businesses and individuals to collaboratively transform conflicts into positive growth opportunities. She is a mediator and coach who believes dysfunctional communication is the real path to the dark side. Danielle lives in Florida with her family and two rescue Ewoks.

Alon Burstein is a Visiting Assistant Professor in the Department of Political Science at the University of California, Irvine. His research, focusing primarily on terrorism, political violence, and insurgent mobilization, stems from one unanswered question he had as a teenager: why do we implicitly accept the certain point of view that the Empire is "evil" and the rebels are "good"? His work on religious terrorism, White Supremacy terrorism, and the Israeli-Palestinian conflict has been published in journals ranging from *Terrorism and Political Violence* to *Studies in Conflict & Terrorism* to *Israel Studies*—but he has yet to grow strong enough with the Force to answer that question.

Deborah A. Cai, PhD (Michigan State University), is professor and senior associate dean in the Klein College of Media and Communication at Temple University, and she is a faculty member in the Media and Communication doctoral program and in the Department of Communication and Social Influence. She is an international researcher with scholarly and professional expertise in intercultural communication, negotiation and conflict management, and persuasion. Deborah is a Fellow in the International Academy of Intercultural Researchers and a Fellow and Past-President of the International Association for Conflict Management.

Emily A. Cai, MA (Sciences Po), is a farmer working to mitigate the climate crisis and promote food access efforts. They have a master's degree in Human Rights and Humanitarian Action from the Paris School of International Affairs, with concentrations in Diplomacy and Global Risks. Emily has previously worked to fight against extreme human rights abuses, including the U.S. death penalty and the practice of lethal injection. Emily formerly studied in Beijing, where they were a recipient of the Chinese Government Scholarship-Bilateral Program. Emily has an undergraduate degree from Temple University where they studied theater, French, and Chinese. They currently reside in Vermont.

Jeroen Camps is a lecturer in Organizational Behavior and Human Resource Management (HRM) at Thomas More University of Applied Sciences. He also teaches at the University of Fribourg on topics like organizational justice and negotiations. In addition to his academic work, he works for the Police Department of Antwerp as advisor on leadership and evidence-based HRM. He eagerly awaits the day that he will finally succeed at lifting objects with the Force.

Michael T. Colatrella Jr. is the inaugural Tracy A. Eglet Chair in Alternative Dispute Resolution and Professor of Law at McGeorge School of Law, University of the Pacific. He teaches and writes in the areas of negotiation, mediation, and conflict management. He is also a mediator. Although Michael dreams of traveling to distant galaxies to resolve intergalactic disputes, thus far he has been content traveling throughout California in his gently used landschlepper assisting various humanoid species to work through their conflicts productively. In these pursuits, he is often accompanied by his golden retriever, Leo—whose long golden fur, prodigious strength, and appetite for adventure leads Michael to suspect that Leo is at least half Wookiee.

Noam Ebner was in the wrong place at the wrong time. Naturally, he became a lawyer. Reprogrammed like IG-11, he is now a professor of negotiation and conflict resolution at Creighton University, where he teaches that wars not make one great. Noam lives in New Dagobah with his wife and their four younglings. He swears by the Maker that everything in this bio is literally true.

Maja Graso researches the impact of visible and invisible harms in social settings. She investigates how different threats, whether a visible crisis like a fire or invisible issues like workplace conflicts and Covid-19, are perceived and addressed. These invisible harms often lead to division due to their ambiguous nature. Maja approaches her research from a perspective that there is no dark side of the Force, really.

Sherrill W. Hayes is a professor of conflict management and an Assistant Vice Provost at Kennesaw State University, where he can often be heard muttering "it's not my fault" from behind his console. He was apprenticed to Jedi Masters in the US and the UK and successfully faced the trials to receive his PhD from Newcastle University in 2005. His missions have since included practicing conflict resolution with families, businesses, refugee communities, and in higher education. Although his office has been called a *Star Wars* museum, what he really loves is playing music and is still waiting on a call from Max Rebo.

Olivia Hernandez-Pozas is an enthusiastic apprentice of Jedi Master Yoda. She truly believes that "when in a dark place we find ourselves, a little more knowledge lights our way." Thus, she spends most of her time producing new knowledge by doing research at the Institute for the Future of Education of Tecnologico de Monterrey. As an associate professor, she unlocks her Padawans' full connection to the Force at the School of Business in the same university. Olivia recently served as research coordinator for the Management Education and Development Division of the Academy of Management and as advisor for Blue5PL, an innovative start up in cross-border logistics and transportation.

Kimberly Y.W. Holst was raised on a family farm in Tatooine and is now a Clinical Professor of Law and Dean's Innovation Fellow at Arizona State University, Sandra Day O'Connor College of Law. She teaches Legal Writing, Feminist Judgments, and legal skills courses. She is the mother of three daughters and looks forward to seeing them develop into the princesses, Jedi, or warriors they need to be in order to lead future rebellions with wisdom and hope.

Dr. **Orlando R. Kelm** is an Associate Professor of Hispanic Linguistics at the University of Texas at Austin, where he teaches courses focusing on business language and the cultural aspects of international business communication. He serves as the Director of the Portuguese Language Flagship Program, sponsored by the National Security Education Program (NSEP) of the Department of Defense. Upon retirement in 2024, his plan is to do a Kessel Run, hopefully taking the longer and more scenic 20 parsecs route to get there.

John Martin, Esq., MBA, MSCM, is a successful attorney, mediator and arbitrator concentrating in commercial and family conflict resolution with practices in Georgia and Louisiana. John earned a MS in Conflict Management from Kennesaw State University's School of Conflict Management, Peacebuilding, and Development, and serves as a primary trainer of Domestic Relations mediation at the KSU Conflict Management Center. In addition, John is an adjunct instructor at Johnson University, teaching business law and ethics to young eager minds in the BS and MBA programs. Happily married with three teenage children, John bleeds LSU purple and gold, is passionate about singing despite his family begging him to stop since he doesn't know the words, and loves all things chocolate.

Avideh K. Mayville, PhD, is no Jedi. She is a nonprofit leader with experience in the peacebuilding, veteran reintegration, and climate transformation realms. With a background in Sociology and International Peace and Conflict Resolution, she has spent her career as a Force wielder seeking balance within the practitioner and scholarly dimensions of the social sector. She currently oversees a squadron of Program Operations Managers and Leads at RMI, driving the implementation of global energy system transformation programs. Avideh's scholarly background is at the intersection between violent conflict and international aid, specifically the multilateral and bilateral capacity development of conflict zones.

Amanda Reinke is an associate professor at the Kennesaw State University School of Conflict Management, Peacebuilding, and Development, and Director of its MS in Conflict Management degree. Like Kylo Ren turned Matt the radar technician, Amanda enjoys the immersive experience of ethnographic work in bureaucratic environments to better understand the dynamics of everyday forms of violence and resistance. In her spare time, she makes special modifications to her galactic hunk of junk and backpacks in nature with her furry Ewok friends.

Josefina M. Rendón has been a judge in Texas for over forty years. Long, long ago, at the request of a prosecutor, she referred an assault case to a rather new concept called mediation. After seeing the parties' creative agreement, she soon became a mediator herself and began teaching about dispute resolution to many groups including the U.S. military. Luckier than Chewbacca, she has received many recognitions for her work in the field of Alternative Dispute Resolution. She has also been President of Texas Association of Mediators and editor of *The Texas Mediator*.

Jennifer Wenska Reynolds is an award-winning professor at the University of Oregon School of Law, located on the forest moon of Endor. She has written and published extensively on alternative dispute resolution, and she is dedicated to training legal Padawans to become wise and thoughtful leaders. Jen believes that helping each other is the solution to the biggest problems in the universe.

Jan Smolinski is a lifelong *Star Wars* fan and a Padawan at Copenhagen Business School. He is pursuing his master's degree in Innovation and Business Development and works at the university's student union to improve the Jedi Academy for future students.

Remi Smolinski is a negotiation professor at HHL Leipzig Graduate School of Management and the Academic Director of the Center on ~~International~~ Intergalactic Negotiation, where he has mentored numerous Padawans and instructed them in the art of negotiation, helping them bring peace to the galaxy. *Return of the Jedi* was the very first movie he watched in a theater, and it was there that the Force bestowed its presence upon him, remaining with him ever since.

Troy Stearns was a Padawan to Professor Noam Ebner at Creighton University's MS in Negotiation and Dispute Resolution program. Troy started off as a scruffy-looking nerf herder and eventually earned his Doctor of Education degree in Interdisciplinary Leadership, later becoming a Special Faculty member working alongside Professor Ebner at Creighton University before departing through Mos Eisley's spaceport. He currently teaches conflict resolution at the Doctorate of Education Program for Concordia University Texas, and he also uses his conflict resolution skills within the biotechnology industry.

Paul Story is an associate professor of psychology at Kennesaw State University. When he isn't arguing with his nephew about who is the real chosen one (it's Matt BTW), he is teaching undergraduates about the dark side of the Force (statistics) and collaborating with them on research projects. Paul enjoys exposing anyone he can to the benefits of positive psychology and how it can help them have happier and healthier lives.

Jill S. Tanz has been a mediator, mediation trainer, and adjunct professor at DePaul University College of Law in Chicago. She has been speaking and writing about mediation and neuroscience since 2014 and has lived with a *Star Wars*-obsessed husband since 1977. She hopes to emulate Jedi calm in her retirement. She regularly rides her new e-speeder along the Chicago lakefront.

Robert R. Tanz, Professor Emeritus of Pediatrics at Northwestern University Feinberg School of Medicine, is one with the Force and the Force is with him. The rumble of the Imperial Star Destroyer passing overhead as it fired on Princess Leia's starship after the opening text crawl in 1977 released cortisol and adrenaline (also dopamine and serotonin) into his system, and it still does today. Although retired, he supervises and teaches pediatric Padawans several times each month. He has never treated a patient with a wound from a lightsaber or blaster.

Zach Ulrich has mediated disputes both galactic and domestic. He is a former research fellow at Pepperdine Caruso School of Law, situated on the ice planet Hoth, and has published numerous survey studies on mediation and arbitration. Zach is currently in 2-1B training and plans to open a therapy practice. He enjoys riding his tauntaun through the ice fields around his settlement and training his dogs to sniff out any wampas lurking about.

Rachel Viscomi is a clinical professor at Harvard Law School where she works with the Rebel Alliance to build dispute systems that further justice. She trains Jedi how to avoid answering power with power, and to guard against the danger of losing who we are. In her free time, she studies the energetic dynamics of health and conflict, using the power of the Force to bring balance to the universe.

Made in the USA
Monee, IL
28 May 2024